SIMON AND SCHUSTER
NEW YORK TORONTO LONDON SYDNEY TOKYO

MURDERS & ACQUISITIONS

A REUBEN FROST MYSTERY

HAUGHTON MURPHY

Copyright © 1988 by Haughton Murphy
All rights reserved
including the right of reproduction
in whole or in part in any form
Published by Simon and Schuster
A Division of Simon & Schuster Inc.
Simon & Schuster Building
Rockefeller Center
1230 Avenue of the Americas
New York, New York 10020
SIMON AND SCHUSTER
and colophon are registered trademarks
of Simon & Schuster Inc.
Designed by Bonni Leon
Manufactured in the United States of America
1   3   5   7   9   10   8   6   4   2
Library of Congress Cataloging in Publication data
Murphy, Haughton.
Murders & acquisitions/Haughton Murphy.
p.   cm.
ISBN 0-671-63735-5
I. Title.   II. Title: Murders and acquisitions.
PS3563.U734M88   1988
813'.54—dc 19   87-31004
                                                CIP

ISBN 0-671-63735-5

This novel is dedicated to my friends Nick and Nora, who were married while it was being written.

THE ANDERSENS

1 "Don't get angry with me, Reuben, but I've got a question for you," Cynthia Frost said to her husband, as they finished their dinner in the dining room of their New York City town house.

After forty years of marriage, Reuben Frost could recognize trouble when it threatened. He knew from experience that the words "don't get angry" meant that his wife was about to bring up a subject calculated to provoke him.

"Of course I won't get angry," Reuben answered. "What's the question?"

"Darling, do we really have to go to the Andersen family weekend?" Cynthia asked, referring to the annual late-August gathering of the heirs of Nils Andersen—the principal owners of the Andersen Foods Corporation.

"I don't see any way out of it," Reuben said. "We've been going for so many years we can't stop now. We're expected."

"Reuben, dear, I understood all that while you were in charge of the Andersens' legal work at Chase & Ward. But now that you're retired as a partner, I don't see why we've got any obligation to be there. One of the young couples should have to suffer through it."

"You forget, Cynthia, that even though I'm no longer a partner, I'm still of counsel to the firm and have to do my share. For better or worse, going to the Andersen weekend is one of the ways I can do that. Besides, Flemming and Sally expect us. And you *do* like Sally."

Frost, making his case, referred to his wife's affection, or at least affinity, for Sally Bryant Anderson, whose career as a professional tennis player had paralleled Cynthia's own as a leading American ballerina.

"Yes, I do like Sally," Cynthia said. "And Flemming and Sally are a fine couple. But *three days* with someone else's family, most of them strangers, is really too much. And by the end of August the Mohawk Inn's like the North Pole."

"I know, I know. But Flemming called me just the day before yesterday to make sure we were coming. I can't turn him down."

"I knew that's what you'd say. So we'll go, and watch the water-balloon tag and see Billy O'Neal get drunk—if he's in the mood for one of his drunken fits—and . . ."

"Don't go on, Cynthia. After all these years, I know the drill as well as you do," Reuben said, with resignation.

"And I really do think someone else from the firm should take over," Cynthia declared.

"It's not that easy. Since I retired, I haven't had much to do with AFC—officially at least. You're right about that. But Flemming's still Chairman of the Board and he consults me from time to time."

"Who's in charge of AFC at the firm now? It's Ernest Crowder, isn't it?"

"Yes it is. So you see the problem. Ernest's a wonderful lawyer, but a total social misfit, as you would be the first to point out—a crabby bachelor with no patience, no small talk and a willingness to tell the world what he doesn't approve of. Such as drinking. Can't you see Ernest and Billy O'Neal squaring off?"

"It might be amusing having him around, though. Just think how *he* would react to the water-balloon nonsense."

"You think he'd disapprove?" Reuben asked.

"Of course."

"You're wrong. Ernest Crowder would see the water-balloon matches for just what they are: good, clean Protestant fun. Innocent, sublimating and thoroughly virtuous."

"Oh, God," Cynthia said, with a sigh, "I guess Andersen Foods did enough for you and the firm so that we have to go. Mature and mellow Reuben Frost and his sweet wife, Cynthia."

"Afraid so, my dear. But cheer up. You never can tell, maybe this year there'll be some excitement."

"Doubtful."

It might be possible for an American to go through life without coming into contact with a product of the Andersen Foods Corporation—AFC. But not very likely, unless this strange, atypical citizen somehow avoided eating. Scores of AFC products were favorites of the consuming public and made AFC a leader in the so-called "food-at-home" market. There were chopped-up vegetables for the baby and salt-free ones for its grandparents; frozen low-calorie concoctions for those on diets and high-calorie candies and ice creams for those not so inhibited; cereals for breakfast, packaged meat for lunch and TV-dinners for the evening. And all washed down with an AFC soft drink, a cup of AFC coffee or—more recently—a beer made by a brewery acquired by AFC.

Like many successful American enterprises, AFC had started modestly. It had been founded in 1898 by Nils Andersen, a Dane who had migrated with his family to Duluth, Minnesota. Andersen was both a farmer and a tinkerer, and the process of storing fresh products in metal cans, then coming into common use in the United States, intrigued him.

Starting in a workshop at the back of his barn, Andersen succeeded in bettering the canning methods then in use, taking advantage of the research on canning spoilage being done by Professor Henry Russell at the University of Wisconsin.

Andersen's improved techniques not only cut down on the number of cans that exploded from defective process- ing, to the delight of retailers, but better preserved the flavor of what was inside them as well, to the satisfaction of consumers. Soon the immigrant tinkerer had a thriving processing plant, canning and distributing corn, peas and other vegetables grown in the midwestern heartland.

As the business prospered, Nils Andersen showed a talent for expanding its operation and scope, building new canneries in California and Baltimore before he retired in 1920. His son, the first Laurance Andersen, continued the business with even greater success. He led the ex- pansion of AFC's product line out of canned goods, add- ing breakfast cereals and other dry foods. But his great- est success, pursued all his life, was supervision of AFC's advertising program. The Company's direct but low-key promotions succeeded in creating an image of quality— a deserved image of quality—with the consumer. The American public became comfortable with AFC's prod- ucts, if not downright proud that it was consuming them.

Flemming Andersen, the first Laurance's only son, stepped into the presidency of AFC when he returned from World War II. Although only thirty-five at the time, he justified in short order the confidence his father had shown in turning management over to him. He combined the talents of both his practical grandfather and super- salesman father. Taking AFC public in the early 1960s was a major accomplishment, requiring him to convince other members of the family that it was a good thing for the nation's widows and orphans—and pension plans and giant insurance companies and other impersonal investors—to have a majority interest in AFC (but with actual control of the Company safely vested in the Andersens).

The family battle over going public had left scars or, more precisely, had deepened at least one old wound. Laurance Andersen, an otherwise enlightened man of his time, had seen fit to divide ownership of AFC into two parts—two unequal and discriminatory parts. After giving effect to Laurance Andersen's will, his son, Flemming, owned two-thirds of the shares of AFC and his daughter, Christina, owned one-third. This was not done out of any animosity toward Christina; Laurance had certainly been as fond of her as of his son. It simply reflected a chauvinist notion of preserving family stability through favoring the male line of succession.

At the time AFC went public, Christina—or more precisely, her husband, Jarvis O'Neal—had tried to have the imbalance corrected. But Flemming Andersen had resisted his brother-in-law's effort. Not because his arguments were without merit but because the division between the O'Neal branch of the family and Flemming's own seemed roughly equitable, since Christina and Jarvis had only one child and he and Sally had three.

Christina Andersen O'Neal never in her lifetime held Flemming's action against him. Her husband did, and there was bad blood between the two men until Jarvis died in 1970. His death did not end the feud, however. The O'Neal son, William, known to one and all as Billy, was more than eager to take it up, watching and criticizing Flemming from his position as Executive Vice President of AFC.

The feud never got out of hand because the Company was an enormous success, and the profits it produced were a balm to hurt feelings. Annual sales hit the billion-dollar mark for the first time in 1972, and had reached five billion a decade later. This volume had most recently produced earnings of over $175 million a year, enabling AFC to pay very comfortably an annual dividend of ninety cents on each of its 80 million outstanding shares.

For the Andersen family itself, and the Andersen Foundation, begun by Laurance Andersen, this meant annual dividend income in excess of $33 million—not huge by the megabuck figures of the 1980s, but more than enough to make one and all very comfortably off.

As he neared retirement, Flemming Andersen was especially pleased at the highly profitable outcome of two developments he had encouraged. One was branching out into pet foods, a new departure for the Company. Through shrewd advertising, AFC had been able to capture a modest but profitable share of the pet market; enough of the country's 56.2 million cats and 51 million dogs were being fed the AFC products to make HEART O' GOLD pet food a thoroughgoing success.

Andersen's other innovation had given him even more satisfaction. He was a competitive person by nature, and it pleased him that AFC had taken on a tough rival— Campbell Soups—and managed to more than hold its own. Many other food processors had tried over the years to compete with Campbell's in soup selling, but their efforts had usually ended in costly failure, or at least without capturing a profitable share of the market.

Those around Flemming Andersen—not least Billy O'Neal—had tried to discourage his move into soups, citing this bleak history. But he would not be deterred. Correctly, he sensed that the country was ready for a line of soups containing only natural ingredients—no monosodium glutamate, no artificial coloring, no mysterious junk. And he also sensed that AFC's reputation for quality would enhance its ability to emphasize the all-natural character of its new SUPERBOWL varieties.

The results had been sensational beyond even the Chairman's expectations, and Joe Faxton, the AFC Treasurer, would be able to report, at the family meeting at Mohawk Inn, that the Company was headed for another year of record earnings.

It was slightly after noon on the last Friday in August when Flemming Andersen left the AFC Building on Park Avenue, climbed into a waiting Company limousine and departed for the Marine Air Terminal at La Guardia Airport. He was accompanied by Casper Robbins, the President of AFC and an obligatory (if not necessarily willing) participant in the Mohawk weekend. The two men would meet their wives, Sally Andersen and Ditsy (*née* Elizabeth) Robbins, at the airport. Andersen would also meet his son, Laurance (named after his distinguished grandfather), a forty-five-year-old bachelor at the moment (after shedding three successive wives in disastrous and costly divorce proceedings, the most recent within the past year).

Flemming's relatives would be coming in from what the family jokingly called the "compound" in Connecticut. (While the Andersens vigorously denied that this estate bore any resemblance to the cluster of Kennedy homes in Hyannis, the fact was that Flemming, Laurance and Flemming's daughter Sorella all had adjoining properties in back-country Greenwich.) At the Marine Terminal, they would take an AFC corporate plane to the Adirondacks.

As the car moved up the F.D.R. Drive, Casper Robbins sensed that his colleague did not want to talk (part of his success as a nonfamily survivor at AFC could be attributed to his instinctive, and correct, impulses as to what the wishes of members of the Andersen family were). Flemming, for his part, wondered how many more years the August reunions would go on. They had been started in the 1920s by his father. The first Laurance had been a willing immigrant from Minnesota—decamping from Duluth within months of his own father's death, moving his family and the AFC corporate headquarters to New York City. He nonetheless had a nostalgia for woods, mountains and bracing weather that the Adirondacks satisfied.

As originally conceived, the outings had been for the Andersen family, ranking management of AFC and outside advisers like Reuben Frost, and their spouses. (Old Laurance, with only one son and one daughter, could hardly have had very festive weekends had they been confined to blood relatives.) Flemming, who somehow became aware that the Company's managers might have other things to do on the last weekend in August, had several years earlier made it clear that management personnel, other than essential figures like Robbins and Faxton, need not attend. The result had been an indecently swift attrition in the number of those coming to the Mohawk Inn. Now, in the mid-1980s, attendance was limited to Flemming and his children; Billy O'Neal; Casper Robbins; Reuben Frost; Randolph Hedley, legal counsel to the Andersen Foundation; and several members of the AFC headquarters staff who arranged the weekend's events and logistics. And, of course, spouses and (very occasionally) spouse substitutes, and a bevy of Andersen grandchildren.

The small attendance made the weekends very expensive, even by bargain Adirondack prices; not only did Flemming Andersen have to pay for those who attended— he was far too scrupulous to attempt to saddle AFC with the bill—but for the Mohawk Inn's weekend expectancy as well. He felt the privacy he purchased was worth it; his only doubts were about the value of the underlying event itself. But tradition was tradition, and he intended to carry this one on at least until protests from the younger generation grew too loud.

(It was also one of Flemming's ways of dealing with his grandchildren. The weekends gave him a chance to get to know them—at least this had been true until the grandchildren had grown into sullen and antisocial teenagers—and he saw it as a means of impressing upon them the existence of a special family, and corporate, ethic that they would be expected to uphold.)

Given AFC's rosy condition, Flemming Andersen should have been in a contented mood as he started the weekend. But he was not. Two recent events intruded into his consciousness as he looked out at the East River from the back seat of his car.

The first had been a scare three weeks earlier when he had had pains in his chest for the first time ever. The pains, which occurred in early afternoon in his office, startled him and sent him scurrying to Michael Odell, his doctor for many years. Odell tried to calm his patient's anxiety, insisting—quite truthfully—that Andersen's cardiogram showed nothing amiss and that he almost certainly was suffering from something no more severe than a slight case of indigestion.

Andersen was reassured—almost. He realized that, at seventy-five, pains or aches—or worse—were inevitable; and, while he had almost literally never been sick a day in his life, he could not deny the existence of occasional but brief spells when he felt weak and below par. This self-knowledge, and the recent heart scare, had made him focus reluctant attention on the question of his succession at AFC. Since the beginning, the Company had always been run by a member of the Andersen family. But now succession by a family member did not seem realistic.

Years before, he had thought that Laurance would be his heir-apparent. After a volatile college career at Yale, during which he was elected editor of the campus humor magazine on one day and threatened with expulsion for gambling the next, Laurance had joined AFC. Despite a collegiate reputation as a playboy that did not diminish as he got older, he took his work at AFC seriously and got a broad experience in every aspect of the Company's business. He was a handsome, athletic man and mostly well liked by those he worked with at AFC.

But Laurance always seemed to be at odds with his father about Company matters, often of the most minor sort. Flemming had been dismissive of his son's ideas, and Laurance had gradually seemed to lose interest in AFC. He was a member of the Board of Directors, but had resigned in the early eighties as one of the Company's two Executive Vice Presidents, a title he had shared with his cousin Billy O'Neal. After his resignation, he had invested heavily in a Colorado ski resort, which in short order had brought him to the brink of personal bankruptcy, from which his father had grudgingly rescued him.

His latest enthusiasm was involvement with a group of young wheeler-dealers in a venture capital partnership based in California—a partnership that Flemming dearly hoped would prove both solvent and successful.

As for his nephew Billy O'Neal, there was no doubt about his desire to take over AFC's management. With justification, he demanded some of the credit for AFC's recent prosperity. As Executive Vice President, he had engineered the Maxwell beer acquisition and his hands-on management had rejuvenated the declining Maxwell brand. One in four Americans still said "Give me a Bud," but now almost one in ten said "Make it Max."

O'Neal's problem, aside from his antipathy to Flemming's branch of the family, was that he was a more than occasional user of his own product—or at least other alcoholic beverages. He was an odd sort of drinker. Most of the time he was fully capable of functioning in his job with both intelligence and genuine Irish charm and wit. But every so often he would disappear on a monumental bender that might last a few days, or a week, or (as had happened at least three times) a month. All of which did not matter too much as long as his responsibilities were limited and he had good assistants. But it was conduct that was simply not suitable, in Flemming's view, for the Chairman of the Board of Andersen Foods.

(Flemming was a realist, not a moralist, in these matters of human failing. While he had grave reservations about his nephew's drinking, he did not think of Billy's tawdry and frequent adulteries as a disqualification. Billy's wife thought otherwise and was now separated from him.)

The only other male that could be considered family was Nathaniel Perkins, the husband of Flemming's daughter Sorella. A failed novelist who bitterly resented anyone else's success, he had never shown any interest in becoming a part of AFC's management, for which his father-in-law had always been grateful.

With the men ruled out, there were, of course, the family women. His wife had always been interested in Company affairs, but this interest had been confined to dinner conversation and pillow talk at home; she had never expressed any desire to participate directly in running AFC.

As for his daughters, Sorella and Diana, Flemming was ambiguous. He was (at least he told himself he was) certain that he was open-minded about the role of women in business. Indeed, he had insisted that Sorella be the head of the family Foundation. This was a not inconsiderable job, given the half-billion dollars in assets the Foundation possessed, and she had handled it both efficiently and graciously.

Diana was quite another matter. She was deeply committed to a highly militant feminist organization called Concerned Women. As a national officer of Concerned Women, she had demonstrated so-called "leadership qualities," but Flemming was not certain that they were of a kind transferable from militant political action to a corporate boardroom. In any event, neither daughter had ever proposed taking an active part in AFC's management—in view of their grandfather's legacy, they had perhaps been afraid to ask—and Flemming had never pressed the issue, though now he thought perhaps he should have.

This brought Flemming Andersen's thoughts to the man sitting beside him in the limousine. Casper Robbins had been recruited by Flemming over much family opposition. The idea of an outsider as President, and very possible heir-apparent, had been alien to the Andersens, either selfishly (in the case of Laurance and Billy O'Neal) or sentimentally (in the case of Sorella and Diana). Only Sally had supported his effort, five years earlier, to transfuse new, outside blood into the AFC body corporate. She actually had known Robbins—the two of them had met playing tennis and had become occasional tennis partners—and had encouraged her husband to hire him after he had been recommended to AFC by an executive search firm.

Robbins had been the second-in-command at a leading communications company, where he had been unexpectedly passed over for the top job just at the time when Andersen was looking for a President. But there was more than timing that drew Andersen and Robbins together. Smooth and articulate, Robbins had nonetheless begun life as a poor boy in the remoter reaches of New Jersey. He had advanced through Williams College waiting on tables. His charm and athletic skill—he was captain of the tennis team—had been sufficient to overcome his deficiencies of background, and he had both the social distinction of membership in St. Anthony's and the academic distinction of graduating with high honors. The Harvard Business School had followed, then an upwardly mobile career at HAG Communications—upward, that is, until he was unceremoniously turned down for the chief executive officer's job.

Flemming Andersen had instinctively liked Robbins. As the scion of inherited wealth, the poor-boy-makes-good image of the younger Robbins both intrigued and appealed to him. Besides, Robbins had talent: a rigorous, tough mind, yet a capacity to conceal the toughness with great charm; an extraordinary articulateness in conveying his thoughts without being cutting or condescending to those he was addressing; a razorlike efficiency, but unaccompanied by the impatience that efficiency often brings along with it.

Robbins had been a good President, carrying out Flemming's orders without complaint, acting with executive authority in those areas in which Flemming was not interested (dealing with AFC's labor relations, for example) and, in general, learning the considerable differences between a communications company, eager to dominate the nation's newsstands, and one dealing in foodstuffs, eager to dominate its grocery shelves.

Flemming Andersen had no reservations about the prospect of turning over control to Robbins; his only regret was that his own family had been unable to serve up an eligible heir. Indeed, as insurance, Flemming (albeit at the insistence of Robbins) had been instrumental a year earlier in constructing a "golden parachute" for the AFC President—a lucrative bundle of payments and fringe benefits that would snap into Robbins's possession if and when AFC were taken over by outsiders and Robbins were fired or demoted. The thought was to show the family's confidence in Robbins, to insulate him from the distraction of any threatened takeover and to put him on an economic and psychological parity with his well-protected colleagues in other corporations.

The idea that anyone could take over AFC had never

really occurred to its Chairman; it was a farfetched pipe dream as far as he was concerned. Or at least had been until ten days earlier when he had met Jeffrey Gruen, the most notorious and perhaps the most ruthless of the corporate raiders still at liberty. Like the pains in his chest, his chance encounter with Gruen had probably been without significance. But . . .

The meeting had taken place at a cocktail party for Dartmouth College fund-raisers that Andersen, as an active and loyal Dartmouth graduate, had attended. Gruen, the father of a Dartmouth underclasswoman, had become as enthusiastic a booster of the college as the most loyal alumnus. (Having gone to work on the floor of the American Stock Exchange after high school in Brooklyn, Gruen had never gone to college himself.) More Catholic than the Pope (or at least more green than any Hanoverian), he circulated at the party as if he were a direct descendant of Daniel Webster.

As Andersen now remembered the encounter, Gruen had come up and introduced himself.

"I'm a great admirer of yours," Gruen had said. "And an even bigger admirer of AFC. It's the greatest food company in the world."

Flemming Andersen recalled thanking him for the compliment.

"Fact is, Mr. Andersen, if I ever want a food company, it would certainly be yours," Gruen had added.

That was all there had been to the conversation. No threat of a raid, not even a veiled hint of one. But still and all, Gruen had certainly been deliberate in seeking out the AFC Chairman at that party. And possibly, just possibly, might have put a playing piece on the starting square of that popular Wall Street game called TAKE-OVER.

Andersen kept telling himself that the twinge of worry he felt was utterly unfounded. At any rate, he was not going to discuss the matter with the tanned, athletic man sitting beside him reading the London *Financial Times*. For reasons the Chairman could not explain, AFC's President had not been a good listener of late and had not paid his customary deferential attention to the Chairman's pronouncements. At the best of times Robbins probably would have found his worries silly, Andersen thought; in light of his recent attitude, he surely would have done so.

Andersen's anxious thoughts—and almost any other kind, for that matter—were banished at the Marine Terminal, where a larger group than he had expected waited to board the AFC plane. Sally had come in from the country not only with Laurance but with Laurance's teenaged daughter, Dorothy. Plus a frisky Rottweiler puppy that seemed attached to Dorothy. Ditsy Robbins and the Frosts also waited in the cheerfully restored central room of the terminal, with the artist James Brooks's splendid *History of Flight* looking down on them.

Flemming greeted all except Reuben and his son with kisses. For Reuben he had a warm handshake.

"Remember when we used to take the old propeller planes from this terminal?" he asked Frost, as they waited to be shown through the gate.

"Of course I do," Frost replied. "Hard to believe, isn't it? Endless trips to California with stops about every hundred miles. And on planes smaller than those private jets outside right now."

"I think that's our pilot over there," Andersen said, pointing to a uniformed figure at the arrival desk. "Yes, he's gesturing to us. Let's scoot."

Andersen gathered the group and its luggage together and they followed the pilot out the exit.

"Reuben, would you sit with me on the way up? There's something I want to run by you," he said, bringing up the rear behind the women, children and dog.

"Of course, Flemming. Something interesting I hope?"

"I hope *not*," Andersen replied.

Once they were airborne, an attendant served drinks aboard the Grumman G-IV, the brand-new and more luxurious of AFC's two aircraft; lunch would wait until their arrival at the Mohawk Inn some fifty minutes later. All of the group except Flemming, Reuben and the dog (whose name turned out to be Winston) sat in facing seats in the middle of the plane. The two men were in adjoining armchairs at the front, far enough away so that they could talk discreetly without their conversation being heard by those behind them. (Winston sprawled benignly in the aisle. His conversation, or more precisely his breathing, could be heard throughout the cabin.)

Frost and his client both had Bloody Marys.

"What's your problem, Flemming?" Frost asked.

"I'm not sure I have one," Andersen responded. "In fact I'm almost certain I don't. But I want to get your opinion."

"Fine."

"I suppose your meter's running for this," Andersen said.

"Why, Flemming, I'm glad you reminded me. I never would have thought to turn it on otherwise," Frost answered, in a slightly acerbic tone.

Frost realized that many of his colleagues would consider an obligatory weekend with a client time for which that client ought to be charged—indeed, perhaps even charged at a premium rate. But Frost was less prone to charge others for his time (especially now that he had so much of it). He was, however, sick of a lifetime of kidding by clients—even as good a one as Flemming Andersen—about hourly rates, meters running, inflated bills and countless other cheap shots carrying the implication that lawyers overcharged as a matter of course.

Seeing a slightly puzzled look on Andersen's face, Frost

realized that his ironic remark had perhaps been mis-
understood.

"No, Flemming, this consultation is on the house,"
Frost said quickly.

His colleague described his encounter with Jeffrey
Gruen. Frost listened noncommittally, then assured Andersen that his fears were almost certainly groundless.

"Flemming, I don't think AFC's a very likely target. I
know you gave Casper his parachute just in case, but the
real reason for that was to show how much you loved him.
No, Gruen and his kind want to raid companies that are
badly run, where the management is vulnerable when
attacked. Whatever your shortcomings, AFC is undeniably
well run.

"And another thing," Frost went on, "these raiders want
operations that they can chop up and sell off in pieces.
AFC's far too integrated for that. I can't believe you have
anything to worry about."

These assurances seemed to cheer Andersen up greatly.
He ordered a second drink and began moving about the
cabin, tousling the head of his granddaughter, flirting
with Cynthia and petting Winston. This last move was a
mistake; once roused, the dog exhibited a strong case of
cabin fever, moving furiously around the confined passenger area and barking loudly. Dorothy Andersen tried
to calm him without success; finally her father shouted
"Sit!" in a commanding voice and Winston returned to his
benign, though loud-breathing, state.

Frost turned his swivel chair around to observe the pre-
weekend festivities. He was glad he had buoyed up Flemming, and hoped he was right. But once the idea was
planted, it would not go away. Maybe Gruen *would* be
interested in AFC. Under Flemming's careful and conservative management, it was certainly cash-rich, and
cash was catnip to raiders like Gruen.

But it was all very unlikely, except that . . . Frost,

with an effort, cut off his own speculation; there was no obvious "except that," and the annual celebratory Andersen weekend, about to begin when the plane landed, was no time to dream one up.

FAMILY GATHERING: I

2 Saturday was a bright, clear day, more remindful of autumn than summer, but hospitable to the athletic activities that accompanied an Andersen outing. With golf and tennis behind them, the participants gathered on the vast green lawn behind the main building of the Mohawk Inn for a late-afternoon bout of water-balloon tag.

The origins of this odd custom were clear—the elder Laurance Andersen had decreed that it was to be a part of the schedule. Why it continued year after year was more obscure; the silly game did not appear to have any ardent devotees. Yet most of the visitors uncomplainingly went through the ritual.

The older guests, like the Frosts, were excused. (Reuben, even as a young man, had treated the tag matches with the contempt he reserved for all athletics. And Cynthia, an active ballerina in those earlier years, had begged off on grounds that the whole thing was too dangerous to her body.) So the tag matches were a contest between the next two generations.

The rules of the game were simple—profoundly so. The contestants divided into two teams. One defended a flag—picturing a bogus Andersen family "crest"—while the other tried to capture it. The players on each side had access to a large supply of water-filled balloons, supplied by the hotel. The object was to tag a member of the opposition with one of the rubber missiles; if the effort was successful, the tagged player had to leave the game. The first team to capture the flag three times was the winner.

The most vigorous player of all, who actually seemed to enjoy the whole exercise, was Randolph Hedley. A lawyer, like Frost, he was a middle-aged trust and estates partner in the sedate and proper New York firm of Slade, Beveridge & Dalton. As the lawyer for the Andersen Foundation, he was a fixture at the annual outing.

Reuben Frost seldom saw Hedley except at the Mohawk Inn. The other lawyer was at least thirty years younger, and they were not social friends. And while he knew Hedley was a good, solid attorney, Frost nonetheless had reservations about him. Hedley was a model of rectitude, there was no question about that. But Frost sometimes felt, to use his old-fashioned phrase, that Randolph Hedley had a screw loose.

How else did one account for the younger man's current behavior? Frost thought, observing the water-balloon struggle from his rough-hewn Adirondack chair. How else did one make allowances for a grown man getting a kick out of tossing balloons filled with water at people?

"Aha! Got you, Dorothy!" Hedley shouted maniacally, as he tagged Laurance Andersen's daughter almost on top of Reuben's chair.

To each his own, Frost concluded. And if Hedley was a comfort to Sorella Andersen Perkins, who had the heavy responsibility of running the Andersen Foundation, let him be.

As if summoned by his thoughts, Sorella Perkins came up beside Frost's chair and sat on the arm.

"Quite a sight, don't you think?" the woman said. "I must say it gives you great confidence in the legendary

New York Bar—look at Randolph Hedley, solicitor to the rich and famous! Look at him!"

Hedley was now chasing Sorella's young daughter.

"Do you think he sees something sexual in this little game, Reuben? Look! He's absolutely crazed, trying to splash young Kate."

"Just a game, Sorella," Frost said calmly. "Randolph plays to win, whether it's Foundation business or balloon tag."

"I suppose you're right," she replied. "But it's a little hard to reconcile this frenzied man with our calm legal adviser at the Foundation."

"Any harder than to realize that the man over there in the Harry Truman shirt is one of the captains of American industry?" Frost asked, pointing across the balloon-tag playing field.

"Oh, Father, you mean? Yes, I can believe it. Appearances are deceiving, after all. Don't you think there are people around who say, 'Does *that* mousy little creature run the Andersen Foundation?' I've been in meetings where I've heard whispers that I'm sure were saying just such things."

"I doubt it, my dear," Frost said. "Or at least, they didn't say it after dealing with you for more than about two-and-a-half consecutive minutes."

Sorella protested modestly, but Frost was right. In outward appearance, Sorella Perkins was an unlikely candidate for running a multimillion-dollar foundation. She was athletically built, like her mother, but was bespectacled and, although she was thirty-eight, freckle-faced. She was reticently shy and was even quite capable of blushing in group conversation.

Yet when Sorella Perkins felt at ease with a person she could kid and speak with the assurance she had just shown in talking with Reuben.

They concluded their conversation as the tag match
broke up—Hedley's team, despite his strenuous exertions,
had lost to the one headed by young Dorothy—and a
sweating, exhausted group shuffled its way toward the
locker rooms in the basement of the main hotel building.

"See you at dinner," Sorella said. "Let's hope none of
our players has overdone."

Saturday dinner was the main social event of the weekend. Unlike the informal Friday night buffet, Saturday's
dinner was black tie, and place cards (prepared and set
out by the AFC staff in accordance with Sally Andersen's
strict instructions) dictated where each person sat.

Reuben Frost, in a white dinner jacket, and Cynthia,
in a fire-engine-red linen dress, mingled with their fellow
guests at the reception preceding dinner. The cocktail
hour was always long and amply catered; a Scandinavian
appreciation for strong drink had not been bred out of the
Andersen genes, though Black Label had long since replaced aquavit as the drink of choice.

Reuben moved easily in the crowd. As a general rule,
he had always tried to avoid social and personal involvement with his clients. Flemming Andersen and his family
had been the exception, with Flemming insisting that the
attorney-client relationship be warmed up. Frost knew all
the family, though the grandchildren had an uncanny
way of changing their shape and size—not to say mode
of dress—from year to year.

By the time dinner was announced he had made the
rounds, drinking two gins-and-tonic in the process. Dinner
was served at a series of round tables for eight. Frost
found himself between Flemming Andersen's younger
daughter, Diana, and Dorothy, the winning water-balloon
captain.

Diana Andersen was not Frost's favorite family member. She was, to put it most charitably, an ugly duckling.

In her mid-thirties and unmarried, she had been known to denigrate loudly both the institution of marriage and men in general. Frost had not himself been treated to such an outburst, but he had heard about them from the woman's father, who had become increasingly disturbed in the last year or two over Diana's militant feminism.

"I'm all for women's rights," he had told Frost just recently. "Didn't I marry one of the original feminists— Sally Bryant, the tennis star? And look at AFC's record, for God's sake. But I find it harder and harder to tolerate Diana's stridency and that Concerned Women's outfit." He was convinced that the "militant loudmouths" in Concerned Women were bleeding his daughter for money.

"You having fun, Mr. Frost?" Diana asked, as Reuben pulled out her chair for her.

"It's passable," Frost said, smiling.

"I'm glad—and you with no family ties to drag you here. Family loyalty's a wonderful thing when it can get the likes of me up here to the mountains. I hate the climate and this creepy inn—and I'm not madly in love with most of my family, either." The woman laughed loudly, pulling a cigarette from the pack she was carrying as she talked to Frost. He instinctively reached for a match, but there were none at hand or in his pocket.

"Never mind, I've got it," Diana said, flicking on a Bic lighter. She was a chain-smoker and always traveled fully equipped.

"They usually don't let you smoke here, you know. Very prudish. But since Daddy rents the whole place, there's not much they can do about it," she went on, laughing again.

During the first course, a new variety of SUPERBOWL mixed vegetable soup, Diana Andersen explained to Reuben that she really came to this August weekend to attend the family business meeting held each year on Sunday morning after church services and breakfast.

"When you're a woman in a big, rich family, you never know anything that's going on," she said. "The boys run the business, of course, and know what's happening. But the women—they're second-class citizens. Seen and not heard—that's what's expected."

"I'm sure that's true in a lot of families," Reuben answered. "But is it true of your father? I've always thought he was fairly open about the Company."

"Oh yes, he's better than most. We have this annual meeting, and he's always willing to answer questions— but don't try to exert any power, or to express any opinions."

"Have you ever pressed him on that?" Frost asked. "Have you ever asked him if you could sit on the AFC Board?"

Diana looked startled, then cross. "Of course not. Why would I? I know what his answer would be. I wouldn't humiliate myself by asking."

Roast beef—good, simple, slightly overcooked roast beef—had arrived, and Diana Andersen turned her attention to it. She had not liked having her set view of her father challenged, and her displeasure showed.

Frost was relieved to be able to turn to Dorothy Andersen on his left, although he had slight trepidation there, too, remembering from an encounter the year before, or perhaps two years before, that the girl spoke in expressionless monosyllables.

But the young woman had changed radically since then. All Reuben had to do was turn in her direction, press an invisible "on" switch, and she was off on a free-form monologue. Frost heard about her summer in Spain, her freshman year at Brown before that and her plans for the coming fall in Providence. The talk was so unremitting that her listener had to urge her to eat.

The girl took two hurried bites of her dinner and then

veered into still a new subject. "Do you like dogs, Mr. Frost?" she asked.

"Mmn. I guess so. Cynthia and I have never owned one, though," he replied.

"They're really wonderful. Do you know . . . Rottweilers?"

Frost was amused. Not at the question but at the sing-song of her voice, which rose on the last word of each sentence—typical teenage inflection, he thought, and a throwback to the lilting speech of her Danish ancestors as well.

"I think I do," Frost said. "Winston—isn't he a Rottweiler?"

"Yes! How do you know Winston?"

"I made his acquaintance on the plane yesterday, if you recall. And I believe I saw him around here today."

"Oh yes. He's here all right. I love Winston. I've been training him since I got back from Spain. You can teach a Rottweiler *anything*."

"That's interesting," Frost said, thinking of the wet, amiable presence that had been at his feet the day before.

"Have you been up to Connecticut?" the girl asked. "It's not only full of Andersens, but dogs as well. Grandma has two poodles, Daddy has his Rottweiler and Aunt Sorella has two Dobermans. I don't like them."

"What's wrong with them?"

"Oh, I don't know, they just seem mean to me," the girl answered.

The discussion of canines was interrupted when Flemming Andersen rose, tapped on his glass and began speaking.

It was time for presenting the sports trophies—an interminable process, Reuben knew. (Cynthia, catching his eye from an adjoining table, rolled her own, being another veteran of past trophy ceremonies.) There were endless prizes for golf and tennis, awarded in most cases to repeat winners such as Sally Andersen and Casper Robbins, who invariably won the doubles competition in tennis. (They were the only really good players in the entire group and had the added advantage of playing together regularly during the year.) Then, finally, there was a trophy for Frost's dinner companion, Dorothy, as the captain of the winning water-balloon team.

"Congratulations," Frost said to her as she returned to her seat after receiving her trophy from her grandfather. It was a statuette of a person tossing a water balloon underhand. (Or so it appeared. On closer inspection, it turned out to be a figure of an ordinary bowler.)

"Not exactly an Oscar, is it?" the girl said, giggling.

Before she was settled in her seat she was up again, heading with the other grandchildren toward the piano, where they would perform another annual ritual, the singing of a satiric song about the Andersens.

As she had done for several years now, one of the Andersen granddaughters, a music major in college, had written the song, a mildly humorous parody of "Ol' Man River" directed to foibles of the family and of AFC. The grandchildren had rehearsed their performance in great secrecy that afternoon and the audience waited eagerly to hear the result.

While the singers were assembling, a waitress came into the room and delivered a whispered message to Flemming Andersen. He got up immediately and walked purposefully toward the door, presumably to take a telephone call.

Since Flemming was the principal target of this year's song, his granddaughter hesitated about continuing when she saw him leave the room. But she decided to go ahead anyway, and the grandchildren began singing.

Flemming Andersen returned during the applause that followed. He had the look of one trying to project a neutral countenance—always a sure sign that something is wrong. Frost soon found out what it was, after Flemming had delivered a few extremely perfunctory remarks to bring the dinner to an end.

Andersen headed straight for Frost's table and all but propelled him out of the room. They ducked around a corner and found privacy in an adjoining hallway.

"I assume you saw that I was called outside a few minutes ago," Flemming said.

"Yes."

"It was Jeffrey Gruen, making a friendly little call. Friendly little call in the middle of Saturday night to tell me that he wants to buy AFC."

"Good God!" Frost exclaimed. "What on earth did he say?"

"He read me a letter he's had delivered to the apartment in New York. It says that he's interested in buying AFC and that he wants to sit down and talk about it—before Tuesday next week, when he says he'll make a tender offer for the Company if he doesn't have an answer from us. He says he'll be filing some goddam form with the Securities and Exchange Commission on Monday . . ."

"A 13D, I believe."

"That sounds right. He's bought eight percent of the Company in the open market already, so he said he had to file this form. He wants to talk on Monday. He says he's thinking of a price of forty dollars a share if everybody cooperates, thirty-eight if they don't."

"What's the stock selling for now?" Reuben asked. "Thirty?"

"Around that, thirty or thirty-one. It was thirty at the close yesterday."

"That's not much of a premium," Reuben said.

"I'll say. And it's not going to get him AFC. There's no way that can happen."

"So you'll fight him?"

"Absolutely. And we need to start right away. You've got all kinds of hired guns at Chase & Ward, don't you? At least that's what I read in the papers. I want the biggest goddam gunner you've got and I want him tomorrow morning."

"That would be Marvin Yates. He knows every in and out of this modern takeover business—unlike old-fashioned types like Ernest Crowder and me."

"Get him up here. I'll send one of the planes for him."

"I'll try to get hold of him," Frost said. "What about Ernest? Shouldn't he be here too? After all, he knows more about the legal side of your business than anybody."

"Of course. See what you can do, Reuben."

After twenty-five minutes of telephoning, Frost reached the two Chase & Ward partners, who reluctantly agreed to take one of the AFC planes Sunday morning. That accomplished, Flemming and Reuben sought out Randolph Hedley to tell him the news. The three decided that there was no need to disturb everyone else's Saturday night and that Flemming could break the news at the next morning's family meeting.

As they went back to join the main group, now reassembled in the hotel bar, Frost turned to Flemming. "You know, these mergers-and-acquisitions types have jargon for everything—even, Marvin Yates tells me, for the little overture you just got."

"Well, what is it?" the Chairman asked.

"It's especially appropriate up here in the Adirondacks," Frost said, chuckling.

"Okay, okay, Reuben, what's the term?"

"Flemming, you just got a great big bear hug."

Sunday Meeting: I

3

The annual Andersen family business meeting took place at eleven o'clock Sunday morning. It was a small assembly, held in a sunny parlor in the main building of the Mohawk Inn. Flemming Andersen presided, as was customary, and his studied, calm demeanor did nothing to hint at the startling turn of events of the night before.

He began the proceedings by calling on Sorella Perkins to talk about the Andersen Foundation. She read a short, businesslike report which informed her audience that the Foundation had made grants of $15 million during the most recent year. In accordance with the Foundation's traditional practice, most of the funds expended had gone for nutrition research and for programs to feed the hungry and homeless.

Her prepared report completed, Sorella, rather hesitantly, asked for questions. Her sister Diana put up her hand at once.

"Sorella, I'd like to know what the Foundation is doing to address the concerns of women," she asked. "I know there are all those nutrition projects you mentioned, but those don't really deal with the issues troubling women today."

Diana then launched into a speech about women's

problems at work; the pay differential between the sexes; the lack of day-care facilities and other problems of the single parent; sexual harassment in the workplace, and on and on down the Concerned Women's agenda.

It was clear that Sorella did not know how to stop her sister's tirade, which was not really an attack on the Andersen Foundation as much as it was a litany of every contemporary female grievance. Sounding a bit like a talking *Statistical Abstract of the United States*, Diana reeled off figure after figure to show the injustices being done to women by American capitalist enterprise.

Her listeners became edgy as she went on without showing any signs of letting up. Finally Casper Robbins, the consummate diplomat, came to Sorella's deliverance.

"Diana, obviously you raise some very important issues here. They are issues that I know interest the Company—my Lord, if the women of this country aren't prosperous, there's very little hope for our business—and I'm sure the Foundation is interested in them, too. Wouldn't you agree, Sorella?"

"Absolutely. The only problem is, the Foundation can't solve all the problems of this country, or even of the women of this country. I think we're better off doing things rather intensively in one area—nutrition and hunger. We've gotten pretty comfortable with those subjects and I think we know how to make a real impact."

"I disagree with that," Diana said emphatically. "We all know the Federal government won't do anything to help women—it's all we can do to keep them from making things worse. So it's up to foundations like ours to provide solutions, to make services available, to . . ."

"Diana, the Foundation is always willing to listen to new ideas," Sorella said quietly. A moment before she had spoken with authority, even eloquence, about the Foundation's work; now, challenging her sister, she appeared much less sure of herself. "If you have any concrete proposals, why don't we sit down and talk about them?"

"You're on, sister, you're on," Diana replied. "And while I'm at it, Mr. Robbins, I'd like to find out a little more than I know now about the situation of women at AFC."

She started repeating her tirade once more, but Robbins again interrupted.

"As I said a few minutes ago, Diana, AFC *must* be attentive to women's issues. Any other course would be downright foolish. I think we're doing a good job at AFC. What we can do, and what we are doing, is making sure that the women who work at AFC are treated fairly. I think we've achieved that. Margaret Holmes, who used to be one of our directors—and not exactly a shrinking violet when it comes to feminist issues—thought so, too . . ."

"Margaret Holmes! Are you kidding?" Diana interrupted. "She's the Uncle Tom of the women's movement! Always saying the correct thing, but always agreeing that management is right. She was just using you as a stepping-stone anyway, going on to bigger and more glamorous boards just as soon as she could. Try again, Mr. Robbins!"

Diana Andersen's tone was more suited to a political meeting of the most confrontational sort. But Robbins refused to be baited.

"I grant you, Diana, no one ever said Margaret Holmes was Mother Teresa . . ."

"Mother Teresa! Don't mention her to me! With her stand against abortion!" Diana sputtered.

"Fine. Leave Mother Teresa and Margaret Holmes out of it," Robbins shot back. "But the reality is that Andersen Foods has a darn good record with respect to women. If you come over to the office in New York some day, I'll show you the facts and figures that prove it. And I'll even buy you lunch. Is that a deal?"

The group laughed, and some applauded. Diana, realizing she was temporarily beaten, did not continue her questioning.

Before Diana could reconsider, Flemming Andersen said that it would next be in order to hear reports about AFC. Following a ritual pattern, he cautioned his listeners at the outset that much of what they would be hearing about the Company was "inside" information not then available to the public. They would be expected to keep it confidential, he said, and could not trade in AFC common stock without seeking the advice of Chase & Ward, as AFC's counsel.

The "inside" information the group heard from Joe Faxton, the AFC Treasurer, was pleasant indeed. Earnings of the Company for the fiscal year then in progress were projected to be up over the prior year by as much as twelve percent, and the long-term outlook seemed very strong.

Making the right obsequies, Faxton attributed the strong projected increases to record sales of SUPERBOWL soup, HEART O' GOLD pet food and Max beer.

Robbins, who spoke next, noted the favorably low commodity prices that were benefiting AFC (except for butterfat prices, which had put pressure on ice cream profits), prices that were expected to remain low because of the bountiful harvests that were projected around the world. He reiterated Faxton's cheerful predictions and expressly mentioned the role of Flemming Andersen in conceiving the soup and pet-food lines, and of Billy O'Neal in developing the beer business.

"If this is what having a family-owned company means, then there are plenty of corporations that could use a little more family," Robbins said, to applause from the group.

"I certainly appreciate the nice things Joe and Casper had to say about SUPERBOWL, HEART O' GOLD—and Max," Flemming Andersen replied, as he got up to speak.

"But with all due modesty, there are some other things that ought to be mentioned.

"First and foremost is our name. 'Andersen' means something to the American consumer. It stands for quality, and people are very much aware that it stands for quality. Now I know some people—perhaps even some in this room—have said that quality is too expensive, that we should be less insistent on using only the finest ingredients in our products, that we should take shortcuts by using more taste-enhancers and preservatives.

"In my considered opinion, that view is shortsighted. The way it is now, our reputation for quality makes introducing a new product much easier—because of our reputation, people will have confidence in it. Now maybe that wouldn't work if we started selling pizzas or chop suey, but it's certainly been true with SUPERBOWL.

"And look what it does to advertising costs. We spend about four percent of sales on advertising. Some of our competitors spend double that. The public knows the Andersen name—we don't have to build a reputation. And the advertising we do can focus on the *new* Andersen products, not the old established ones.

"But you've heard my quality speech before," the Chairman concluded. "So let's go on to any questions you might have for any of us."

Diana Andersen again put up her hand. "With all these profits, when is the dividend going to be raised?" she asked.

"I'll try to answer that, my dear," her father said, from his armchair. "The Company now pays ninety cents a share—roughly one-third of profits. Absent any great demands for cash, which I don't now foresee, I'd expect there would be a modest increase sometime in the next twelve months, possibly to a dollar. But I don't see going above the one-third line. We have to make capital expenditures on our plants and we must spend unsparingly on research and development. All this takes money, and it means we can't be paying out all our earnings to the stockholders."

"But other companies manage to pay out more," Diana pressed.

"Of course they do. Eat, drink and be merry, for tomorrow you may die. And that's exactly what companies that fail to reinvest may do. Die. Die a slow death trying to operate without any innovations. Besides, Diana, I don't quite see what your concern is. At a dollar a share, you'll collect annual dividends of about two point four million. That really ought to be enough to live on, my dear. Unless, of course, you've sold off some more of your stock."

Flemming Andersen's veiled reference was to the fact that Diana had sold a portion of her AFC holdings. She had originally held the roughly 3.2 million shares her father had given her. But citing the needs of Concerned Women and her other causes, she had sold 800,000 shares in the public market over time, freeing up (after taxes) some $15 million for her good works.

Diana's parents had been furious at her disloyalty; it was a firm, if unspoken, Andersen rule that family-owned shares were not to be sold. Laurance and Sorella, unlike their parents, probably would have been tolerant of Diana's sales, except for her high-minded exhortations to them about being too rich and about not caring for the poor and unfortunate (Diana making her own moral superiority in this regard quite clear). As a result, her brother and sister were as displeased with her as Flemming and Sally, and they now quite enjoyed their father's dig.

"Thank you, Father, for your help," Diana said sarcastically. "I think that even little impractical me could have figured out my dividend income—multiply the number of my shares by one dollar, right?—but thanks for doing it for me."

When Flemming Andersen again rose from his chair, his audience assumed that this signaled the end of the proceedings. But instead, he began speaking, his countenance no longer placid but stern and angry.

"After all the good news you've heard this morning, I'm afraid I have some bad news. Or at least disturbing news," he began. Several of his listeners looked at each other, puzzled.

"Last night I received a call from Jeffrey Gruen. Now you all know who he is—the raider, the financial Dracula who takes over corporations and sucks out their lifeblood. Gruen told me that he's bought eight percent of AFC's common stock and he wants to buy the rest.

"The man is a blackmailer, in addition to everything else. If the Company Board of Directors approves a deal with him, he says he will propose forty dollars a share. But if he has to make a hostile tender, the price will be thirty-eight.

"Mr. Gruen asked to meet with me tomorrow morning. I'm going to do that. But I'm also going to tell him that there is no way that he is ever going to take control of AFC, because this family will never sell to him, no matter what his tender price.

"I assume that I have the concurrence of all of you in this—that AFC should oppose Gruen by every honorable means at its disposal. Is there any dissent from that proposition?"

The room was silent and no hands went up. Flemming looked directly at his daughter Diana and his nephew Billy O'Neal—the most likely potential defectors, in his judgment—but they sat impassively.

"Very well. Our esteemed counsel, Reuben Frost, tells me that we have been given what is known in the mergers-and-acquisitions trade as a bear hug. Well, ladies and gentlemen, I can tell you here and now that if it is legally possible to do so, we will extricate ourselves from that hug, whether we tickle the bear under the armpits or do something dirtier and more drastic."

"Who's going to this meeting tomorrow?" Billy O'Neal asked, from the back of the room.

"Whoever wants to," Flemming replied. "If you want to come, that's fine. You or Laurance or anybody else."

"I do," O'Neal said.

"I do, too," Laurance Andersen added.

"All right. I might also tell you that two of Chase & Ward's lawyers are coming up here this morning and will fly back with us this afternoon. Reuben, let's go find out if they're here yet. I'll see the rest of you at lunch."

The family meeting was over. Flemming quietly circulated in the group and approached those he wanted to go back to New York with him on the first flight leaving after lunch. There would be a second flight soon after, so the others would not have to wait long, though Flemming's arrangements would separate husbands and wives (including Reuben and Cynthia).

"Reuben, what do we do about the Board?" Andersen asked, when he had found Frost in the crowd and after asking him to come back on the first flight. "Shouldn't we be setting up a special meeting?"

"Yes, you should," Frost answered. "As soon as you can."

"I'm sure everyone's scattered to the four winds today. So I guess it'll have to be tomorrow. Gruen wants to see me early, if possible. So do you think the Board can wait till afterward?"

"That depends on what you're going to say to him."

"I'm going to tell him to go straight to hell."

"That's what I suspected, from what you just said inside. But I don't think you ought to do that without the Board behind you. If they agree to tell him to go to hell, that's fine, but I don't think you should do it on your own, no matter how strongly you feel as an individual."

A look of impatience appeared on Andersen's face, then as quickly went away. He knew the rules, knew that he was not the sole owner of AFC, but he did not especially like to be reminded of this actuality. He was sure in both heart and mind that he would only act in AFC's best interest and did not need the Board of Directors—or his lawyer—to tell him how to go about it. But this was no time to be autocratic.

"What are you saying, that I should be noncommittal?" Andersen asked.

"Yes. And if that's your approach, the Board meeting can certainly wait until afterward."

"I'm going to try and call them all now. And I'll tell Gruen we'll see him at nine o'clock. Okay with you?"

Frost thought briefly of asking whether Andersen really wanted a superannuated retired lawyer to accompany him. But he thought better of it. After all his years dealing with AFC affairs, why shouldn't he go along? Besides, he had to admit to himself that it might be interesting.

"Fine. While you're calling, I'll see if Yates and Crowder have arrived."

4

Frost found his colleagues from Chase & Ward at the hotel's front desk, where they were inquiring about him.

"There you are," Ernest Crowder said. "We were just trying to find you."

"Where's Flemming?" Marvin Yates demanded of Frost, in his rapid-fire, no-time-for politeness manner; Reuben might as well have been Chase & Ward's greenest legal assistant as far as Yates was concerned.

"Let's review the bidding for a couple of minutes and then I'll introduce you to Mr. Andersen," Frost said pointedly, trying to underscore the reality that Yates had never met the man he referred to with such familiarity. "Let's go out here," he added, leading them outside to a remote corner of the hotel's terrace.

As they went outside, Frost could not help noticing the differences between his two former partners. They were a study in contrasts. Crowder, at forty-three, was roughly the same age as Yates, but appeared to be at least a decade older. Never married and a gravely celibate bachelor, he was dressed in a severe dark suit, complete with white shirt and quiet striped necktie. There were several red spots on his face and balding scalp, indicating that he had been in the sun but that he was not particularly used to it. As he walked outside, he looked around disdainfully at the hotel and its grounds, his narrow, pursed lips sloping downward in disapproval.

Yates, by contrast, was oblivious to his surroundings. All nervous energy, he was interested only in hearing about the problem that had brought him to the Mohawk Inn. In contrast to the fastidious Crowder, he had not shown much interest in his attire: bright green golf slacks, a pink alligator polo shirt and a light blue linen blazer. Frost knew that this apparent lack of sartorial attention was deceptive; when required, he could show extraordinary sensitivity and patient observation, as when he devoted himself to his four young, attractive and intelligent children, one more gifted than the next, or when he participated, as a very good amateur violist, in chamber-music evenings organized by his wife, a pianist of near-professional standing and a graduate of Juilliard. And when it came to professional business, patience and politeness might disappear, but a dedicated, laserlike concentration on the legal problem at hand always remained.

Since Frost was the only one who was up-to-date on developments, Yates and Crowder of necessity had to hear out his recapitulation, though Yates's impatience, as he listened to his former partner, was palpable. Frost reviewed the call from Gruen and the prospect of a Monday morning meeting. He also told his colleagues of Flemming Andersen's repeatedly announced determination to fight Gruen's tender offer, if it came.

"How does the stock break down, Ernest, do you know?" Yates asked his partner Crowder, ignoring Frost.

"Unless things have changed, and there's no reason to think they have, the family has about twenty-six percent and the Foundation another thirteen percent."

"And can Flemming truss up his family?"

"Hard to say," Crowder said. "One daughter has already sold some stock and I'm sure wants to sell more. The others have held on to theirs so far, but I can't say what they'd do if Gruen's money were flashed in front of them."

"What about the Foundation?" Yates asked.

"It's pretty much run by Flemming's daughter Sorella, though I think Randolph Hedley manages to intrude in its affairs pretty heavily."

"You mean that prig from Slade, Beveridge?"

"That's not fair, Marvin," Crowder said. "He's not a prig."

Crowder and Hedley probably go to the same church, Reuben thought as he listened.

"Okay, okay, Ernest. But he's not my idea of a companion for a desert island."

"Sorella's important," Crowder observed, ignoring his partner's dig about Hedley. "She owns four percent outright. And she and her father and Hedley are the trustees of the Foundation. If she votes with her father, the two of them can deliver the Foundation's thirteen percent."

"What does the husband do?" Yates asked.

"He's a failed novelist," Crowder answered, leaving unclear whether he regarded "failed" or "novelist" as the word of greater opprobrium.

"It looks to me as if the family should be in pretty good shape if they put up a united front," Yates concluded.

"Here comes Flemming Andersen now," Frost interrupted. Andersen greeted Frost and Crowder, and was introduced to Yates.

"You're the expert who's going to save us from perdition, is that right?" Flemming asked Yates.

"We're going to try, sir."

"Good. Let's have some lunch and we can talk the whole thing over on the plane, which is leaving at two o'clock."

"Before we do that," Yates said, "have you got your investment bankers on board for this? Hughes & Company, isn't it?"

"That's right. Jack Hilliard," Flemming replied.

"Has anyone called him?" Yates asked, looking pointedly at Frost.

"Not yet," Andersen said.

"Well, you should. They should be analyzing the terms Gruen outlined to you, because you're sure going to want them to tell you whether he's being fair or not."

"I'll do it right now," Andersen said, almost obediently. Frost regretted that he had not thought of this detail himself—Yates's glance had convinced him that he should have. But his lapse had been rectified and no great harm had been done.

The alert AFC staff members had cars at the Mohawk Inn promptly at one forty-five to take the working party to the airport. Reuben Frost, after fleetingly commiserating with his wife, who would have to return on the plane for women and children leaving an hour later, joined the group at the front entrance: Flemming Andersen; Casper Robbins; Randolph Hedley; Crowder and Yates; Laurance Andersen; and Billy O'Neal. Sorella's husband, Nathaniel, and the more junior Company officers, such as Joe Faxton, were not included. Nor were Sorella and her sister.

Whisked off to the airport, the chosen party boarded the waiting G-IV, which took off promptly at the appointed hour of two.

"I'm glad we're going back on this," Yates muttered to whoever was listening as they boarded the plane. "We came up on their Westwind, which is like riding sidecar on a motorcycle. But at least it wasn't a Lear."

Frost didn't know what his former partner was talking about, though he assumed Yates had acquired great expertise about the private aircraft used by corporate America in his M&A travels. He did not like the sound of the Westwind, on which Cynthia would presumably be stuck an hour hence.

Once aboard, the eight passengers sat in two clusters

of four across the aisle from each other. Flemming Andersen began a dialogue with Marvin Yates, who was sitting
on the armrest of a seat with his arms crossed in front of
him. Coat off, he was ready to operate. The others paid
rapt attention and only occasionally interrupted.

"Mr. Yates, I assume Reuben has told you about our
bear hug, as I believe it's called."

"Yeah, he has."

"So what can we do to stop Mr. Gruen?"

"Before I get into that, I think there are a couple of
things I ought to review for you. They may be obvious,
but it doesn't do any harm to go over them," Yates began.
There was a sense that he was starting a speech he had
given to troubled executives before—which was true—but
his hearers didn't care; his sermon could be hackneyed as
long as it promised deliverance.

"Let's assume Gruen offers to buy AFC at a price well
above market—thirty-eight, forty, you name it. Can the
Company—that is, the Board of Directors of the Company—fight the tender? Not necessarily. You must not
forget, my friends, that directors have a duty to act in
the best interests of the Company *and* its shareholders. If
they reasonably believe they are so acting, they should be
protected from stockholder lawsuits. That's the so-called
'Business Judgment Rule,' which protects directors if they
act responsibly and reasonably. Incidentally, where is
AFC incorporated? Did I read Minnesota?"

"That's right," Flemming said. "My grandfather set the
company up there and nobody's ever seen any reason to
change."

"Good," Yates said. "You won't be stuck with all the
complications about business judgment that have occurred in Delaware. But let's get back to reasonableness,
and what it is. Opposing an offer just because it would
unseat existing management is not reasonable behavior.

But if there are other factors to consider, then you may have a basis for opposition—a *reasonable* basis for opposition. For example, would the raider endanger the Company's effectiveness or seriously alter its corporate policies? Would he be interested in breaking up an entity that has had a proven track record operating as an integrated whole?

"From what I've heard about AFC over the years from Ernest, and what I read last night and on the plane this morning, it seems to me the Company's unique—an efficient, smooth-running, integrated operation with a classy reputation. That's something worth protecting, and Jeff Gruen isn't exactly known for keeping companies in one piece, or enhancing their reputations, once he takes them over."

"Mr. Yates, why on earth does Jeffrey Gruen want AFC?" Casper Robbins interjected. "Any theories?"

"Sure. Gruen's got a big reputation. He's made himself a billionaire in the takeover game, at least on paper. He's bought corporations cheap and sold off the pieces for big prices. In some other situations he's taken positions in companies, scaring the bejesus out of their managements, and then accepted an inflated price to go away. Otherwise known as greenmail.

"Then there've been the leveraged buyouts—LBOs— like United Dresses. He and the management of UD borrowed the money to buy out the public stockholders. Then he and his newfound buddies in the UD management held the stock for a little less than two years, when they unloaded it on the public once again—at a much higher price, needless to say.

"Whatever the game, Gruen's been right there, becoming a paper billionaire in the process," Yates continued. "And he's made a whole stable of investors rich, too. Including almost certainly some silent partners."

"Is that true, Marvin, silent partners?" Crowder asked.

"That's the rumor."

"Who are they?"

"Depends who you talk to. Arab sheiks. Texans bailing out of the oil and gas business. South American dope dealers. The Rockefellers. Who knows?"

"I don't understand," Randolph Hedley declared. "Surely Gruen has to disclose the sources of his funds in his SEC filings?"

"He's supposed to, Randolph," Yates answered, a touch of condescension in his voice. "But if no one can prove he has silent partners, how can he be made to name them? Rumors over breakfast at the Regency are one thing, proving the facts quite another."

"You still haven't answered my question," Robbins pressed. "What does he want with us?"

"Sorry, I got sidetracked," Yates said. "My guess is that Gruen's under pressure to perform from his investment partners. Don't forget he hasn't been doing so well the last few months: Gene-Some, his genetic-engineering company, is practically bust. The movie company he bought hasn't had a hit since he took over. And he lost his fight for that supermarket outfit—Foodstops—to the Canadians. He needs a win, and the more prestigious the better."

"But what would he get, except an outstanding corporation with good, solid earnings growth?" Robbins said. "That can't be very sexy in his terms."

"Yes, but if you look at the short run and not the long run, there's plenty he can do if he's greedy," Yates answered. "I was looking at your annual report last night and tried to put myself in Gruen's place. What did I see? A fair amount of cash to play around with. Lots of expensive luxuries that can be cut, such as your research and development expenses. Maybe a sale of the beer company, now that it's doing so well."

"That's ridiculous," Billy O'Neal, the beer business's patron, grumbled. No one paid attention.

"So we've got to think Mr. Gruen is serious," Flemming Andersen said. "How do we stop him?"

"Before you get to that, Flemming, the Board has got to decide that Gruen's offer is unfair and inadequate. Only if they do that can you think about defenses."

"I have no doubt the Board will do the right thing on that score," Andersen snapped.

"Okay, then we can consider defenses. There are certain things that probably won't work here—assuming, as I said earlier, that your Board wants to fight. A crown-jewel defense, for example."

Yates motioned to the male cabin attendant and asked for a glass of ginger ale. While he paused to drink deeply from the glass he was given, those around him, less versed in mergers-and-acquisitions argot, tried to parse out what he meant. Frost, sensing the puzzlement—and not being entirely sure himself what Yates was talking about—was bold enough to seek clarification. "Marvin, could you explain that a little further?" Frost asked.

Yates shot an impatient, disapproving look at Frost, but he answered calmly. "Of course, Reuben. No problem. A crown-jewel defense means you sell off a part of your business—preferably the part that a raider wants—so you become a less attractive takeover target. It won't work for AFC because all its businesses are related. There's no obvious, discrete asset you could sell—except possibly the brewing operation, as I said before."

"Mr. Yates, we're not interested in selling *any* of our business," Flemming said icily. "And we're not interested in making the Company less attractive—to Jeffrey Gruen or to ourselves."

"I understand, sir," Yates answered calmly. "That's why I said a crown-jewel defense wouldn't work for you. It probably rules out a poison pill as well."

"Marvin, can you elaborate on that?" Crowder asked. "I'm afraid not everybody is as familiar with acquisition lingo as you are."

Frost was glad he had been spared interrupting Yates's narrative a second time; Crowder had done the dirty work and Yates seemed not to resent it.

"Put very simply," Yates began, "a poison pill is a right given to stockholders to purchase additional shares at a bargain price if certain events happen—like someone buying, say, thirty percent of a company's stock. It's a way of guaranteeing that somebody taking over a company has to pay a fair price."

"Mr. Yates, let me repeat again, we don't want anyone taking over AFC, at any price," Flemming Andersen said.

"I appreciate that," Yates answered. "Given your attitude, Flemming, you're probably not interested in finding a White Knight, either. Though that presents interesting possibilities. I know, for example, of at least three companies that would like to diversify into the food business. Including, or so I'm told on good authority, General Motors."

"Good Christ, Mr. Yates," Flemming Andersen interjected, his temper all but out of control and his face red. "Are you suggesting I should let AFC fall into the hands of those idiots in Detroit? So they can do for me what they did for Ross Perot? They can scarcely bang out cars, let alone run a business they know *nothing* about."

"I agree that GM is a farfetched idea," Yates said. "But there are others, I know, who could be induced to acquire AFC on favorable terms."

"This discussion is getting nowhere," the Chairman said, still quite obviously angry. "I have yet to hear a suggestion, Mr. Yates, that makes any sense whatsoever. Such as some kind of counteroffer to our shareholders. Isn't there something we could do along those lines?"

"I was just getting to that," Yates said, unfazed by

Andersen's anger. "AFC could make an offer to purchase its own stock at a price above what Gruen is willing to pay. Of course, we don't know what that price is, so we don't know how expensive a tender would be. If he's talking forty a share now, he's probably willing to go to forty-five, or even fifty."

"That means the Company would have to go into hock pretty badly to pay for it, doesn't it?" Robbins asked.

"Absolutely," Yates said. "Unless the Andersen family wants to form a group and raise the money on its own. But we're talking big dollars—three billion perhaps."

"I don't like it. Don't like it at all," Flemming said. "We've always operated pretty much independent of the banks. Sure, we've borrowed money, but it's always been on easy terms that we could live with. If we hock everything, the banks will stick us with all kinds of covenants and restrictions. We'd be running to them to get permission to go to the can."

"That's undoubtedly the case," Yates said. "It would really be a question of who you'd rather sell your soul to—Gruen or the banks."

"You mention three billion," Robbins said. "Making some quick calculations here, that assumes that all the stock would be tendered. But that isn't so. I'm sure the family shares wouldn't be tendered, and I'm almost as sure the Foundation and the management shares wouldn't be either. That's well over forty percent right there."

"How does the ownership break down exactly?" Yates asked. "I haven't quite been able to figure it out."

"It's very easy," Flemming said. "My children and my wife and I own seventeen point three percent—six point three percent by Sally and me, four percent each by Laurance here and my daughter Sorella. And three percent by my daughter Diana. She owns less because she sold a quarter of the stock she originally had."

Flemming paused as he revealed this distasteful fact.

Frost, meanwhile, had taken out a pocket notebook and was writing the figures down for future reference.

"Billy O'Neal here owns another eight point sixty-six percent. Or do you and your wife own it jointly, Billy?"

"Jointly," O'Neal replied brusquely, his irritation presumably caused not so much by mention of his estranged wife but the surfacing in the Chairman's figures of the inequitable division of ownership between Flemming's branch of the family and the one his father had married into.

"Then the Foundation, which my daughter runs, owns thirteen percent," Flemming went on. "And management, thanks to our exceedingly generous stock-option plans, owns roughly eight." Andersen looked at Robbins—albeit with a trace of a smile—when he referred to the "exceedingly generous" stock-option plans.

Frost silently toted up the figures he had written in his notebook, realizing that forty-seven percent of the stock was accounted for in what were presumably safe hands:

Flemming & W	6.33%
Laurance	4.0%
Sorella	4.0%
Diana	3.0%
Foundation	13.0%
Billy O'N. & W	8.66%
Management	8.0% (+ or −)
	———
	47.0%

"Can we keep all those holders in line?" Yates asked.

"I would certainly hope so," Andersen replied. "Of course, we have no legal right to stop any of them from tendering, but I'd be amazed if they did. Certainly that's true of the family, the Foundation and at least top management."

"Flemming, I'm afraid I have to say something about

that," Randolph Hedley interrupted, leaning forward from his window seat to be closer to the group. "As far as the Foundation is concerned, it can't just do what the family thinks best. Its trustees are going to have to evaluate any proposal that comes their way—including Jeffrey Gruen's—to see what's in the best interest of the Foundation. The trustees have a fiduciary duty to do all they can, consistent with prudence, to maximize the assets of the Foundation. That might well mean they couldn't turn down the highest offer being made to them, whether by the Company or by Gruen."

The group fell silent after Hedley had made his observation. Frost, with his pen and notebook, quickly calculated that buying out the Foundation shares, assuming a forty-five-dollar price, would cost almost a half-billion dollars.

"Are you saying, Randolph, that the Foundation would *have* to sell?" Flemming asked.

"No, I'm not saying that. I'm just alerting you that my legal advice may be that the Foundation should sell. But that will depend on all the facts, and we don't have those today."

"Let's hope we can find a way around your problem," Flemming said. "What about Gruen? Do we have to buy his stock in AFC, too?"

"I'm afraid so," Yates said. "Unocal got away with excluding Boone Pickens when he tried to take it over. But the SEC now says you can't discriminate against the raider."

With this unhappy news, the group became silent as the pilot signaled from the cockpit that he was about to land in New York. As the eight men buckled up, Flemming Andersen asked Yates how he thought they should approach the meeting with Gruen the next morning.

"I think you'll do better with a small group," Yates said.

"Such as?" Flemming asked.

"Well, on the business side, yourself of course. And you, Mr. Robbins?"

"Yes, I want Casper there," Flemming said. "And Laurance and Billy have expressed a desire to attend. Isn't that right?"

The two men nodded.

"Is he having lawyers there?" Yates asked.

"He said he was."

"Then I guess I should go. And Ernest as well—he knows much more about the Company than I do. On the other hand, I would think, Randolph, as the Foundation's lawyer, that you wouldn't need to attend at this juncture."

"I agree," Hedley said.

As they landed, Frost realized that he was the only passenger not accounted for, which made him painfully aware of his retired, out-of-the-fray status. Fortunately Flemming Andersen sensed this, and repeated his desire, expressed earlier in the day, that Reuben be present also.

Reuben was grateful for the reiterated invitation, and said as much as he and his elderly contemporary walked to the entrance of the Marine Terminal.

"We can't leave everything to the young ones," Andersen said. "This is going to be a real fight, Reuben, and we're going to need every brain cell we can get on our side. I mean business about fighting this damnable upstart. As far as I'm concerned, Jeffrey Gruen will take over Andersen Foods only over my dead body."

WAITING

5 There was a general rush for transportation at the Marine Terminal after the AFC plane landed. Four separate AFC limousines met Flemming and Laurance Andersen, Casper Robbins and Billy O'Neal.

Frost declined a ride with each of the executives—Flemming Andersen was going to Connecticut, Robbins to Westchester, O'Neal to Long Island. Only Laurance Andersen was traveling to an undisclosed destination in Manhattan, but he did not seem eager for company. Frost's two erstwhile partners, Crowder and Yates, were off to the firm's office, downtown at One Metropolitan Plaza, bent on sharpening the AFC antitakeover strategy, and Randolph Hedley was headed for his apartment near Gramercy Park.

The result was that Frost did not share a cab into Manhattan with anyone. This suited him perfectly. It was not that he disliked being sociable—quite the contrary, he was by nature outgoing and extroverted. But, nonetheless, at seventy-five, being "on" for an entire weekend, being in the observing eye of those who were younger and more alert, had been tiring.

Riding in the cab alone, Frost thought sympathetically of Cynthia, stranded with Nate Perkins, Diana, Sorella and assorted wives and children. She would not be happy when she returned to East Seventieth Street; indeed, she might well be furious. Frost went through his mental index of New York restaurants open on Sunday where he could take his wife and attempt to make peace.

Having settled on Vico's, which was a new favorite of the Frosts and which was usually relatively calm on Sunday night, he tried to repress his quiet but very real anger at Yates for consciously or unconsciously humiliating him on the plane trip that had just ended. He thought bitterly of Yates's advice to his new intimate "Flemming"—"You'll do better in a small group." Sound advice, perhaps, but its only real effect would have been to exclude Frost from breaking developments.

Had Yates done this deliberately? Had his younger colleague really wanted to exclude him from the handling of the greatest crisis Andersen Foods had had in the fifty-odd years it had been represented by Chase & Ward? Or had he merely been thoughtless? Reflecting as his taxi crossed the Triborough Bridge, Frost concluded that Yates, in the heat of strategic planning, had not considered Frost's feelings; but he couldn't entirely rule out the possibility that Yates wanted to run his own show and didn't want Frost casting the long shadow of history and tradition over his actions.

Hurt as he was—even after almost persuading himself that there was no cause for hurt—he had to admit, however grudgingly, that both Yates and Crowder, but more especially Yates, had handled themselves well. Neither of the younger Chase & Ward lawyers was a particular favorite of Frost, nor a friend socially. In the old days, when Frost had joined Chase & Ward, it was inconceivable that any individual would have become a partner in the firm without having had some minimal professional exposure to all—or at least almost all—its members. With the firm's growth—standing currently at thirty-nine partners and one hundred twenty associates—such personal vet-ting was no longer possible; one had to rely on the judgments of one's colleagues.

Crowder and Yates had both come highly recommended by the firm's partners with whom they had worked most closely. These assessments, correctly, were made as to professional competence and, to a certain minimal extent, as to whether the lawyers in question could function in dealing with clients. But they were in no sense appraisals of Crowder and Yates as whole men.

But did that matter? If it did, Frost mused, then there would be no legal profession—and no other profession as far as that goes. Whole men were in very short supply; finding those competent in their chosen field was quite hard enough without expecting much in the way of extraneous intellectual or social charms.

Frost might have his grievances against Yates. But look what he had done: interrupted his personal life on the last weekend before Labor Day to gather and immerse himself in every available detail about Andersen Foods and, at Flemming Andersen's beckoning, to fly around New York State giving legal advice as he went. Some would have called Yates a workaholic with a warped sense of priorities. But if corporate raiders were going to make surprise announcements on Saturday night, knowledgeable lawyers like Yates had to be ready to deal with the consequences early Sunday morning.

Then there was Crowder. Often unable to contain his disapproval of the perfidies he saw about him. Given to stentorian and apocalyptic pronouncements. But the possessor of a first-rate mind, capable of penetrating the toughest legal thicket, of tackling the hardest legal problem. And obnoxious in an entirely different way from Yates, Frost thought with some amusement.

No, if clients wanted sweet pears without prickles they could go to the personality boys within the profession, those more skilled at dispensing charm than sound advice. God knows there were plenty of them. But if the premium was on the quality of advice given, the Flemming Andersens of this world would have to endure the eccentricities of the likes of Marvin Yates and Ernest Crowder. Or so Reuben Frost argued with himself, as he silently excused away Yates's injudicious reference on the plane to the "canned crap" produced by AFC and Crowder's gravely intoned statement, to his startled hearers, that "corporate raiders will end the American free enterprise system as we know it."

Frost's mind was at ease over his confreres' utterances when he arrived at East Seventieth Street. Even before he had unpacked his suitcase, he received calls confirming the appointment the next morning with Gruen and the AFC Board meeting. It would be a busy day, and probably a busy week. He and his wife should enjoy their Sunday-night dinner with this schedule in mind.

Frost skimmed through the Sunday *Times* as he waited for his wife, who did not arrive until a good three hours after her husband. Cynthia had been the victim of the great New York one-two transportation punch: air-traffic delays into the airport, immediately followed by road tie-ups into Manhattan. She was tired and slightly cross, but brightened at Reuben's suggestion of an early supper at Vico's.

At the Second Avenue restaurant, the Frosts were greeted effusively by the two owners, Gennaro and Nino, and the two Capri émigrés who were the waiters, Cesare and Enzo. The restaurant was tiny and, when full, as it almost always was, a trifle noisy, but what it lacked in comfort was compensated for by the easy affability of the staff and the extraordinarily high quality of its food (two estimable virtues, Frost noted, that many of the fancier dining spots about New York could well copy).

"How was *your* trip?" Cynthia asked, after she and

Reuben were seated. "I'm afraid I was so busy complaining about my own I never did ask."

"You were on the Westwind, I believe," Reuben said, ignoring her question and eager to show off his recently acquired knowledge about private aircraft.

"What's that?"

"The airplane. A Westwind. Very old-fashioned, cramped and uncomfortable, I'm told," Frost said.

"By whom?"

"Marvin Yates."

"I see. Well, you can tell Marvin he was absolutely right."

"But you were better off than being aboard a Lear."

"And what's that?"

"I haven't the faintest idea. But people like Marvin who ride around in these things all the time say it's even worse than a Westwind."

"I see."

"My trip was fine, to reply to your original question," Frost said. "Marvin read the group the riot act and I think they're ready to confront Gruen tomorrow."

"They're meeting with him?"

"Yes, first thing in the morning."

"Does that include you?"

"Afraid so," Reuben answered simply, seeing no need to elaborate or to inform his wife that he was going along only as the result of Flemming's intervention.

Reuben ordered a bottle of the Amarone from the middle range of Vico's reasonably priced wine list, and both he and Cynthia ordered the *Caprese rustica* and the *linguine vongole,* a very superior pasta with white clam sauce. Cesare, the waiter, and the two owners expressed pleasure at their selection.

"Even leaving the delays aside," Reuben said, ordering completed, "I gather your flight was not exactly the best one you ever had."

"Indeed not," Cynthia answered. "Remember *Rosencrantz and Guildenstern Are Dead?* The Tom Stoppard play? That's the way everyone felt on the plane I was on—minor characters excluded from the main drama. Both Diana and Sorella were seething—Diana could barely contain her remarks about male chauvinism, and Sorella certainly felt that she, rather than Randolph Hedley, should be representing the Foundation at Flemming's little summit."

"They—or Sorella at least—were probably right," Frost said.

"Nate Perkins was annoyed, too," Cynthia went on. "I don't think he gave a damn about what was going on on your flight, but he certainly felt hurt and excluded. He was sitting across the aisle from me and was grousing, or verbally pouting, or whatever you might want to call it, most of the way back."

"He really is a hothouse flower, isn't he?" Reuben said. "If he were ever put in charge of anything at AFC, he'd collapse in an instant. Or for that matter, he'd dissolve if his publisher ever put him on a deadline. But I know that doesn't stop his resentment and general huffiness."

The couple, hours away from a rather skimpy lunch at the Mohawk Inn, quickly devoured their *Caprese rustica*—mozzarella, tomatoes, salami and all.

"I did learn one very interesting thing," Cynthia said.

"Which was?" Reuben asked.

"Did you hear anything about the TV advertisement Flemming is going to make?" Cynthia asked.

"Good Lord, no," Frost replied. "What are you talking about?"

"Apparently Vickery & Carpenter, the advertising agency for AFC, has talked Flemming into doing a commercial for SUPERBOWL."

"I don't believe it."

"As I get the story, Flemming's going to come on, look at the viewers straight on and tell them how wonderful and pure SUPERBOWL soups are. You know, just like Lee Iacocca and Chrysler or that funny chicken plucker, Frank Perdue."

"Who told you this?" Frost demanded.

"Sally," Cynthia answered. "I was sitting next to her on the flight down. She's beside herself. You know how she is about privacy—as far as she's concerned, notoriety and publicity ended the day she quit professional tennis. She's sure Flemming will make a fool of himself. 'You just know what will happen,' she said to me. 'We'll go to the theater some night, minding our own business, when the entire Morristown, New Jersey, Ladies' Club will do one collective swoon and demand to know if Flemming's the soup salesman they've seen on TV.' She's really upset, Reuben, but there's nothing she can do—Flemming believes in advertising and he's going to follow the Vickery advice."

Frost chuckled as his wife described Sally's distress—and his old friend Flemming's apparently new senescent vanity.

"She never said it," Cynthia went on, "but she certainly implied that Flemming should be getting out of AFC. More than implied, in fact. She said she wished there was some way for him to retire gracefully."

"Who would she have replace him? Billy O'Neal?" Frost asked.

"She didn't say, but she certainly had kind words for Casper Robbins. He's obviously a very close friend."

"Close friend? Do you think that's all?"

"I've never been sure. I suppose I think he's her tennis partner and chum, and that's it. But God knows there've been enough rumors about the two of them over the years," Cynthia said.

"Very interesting," Reuben said, by now at work on his linguine. "Maybe Jeffrey Gruen will solve her problem."

"I seriously doubt that," his wife answered. "Sally said Flemming's apoplectic on the subject of Gruen."

"I'm sure," Reuben said, with a sigh. "All of which means we should get home. Tomorrow's going to be some kind of day."

While they were waiting for the check, Reuben looked around the narrow confines of the restaurant.

"What do you suppose was here before, Cynthia, a shoe store?" Reuben asked.

"I don't remember, but it certainly is possible," his wife replied.

"I must say it reminds me of the first apartment we ever had," Reuben said. "That railroad flat in the tenement down on Nineteenth Street."

"You're right, dear. The kitchen would have been right back there, with the bathroom behind it," Cynthia said, pointing to the rear of the restaurant.

"And as I figure it, Cynthia, our table is approximately where our bed was," Reuben added.

"Nothing wrong with that, my dear."

"No indeed. No indeed." Reuben grasped his wife's wrist with affection, then picked up the check Gennaro had put on the table. He paid the check—both Gennaro and his partner Nino knew the Frosts well enough not to protest the omission of dessert or coffee—and the Frosts left, after shaking hands all around.

"There's no justice in the world," Frost said, as he walked home with his wife. "Look at those fellows, running an absolutely impeccable restaurant and making a good, but not huge, amount of money. Then look at Jeffrey Gruen, who's become a billionaire by wheeling and dealing, shuffling papers. Making one batch of *linguine vongole* in that restaurant is a bigger contribution to society than any corporate stew Gruen ever cooked up."

"Why don't you tell him that tomorrow, dear?" Cynthia teased her husband.

"For two cents I would," Frost said. "But Flemming and his crew can hold their own."

Monday Meeting

Reuben Frost slept fitfully and was fully awake when he got out of bed at seven o'clock Monday morning. He had scarcely had time to retrieve the newspaper from the front door when the telephone rang and he found himself talking with George Bannard. Bannard, who now held the post Frost had once occupied, as Executive Partner of Chase & Ward, was not one of Reuben's favorites. He found him bumptious and often ill-mannered—and it had always seemed to Frost that Bannard had perhaps tried to hasten his retirement as an active partner of the firm.

"Reuben, what's this I hear about a takeover of AFC?" Bannard demanded. Frost was startled at the question. Yates or Crowder must have felt some reason to call Bannard over the weekend and tell him the news. But why?

"It's very possible," Frost answered. "But I'm sure the Company will fight it. It's Jeffrey Gruen, you know."

"Yes, yes. Marvin Yates called me last night," Bannard said. Then, after a pause, he asked Frost if he were "going to be involved."

"To some degree, I expect. Flemming asked me to go to the meetings today."

"Fine, Reuben, fine. But just remember, Reuben, you're

an old croak like me—you don't know a goddam thing about this takeover stuff."

"Yes, but I have a modicum of common sense and have worked out tough corporate problems for half a century," Frost felt like answering, but did not.

"Of course, George," he said instead. "As far as I'm concerned it's Marvin's show and I'm just there to help out if and when I can."

"Good, Reuben. I knew that's what you'd say. Good luck." Bannard hung up the telephone without saying good-bye.

So Yates had put him up to that call, Frost thought. Well, the hell with both of them. Of course he wasn't going to run the show any more than his successor as AFC's counsel, Ernest Crowder, was. Yates was the expert, there was no doubt about that. Frost, and Crowder, too, would only speak when spoken to—unless, of course, they felt that circumstances dictated otherwise. Surely there was a First Amendment right of free speech for Chase & Ward partners (and retired partners) that even George Bannard could not abrogate. In any event, Frost had forgotten the Executive Partner's call within seconds of opening up the *Times.*

Reuben Frost actually knew the notorious Jeffrey Gruen. Or more precisely, he had met him several times at meetings of the Board of Directors of the National Ballet, of which Frost was chairman. Gruen was a modest, even retiring, figure at these sessions, conscious perhaps that he had been selected for the Board more for his potential as a donor to NatBallet than as an adviser on artistic matters. (In reality, he should not have been in the least self-conscious; most of his fellow directors had been picked for precisely the same reason.)

There had been nothing in Gruen's outward demeanor

that had evidenced his reputation for both gall and greed. Frost had found him perfectly pleasant, and cooperative in performing the few modest tasks he had been given as a director. All Frost really knew about Gruen he had learned from the public print, though, God knows, there had been plenty to read about, starting with his Horatio Alger rise from being a runner on the floor of the American Stock Exchange to a succession of jobs, none held for very long, at well-known Wall Street houses and then at his own venture-capital firm, started in the mid-1970s.

Gruen had shown savvy in making seed-money investments in small computer companies that tried to fill the interstices of the marketplace not occupied by IBM; the transition from venture capitalist to raider had been easy. His own fortune, and the financial backing of his grateful investing partners, had given him an equity base from which to acquire ever-larger companies.

Marvin Yates had been right in assessing Gruen's current position—that he "needed a win" to reverse a series of unexpected setbacks in his recent corporate forays. But there was no evidence of this as he greeted the delegation from AFC on Monday morning. The group had assembled one by one in the spacious waiting room of the offices of Gruen & Company at 324 Park Avenue: Reuben Frost, Marvin Yates and Ernest Crowder from Chase & Ward, and Flemming and Laurance Andersen, Billy O'Neal and Casper Robbins from the Company. Promptly at nine, they were shown to a spacious, mahogany-paneled conference room, where Gruen stood at the door and shook hands with each of them. Arrayed along one side of the long table in the room were five others, only one of whom Frost had met before—Jason Stockmeyer, the senior partner of Stockmeyer, Browne & Pernis, Gruen's legal counsel. And the greatest expert in New York, at least in point of service, on the legal aspects of mergers and acquisitions; Stockmeyer had been willing to represent clients interested in making unfriendly acquisition proposals when such representation "wasn't done" by the more established and respectable Wall Street law firms and was treated as being in much the same class as ambulance chasing. Time, and the attraction of the splendid fees involved, had changed all that—even Ernest Crowder no longer turned up his patrician nose when "M&A" was mentioned—but Stockmeyer still gained some advantage from the length of his experience. (In addition to which, he was an intelligent and imaginative lawyer and a decent and pleasant person.)

Stockmeyer greeted Frost warmly and introduced him to three colleagues, two male partners and a young woman associate. The fifth person waiting in the room turned out to be Jeffrey Gruen's young assistant, Norman Cobb.

The AFC forces lined up on the side opposite their Gruen counterparts, with Flemming Andersen, flanked by Casper Robbins and Marvin Yates, sitting in the center.

While the assemblage was getting organized, a uniformed butler, working from a large table at one end of the room, served juice, pastries and coffee to those desiring them. Reuben Frost, accepting a Danish and coffee, contrasted Gruen's amenities with those at Chase & Ward. One attending a meeting at the law firm was lucky to get a cup of weak, lukewarm coffee in a serve-yourself Styrofoam cup. Solid food in the morning consisted of cold, leaden pastries wrapped in transparent plastic. By comparison, here at Gruen & Company the pastries were warm and served on china plates, and the fresh coffee was dispensed in china cups with saucers. Ah well, Frost consoled himself, Chase & Ward was in the business of providing legal services, not catered meals.

Jeffrey Gruen sat down directly across from Flemming Andersen. Without a word, the butler brought him a cup of tea, and Cobb placed a single typewritten page in front of him on the table.

Frost could not help noticing how impeccably neat the man was. Not a hair was out of place on his trimly barbered head; his manicured fingernails were immaculate; his expensively tailored suit was well pressed. It was almost as if he had been unpacked from a hermetically sealed tube just before entering the conference room. The only imperfection was the reddish-brown tint of his hair, which was almost certainly from a bottle or a jar.

Gruen introduced those on his side of the table and asked Flemming Andersen to do the same. Then, in an outwardly affable manner, he thanked the AFC delegation for being present.

"I realize this is probably most inconvenient for many of you, coming here on a Monday morning at the end of the summer," Gruen began, speaking slowly and deliberately in an accentless voice. "But I thought it was important that you know where I stand.

"As I told Mr. Andersen Saturday evening, Gruen & Company is interested in buying Andersen Foods—either in a friendly, negotiated deal or, if necessary, through a tender offer. My colleagues and I have been looking at the Company for some time, and we like what we see. . . ."

"Can I interrupt right there?" Flemming Andersen said, in a strident voice.

"If you like," Gruen answered evenly. "I had thought I would make my statement and then give you an opportunity to reply. But go ahead, please."

"I just wanted to say right up front that no one is interested in selling AFC," Andersen said, ignoring the agreed legal advice from the weekend that he would hear Gruen out but remain noncommittal.

"That may be, Mr. Andersen, but I'm interested in buying," Gruen shot back. "And, if I may, perhaps I can tell you why.

"When we first started looking at AFC, we were impressed with how well run it is, how good your employee relations are, yet how trim you are operationally. The more we saw, the more AFC appealed to us as a good, solid investment. We firmed up our plans last week, and I was able to tell Mr. Andersen of the terms we're thinking about last Saturday." He made it sound as if it were the most natural thing in the world to call an executive on a Saturday night and inform him that his corporation was about to be raided.

"I'm sure you all know what those terms are. But to repeat: we are thinking of offering forty dollars for each and every share of AFC common—if the offer is friendly and endorsed by the Board. That's obviously what we would prefer. But if you don't want to be friendly, that's all right, too. Only the price will be thirty-eight dollars."

"What do you see as your timing, Jeffrey?" Marvin Yates asked.

"We've got the financing. We're ready to go. We plan to file our 13D, showing our existing holdings, with the SEC this afternoon. We can be ready to file a 14D, with the exact terms of the offer, very soon thereafter," Gruen said. "Like, for example, tomorrow after the close of the market."

"Can I ask another question?" Yates said.

"Sure."

"I'm a little puzzled here," Yates said. "Flemming Andersen has indicated there's no interest in selling. Now obviously he can't speak for the public holders, but he can certainly speak for a pretty fair number of the private ones—about forty-seven percent, to be exact. I'm sure you know that figure, Jeffrey, but it does lead me to wonder how you think you'll ever get control of AFC."

"Yes, I know the figures," Gruen responded. "But as I understand it, there aren't any voting trusts or voting agreements binding that stock, are there?"

"No, no, nothing like that."

"Well, then, maybe Mr. Andersen can speak for the

holders of that forty-seven percent and maybe he can't. And I'm not sure the legal advisers to the Foundation would permit the trustees to pass up an offer at thirty-eight, forty dollars."

"Jeffrey, I doubt very much that they'll have a problem at your, shall we say, conservative price. Or perhaps I should say downright chintzy price?" Yates said.

"Say what you like, Marvin," Gruen answered, in an unruffled voice. "It's not your money—either going out or coming in."

"Can I have another question?" Yates asked.

"Marvin, you can have as many as you want," Gruen said, smiling.

"Let's put it this way. I'm puzzled about why you want AFC. There's no way that the parts are worth more than the whole—you can't sell off bits and pieces and come out with a profit. The Company's too integrated for that. So what's your interest? I just don't see why it appeals to you."

"Well, there is a reason, which I'm perfectly happy to tell you. Whatever the rationale may have been, the Andersens have kept AFC out of overseas operations. They've concentrated almost exclusively on United States, or at least North American, business. I think the Company's ready for a major, major expansion abroad. I want to buy the Company and push that expansion. Does that make things clear?"

"Now I have a question for you, Marvin," Jason Stockmeyer interrupted. "If I understand Mr. Andersen correctly, he has said the inside shareholders will never sell. Does that mean he won't even take Jeffrey's offer to the Board of Directors?"

Yates was not about to allow his client to be set up for future litigation. "Oh no, Jason. Jeffrey's offer will be given every consideration by the AFC Board, you can rest assured of that. In fact, the Board is meeting later this morning and I think you can assume these discussions will be on the agenda."

"Do you have any questions, Flemming?" Yates asked. The Chairman shook his head no. "Bill? Laurance?" Silently, they indicated they did not have questions either.

"I have only one more thing to say," Gruen added. "We really are serious about starting a tender right away, if we have to do that. So we need to know what the thinking of the AFC Board is. You've got a Board meeting today, you said. Can I get some sense of whether the Board's approach will be friendly or hostile to us? That's something I'd like to know by, say, noon tomorrow. And let me just add that our offer will be a serious one, and I hope it will be received in the friendly spirit in which it is going to be made."

It was clear to the lawyers, if not necessarily to their clients, that it would be best to break up the meeting after Gruen's ultimatum; further comments and questions would exacerbate a situation that could only become more tense. All shook hands politely and correctly, but with no humorous asides or small talk, and the AFC group headed en masse toward the elevators, discreetly holding their tongues until they were off Jeffrey Gruen's premises.

Bringing up the rear of the procession, Reuben Frost silently pondered what he had just seen and heard. Jeffrey Gruen had been supremely confident of his ability to take over AFC. But how could he be, given the holdings of the family, management and the Foundation? What did he know that made him so confident? Frost searched his mind in vain for an answer. The only thing that seemed apparent to him was that there was some lurking disloyalty within the family—and that Jeffrey Gruen knew about it.

THE BOARD

The procession of AFC executives and lawyers that went down Park Avenue from Jeffrey Gruen's office to AFC headquarters must have seemed odd indeed to onlookers. Walking three across, the men were deep in animated conversation about their meeting with the raider, oblivious to the approaching passersby they brushed with their swinging briefcases or forced off the sidewalk into the street.

The group gathered in Flemming Andersen's office, where the Chairman outlined the agenda he thought the meeting of the Board of Directors, which was due to begin in ten minutes, should follow.

"I want all three of you lawyers there," Andersen said. "And Jack Hilliard and his bunch from Hughes & Company when they arrive. What I plan to do is tell the Board what's happened and then leave it to you, Mr. Yates, to explain to the directors what their responsibilities are, after which we'll hear from Hilliard. And then we'll vote Gruen's goddam proposal down. Okay?"

"Just one amendment," Ernest Crowder said. "I know how you feel about Gruen's offer, Flemming, but just to keep the record straight, I think you should emphasize that the directors are free to act as they choose—and even to sleep on it overnight if they want to. After all, we don't have to say anything to Gruen until noon tomorrow."

"I agree with you, Ernest," Yates said. "It's very important, if we get into a cat fight in court, to show that the Board acted prudently and deliberately."

"Reuben, do you agree with all that?" the Chairman asked Frost. "Can't I just tell the directors to reject Gruen's offer or get the hell off the Board?"

Frost did not know whether Andersen was joking or not. But he took no chances and rejected any such behavior.

"My colleagues are right, Flemming. Even *I* know about the *Van Gorkum* case," Frost said, referring to an important recent court decision in which the directors of a corporation were found too willing to bless management's handling of a takeover proposal.

"All right, gentlemen," Andersen said, with a deep sigh. "I'll try to behave. Let's go."

The Andersen Foods boardroom was austere by comparison with the conference room at Gruen & Company. Its windows looked out on Park Avenue, but only at the correspondingly low floor of the building across the street. The principal ornament in the room was a huge wooden table, unscratched and polished to a high sheen. (The directors did not know that a self-important secretary in the adjoining executive offices had made it part of her life's work to save the directors' table from the depredations of lesser mortals. When others used the room, she saw to it, by scolding and surprise inspections, that no food or coffee cups desecrated the table. Not knowing of her devoted if misguided efforts on their behalf, the directors were never properly grateful to the woman, who was universally hated by her fellow employees.)

The first person Frost saw on entering the directors'

room was Marlene Vaughan. Mrs. Vaughan seemed to be at first meeting a flighty Southern belle with no powers of concentration and probably very little gray matter to concentrate with, an image reinforced by her characteristically bright red lipstick and nail polish. This was a very wrong impression, as Reuben had learned from past experience. Not only was Mrs. Vaughan a well-known nutritionist at Emory University in Atlanta, but she had shrewd and tough-minded business instincts as well.

"Well, Reuben, is the fox going to take over the henhouse?" she asked, as Frost approached her and kissed her on the cheek.

"I don't think so, Marlene. But we will see," Frost answered, then greeted the distinguished-looking Weston Greene standing by the windows next to Mrs. Vaughan. Greene, a former United States Senator from Minnesota, had come to New York to work for a management consulting firm after an upset defeat four years earlier. Frost rather liked the man, though during his time in Washington some cynics said that he had been elected only because he looked like a Senator, with his slim, lanky frame and a full head of gray hair. Frost gave the voters of Greene's home state more credit than that, though the former legislator's position on the Board represented nothing more than obeisance by Flemming Andersen to AFC's historic ties to the North Star State.

Nearby was Harry Knight, the retired Chairman of the Board of First Fiduciary Bank. If Greene looked like a Senator, Knight looked like a banker—tall, filling out but not overflowing a double-breasted suit, a rough-hewn face projecting solidity and (if necessary) sternness and discipline, those essential virtues of the commercial banker. He was conversing somewhat uneasily with short and squirrelly Andrew Fordyce, the editor-in-chief of *View* Magazine.

Fordyce had started his career, and gained his public

reputation, as an outspoken left-wing journalist. Even today his manner was that of the gadfly and the agitator,
though ideologically he had long since become an arch-
conservative. His horizontal shift to the right on the political continuum had coincided almost precisely with his
vertical movement upward on the corporate ladder at
Foresight Publications, Inc., the publisher of *View*; he had
become an enrolled Republican the year he was elected a
director of Foresight. As a director, he displayed a talent
for boardroom politics and, when word of that talent
spread, he found himself almost in as much demand for
corporate directorships as highly qualified women and
blacks. Having a real, live journalist on one's board—and
one who understood the trials and tribulations of the Free
Enterprise System at that—was considered a plus by, at
the moment, eight corporations in addition to AFC. (How
much time this left for editing *View* was uncertain.)

Under normal circumstances, the outside directors of
AFC made up a majority of the Board. Today, however,
the fifth outsider, Leonard Snyder, President of a Chicago
corporation with strong holdings in agricultural real estate, was traveling in Europe and could not be reached.
So present were four outsiders—Vaughan, Greene, Knight
and Fordyce—and the four insiders—Flemming and
Laurance Andersen, Billy O'Neal and Casper Robbins.

None of the Chase & Ward lawyers was a director of
AFC, reflecting the wisdom of Charles Chase, one of the
partnership's founders, that the firm's lawyers could not
be truly objective in advising clients if they were also
directors of those clients. Reuben Frost, when he had
been the Executive Partner of the firm before his retirement, had staunchly defended Chase's rule; indeed, he had
carried it to the point, as he did now, of refraining where
possible from sitting at a board meeting at the same table
with the directors. He, along with Crowder and Yates, sat in
chairs placed against the wall. There was no harm, in

Frost's mind, from keeping ever so slight a distance from one's client (not so great a distance as to allow an aggressive competitor to come between lawyer and client, but enough to make one's independence clear). Frost would never, as many lawyers did and as Marvin Yates had done the day before, refer to his client and himself collectively as "we."

While they were waiting, the receptionist announced that the "delegation" from Hughes & Company had arrived. Delegation it was—John Foster Hilliard, the Hughes partner in charge of the AFC account, and five others, together with two more lawyers from Hughes's regular law firm, Rudenstine, Fried & D'Arms.

Frost sighed, he hoped not noticeably, when Hilliard came through the double doors of the directors' room. John Foster Hilliard was personable, white, Protestant, Anglo-Saxon—and smarmy and monumentally stupid; he was a perfect customer's man, never saying no to a client, no matter how absurd the idea being put forward or the request being made (negative answers only came later, from others in the Hughes organization).

The other bankers were introduced, and Frost had hopes that they would be more alert than Hilliard. Frost had heard of two of them, Frederick Stacey and Vincent McDonnell, billed as experts on M&A and "capital markets," respectively. He did not know the other three, a young woman named Jeanne Lowell in a dressed-for-success suit and bow tie; a thirty-ish black, Darryl Gillson, wearing the best approved preppy raiment; and a baby-faced youngster named Edmund Halleck. Halleck promptly took off his jacket (thus signifying his willingness to get down to hard work) and by so doing revealed his full range of yuppie accessories: yellow pastel shirt with white collar and cuffs, red silk paisley suspenders and a blue Hermès tie. He was also wearing a warning beeper, a device Frost had heretofore associated with busy

surgeons and, based on what he had read in the newspapers, street-corner dope sellers. Frost also observed that
all the bankers, save Ms. Lowell, were wearing black
loafers with tassels, recalling the observation of one of his
partners that investment bankers favored this style because they couldn't tie their shoes.

With the full cast now assembled, Flemming Andersen
opened the meeting by describing the sequence of events
that had begun with Jeffrey Gruen's Saturday-night telephone call. He tried to do so calmly, but there was a tone
of indignation in his voice that was not quite suppressed,
though he managed to hold himself in check. His account
finished, he noted that a "full complement" of lawyers
was present—"our regular counsel, Ernest Crowder, I
guess what you might call our counsel emeritus—though
he's the same age as I am—Reuben Frost, and Mr. Marvin
Yates, Chase & Ward's chief takeover expert." He then
asked Yates to "read the directors their rights."

Yates, moving from his chair at the wall, stood at the
end of the table where he could be seen and, in effect, repeated the lecture he had given on the Company plane the
day before, emphasizing the duty the directors had to consider Gruen's proposal within the standards of the Business Judgment Rule.

"Does all this mean the outside directors should have
their own legal counsel?" Senator Greene asked, when
Yates had finished.

A little learning is a dangerous thing, Frost thought to
himself at the side of the room. Greene had obviously
heard the buzzword "independent counsel" as applied to
outside directors, but didn't quite know what that meant.

"I would think not, Senator," Yates responded. "At least
not yet. As of now, there's no dispute between the outside
directors and the inside directors. Nothing's been voted
on. If you and the insiders come to a parting of the ways,
that would be the time to consider getting your own law-

yer." Yates had answered respectfully, concealing whatever impatience with the question he shared with Frost.

Andrew Fordyce then spoke up. "I can't tell you how
this whole thing appalls me," he began, fingering his small
bow tie. "Here is one of the best-run companies in America being threatened by a little *parvenu*. Of course, we
won't sell out to him. I don't care if he goes to fifty-five or
sixty dollars, I'll never approve. AFC has too bright a future
for that."

"Mr. Fordyce, you may well be right," Yates said. "But
I think, frankly, we've got to proceed a little more delib-
erately in answering the question of whether we turn
Gruen down."

Frost noted disapprovingly that his former partner was
again using the word "we" to include both AFC and himself.

"One of the reasons Mr. Hilliard and his colleagues are
here is to give you their assessment of Gruen's offer and
whether it truly reflects the value of the Company," Yates
explained.

"Should we hear from them now?" the Chairman asked.

"Yes," Yates answered.

After the obligatory introductory pleasantries by John
Foster Hilliard—Hughes & Company was "deeply hon-
ored" to be of service to AFC, he said—Frederick Stacey
was asked to evaluate Gruen's offer.

"You all must realize we've had very, very little time to
consider Jeffrey Gruen's proposal," he began. "But we of
course have known AFC for many years, so I think we're
in a position to give you at least our tentative thinking.

"AFC's stock price is now thirty. There's no doubt in our
mind that the Company's undervalued at that price—and
would be undervalued at thirty-eight or forty."

Stacey went on to explain why he and his colleagues
thought AFC was worth more on a long-term basis: the
exponential growth of the beer business, probable long-

term stability in commodity prices, the new but very real entrenchment of the SUPERBOWL and HEART O' GOLD products.

The Chairman began talking when Stacey had finished, speaking in measured and even tones. "Mr. Yates, I want to thank you for your very clear presentation to this Board of its duties and obligations regarding Mr. Gruen's offer. And, Mr. Stacey, I want to thank you for your very lucid— not to say flattering—analysis of AFC and its future. Based on the conversations we've all had in the past few hours, either in person or by telephone, I'm sure my position is clear. I am unalterably opposed to having Jeffrey Gruen take over this Company. My father, my grand-father, my son, my nephew, we've all worked too hard to build AFC to have it fall into the hands of a manipulator like Gruen. But my decision is not controlling. As Mr. Yates has told you, it is a decision all of us, sitting as a Board, have to make.

"So there it is, my friends. What's your best business judgment, as Counselor Yates would say?"

There was silence as Flemming concluded his remarks, thoughtful looks on the faces of those around the table as they mentally blocked out their individual positions.

Andrew Fordyce again was the first to speak, this time saying that nothing he had heard had changed his mind about voting to turn Gruen down. Mrs. Vaughan added a ringing endorsement of Flemming's leadership of the Company and in short order the four outside directors all agreed that the proper course for AFC—and its stockhold-ers—was an independent future, free of Jeffrey Gruen's machinations. Without taking a formal vote, and subject to a supporting Hughes report, all the directors agreed that a Gruen offer at forty dollars should be rejected.

"Mr. Gruen has asked for an answer by tomorrow noon," Flemming Andersen said. "I don't propose to give him the satisfaction of telling him anything a minute before that.

But meanwhile, I think we've got to consider the alternatives if he tries to fight us—as he almost certainly will. One proposal we kicked around very tentatively yesterday with Mr. Yates would be a counteroffer, so that AFC could buy back enough shares to keep majority control out of Gruen's hands. When you count the numbers, my family, Billy O'Neal and his wife, the Andersen Foundation and management own forty-seven percent of the stock. None of those shares will, I am positive, ever be sold to Jeffrey Gruen. That means a buyback of as little as three percent of the stock could keep Gruen out forever. Subject to you bankers telling me otherwise, I think it will work, however much Arab or Japanese or Mafia money Mr. Gruen can throw into the fight."

"You sure you can get the money to do it?" Harry Knight asked.

"Good Lord, Harry, I assumed that First Fiduciary would be good for it all by itself," Andersen replied, as the group laughed nervously. "We don't have much debt, after all, so we certainly ought to be able to raise three hundred, four hundred million with no trouble. What do the bankers say?"

Vincent McDonnell, Hughes's capital-markets expert, took the floor. "We haven't had much time to explore this, as you know, but on the basis of some recent experience, I'm sure the money can be raised," he said. "It really comes down to a question of what kind of financing you want and how much you want to pay for it."

The banker recited the various alternatives—long-term borrowings from insurance companies or pension funds, or borrowings on a short-term basis from commercial banks.

"Given your timing," McDonnell said, "I suspect you'll want to borrow from the banks—they certainly can act faster than the insurance companies—or at least *some* of them can. Then you could roll your borrowings out later with the institutions, when you'll have more time to work out an acceptable deal."

As McDonnell continued talking, young Halleck's beeping device began sounding. He struggled to turn it off, as everyone in the room turned to watch. It apparently was a false alarm, as he did not leave the meeting to find a telephone. "Sorry about that," he said, turning to McDonnell. The latter resumed his explanation of other esoterica of the proposed loan: whether the money should be borrowed domestically, or overseas in the Eurodollar market. Whether an attempt should be made to get a quote for a fixed rate of interest or the interest rate should "float" above the so-called prime rate charged by the banks. Whether the loan should be collateralized with AFC assets or be unsecured.

"We may have to move fast on this," Flemming Andersen said, when McDonnell had finished. "But we certainly should explore just what options we have before we make a decision."

"Exactly so," McDonnell said. "Can I make a suggestion? I think you, Mr. Andersen, Casper Robbins and your Treasurer, Joe Faxton, should sit down with us after this meeting and decide who we want to approach and on what basis. There are about three banks who can put together syndicates for these loans in a hurry and without a lot of nit-picking. One is Mr. Knight's bank, First Fiduciary."

"I'm pleased to hear that," Knight said. "Or are you really saying my bank's a pushover?"

"No, no, not at all," McDonnell replied. "I just meant your people are practical and businesslike."

"Thank you," the banker said.

"I think Vince has a good idea," Flemming Andersen said. "Some of us have some homework to do and all of us have some careful thinking to do. I suggest we recess till tomorrow morning, when I hope we'll have enough information to consider a self-tender. Besides, I know all the out-of-towners and vacationers will be delighted to spend as much time here as possible, in our beautiful late-August weather."

The AFC Board reconvened the next morning at nine o'clock. Frederick Stacey took the directors through the mathematics required to thwart Gruen. He agreed that purchasing roughly three percent of AFC's stock would do it, assuming all the inside holders stood firm. But he recommended that the tender offer be for ten percent of the outstanding Common. He said he thought sufficient stock could be bought in at forty-five dollars per share—though this would have to be raised if Gruen upped the ante. For safety's sake, he told the directors to assume a fifty-five-dollar-per-share price for planning purposes.

McDonnell and Stacey then reported on their quick canvass of the financial markets made on AFC's behalf. Using McDonnell's fifty-five-dollar figure, a total of up to $440 million would be required to purchase eight million shares. Casper Robbins interrupted to say that $40 million of AFC's available cash could be used, so that the Company would be looking to borrow no more than $400 million.

"As we expected," McDonnell said, "there won't be any problem in raising the money. First Fiduciary came through nicely. They will be happy to form a group and to make the loan unsecured. The only problem is that their pricing is not quite as good as Second Interstate's. But Second Interstate will only do the loan secured.

"Obviously there's a lot that's still up in the air. But we have three live bidding groups—First Fiduciary, Second Interstate and Renwick Trust. Darryl Gillson has done a little summary of the three proposals for you, and Jeanne Lowell has done a chart showing the terms of comparable deals done recently with other companies. We'll pass these out to you now."

While the group began studying the handouts from the Hughes representatives, Mrs. Vaughan began questioning the investment bankers.

"I think we're getting a little bit ahead of ourselves," she began. "Have we really decided that a buyback, or self-tender, or whatever you call it, is the way to defend the Company? What do you all think?" she said to the bankers.

"It's really not our call, Mrs. Vaughan," John Foster Hilliard said. "But we think the self-tender approach is viable if you want to do it."

"Do the rest of you agree?" she pressed. "Mr. Halleck, how about you? What do you think?"

Frost, who often had difficulty with names, was impressed that Mrs. Vaughan remembered the yuppie banker's name, since he had been totally silent and had attracted attention only when his beeper had accidentally gone off the day before.

"We've kicked it around pretty well, ma'am, within the time constraints we're operating under," Halleck (today wearing a pink shirt with white collar and cuffs) replied. "It's doable and I think you should go right ahead like gangbusters."

Marlene Vaughan hesitated—perhaps absorbing the volley of clichés directed her way—and then proceeded to quiz the other Hughes personnel, one by one and by name. All agreed with Halleck.

"Have we heard anything more from Gruen?" Senator Greene asked.

"Not a word," Flemming Andersen said. "But I don't expect to, unless we don't get back to him by noon."

"Jesus, I didn't realize what time it was," Laurance Andersen interrupted. It was the first thing he had said in the two days of meetings. "I'm afraid I've got to run. Got to get the noon flight to Los Angeles. But, Dad, you have my proxy. Tell Gruen to go to hell, as we agreed yesterday. And I'm in favor of the self-tender. I'll call you from

L.A." The younger Andersen stuffed his papers in his brief-case and left hurriedly.

"Well, at least someone has spoken up," the Chairman said. "What about the rest of you? What do you think?"

A few minutes' additional discussion followed, most of it irrelevant. Then the Board unanimously agreed in principle, if Gruen should make a tender offer, that AFC should make a counteroffer at up to fifty-five dollars a share for ten percent of the Company's stock. (Harry Knight, whose bank might profit handsomely from loans made to finance the buyback, asked that the minutes show that he did not vote.)

"Very well," Flemming Andersen said, his voice telegraphing his satisfaction with the result. "Unless anyone objects, I'm going to call Jeffrey Gruen right now and tell him we're not prepared to approve his offer. Then I'm going to sit down with Casper, Joe Faxton and our banking friends and get us the best deal we can for the money we would need for a self-tender. Okay? Motion to adjourn?"

The meeting broke up quickly. Flemming Andersen was in an exuberant mood as he left the room. "That bloody little bastard's going to have a fight on his hands," he said to Reuben. "You want to stay around for this bankers' talk?"

"No, I don't think you need me. But Marvin and Ernest will stay," Frost answered.

"Then I'll say good-bye for now," Andersen said. "Thanks for all your help, Reuben. Get some rest, 'cause I want you around when things get interesting."

OLD BONES

8

Things "got interesting" that very night. Sitting quietly at home, Reuben Frost got a call from a nearly incoherent Sally Andersen in Greenwich. Flemming Andersen had been found dead, floating in the outdoor whirlpool bath adjoining the swimming pool on the Andersen estate.

"What was it, a heart attack?" Frost asked his distressed caller.

"I don't know, Reuben," the woman replied, between sobs. "I don't know what to think."

"Had he been swimming?"

"Oh no. He was fully dressed. I found him in that thing, floating on his stomach. *I* found him, Reuben. *I* found him dead, floating in the steaming water."

Frost tried without any success to calm Sally Andersen by long distance. Having determined with difficulty that she was not alone, that Sorella and her husband were with her, and that the police had arrived, Frost told her that he was coming up. "It's seven o'clock now. I'll be there by eight-thirty," he said.

Frost was shaken by the call. The death of Flemming Andersen would have been shocking enough, but the circumstances his widow described were not exactly the equivalent of dying peacefully in bed in silk pajamas.

Within minutes Frost had called a car from the radio taxi service used by his office, written a hasty note of explanation to Cynthia (who was off at a fund-raising cocktail party he had refused to attend) and gone outside to wait for the car.

On the way to Connecticut, Frost tried to picture the scene in his mind. Recalling earlier visits, he remembered that the swimming pool was in a grove of trees, well removed from the house of the senior Andersens on one side and the homes of Sorella and Nate Perkins and of Laurance Andersen on the other.

Frost now recalled with sadness his last visit to the Andersens, the summer before. Flemming had been especially proud of the new whirlpool that had been installed beside the swimming pool that spring. He had refused to call it a "hot tub" or a "spa"—the terms favored by the local salesman of such things—and had more or less decreed that it was a "whirlpool."

"It makes you feel twenty years younger," he had explained to Frost. "I use it every day when I'm here. I'm telling you, it's great for old bones."

At Flemming's urging, Frost had tried the new toy and, indeed, had found it to his liking. The hot jets of water coming out of the lining of the round enclosure were unquestionably invigorating.

As his car approached the fenced-in Andersen complex, Frost found himself hoping that his old friend had died of natural causes. But he realized that being found fully clothed and face down in the whirlpool did not exactly point in that direction.

A young policeman stopped the New York taxi at the gate but allowed it to proceed inside once Frost had identified himself. He was told that Mrs. Andersen was in the library of the main house, so he headed there directly. The sight of him sent Sally Andersen off into a flood of tears. Frost rushed to her, embraced her and tried to soothe her by patting her back. Sorella and her husband, who looked as if he wanted to fade into the wallpaper, stood nearby.

Although time had passed, Sally was still as incoherent as she had been on the telephone. Finally, in despair, he motioned to Sorella and the two went out into the hallway.

"Any new developments?" Frost asked.

"He was murdered, Reuben! Murdered!" Sorella Perkins answered angrily.

"How do you know that?"

"The police. He had a bad bruise on his neck, so it looks like someone knocked him out and then pushed him into that damnable whirlpool. And the heat was on in the thing full blast, so he could have *scalded* to death." The woman's self-control gave way and she, too, dissolved into tears. Then, recovering, she told Frost that there had been a note.

"Note? What do you mean?" he asked.

"An anonymous note. They found it under a rock on the terrace by the pool."

"Where is it?" Frost asked.

"The police have it."

"Well, what did it say?" Frost pressed, impatient.

"You'll have to see it for yourself. It's too unbelievable—the work of a madman," Sorella said.

"Where are the police?" Frost asked.

"Out by the pool," she answered.

"I want to talk to them," Frost said. "I'll be back just as soon as I can."

The normally tranquil area around the Andersens' pool was aswarm with police busily and noisily carrying out the procedures incident to an investigation of suspected foul play. Spotlights had been thrown up into the darkness, giving the swimming pool terrace an artificial midday brightness. A police photographer was taking pictures of the whirlpool from all angles, and another technician was meticulously scraping the slate terrace surrounding it.

When Frost reached the pool area, he was disconcerted to see the spare, limp body of his late friend spread out on a green plastic sheet. The cadaver was still dressed in pants and shirtsleeves, although the shirt had been ripped down, presumably the better to examine the bruise on Andersen's neck, visible even to Frost looking at the corpse from several feet away.

He was also disturbed at seeing the plum-purple color of Andersen's face. If that face had been alabaster, or bright red, or even yellow, Frost felt he would not have been shocked. But he was not prepared for purple.

A large, ruddy-faced man in a dark suit seemed to be in charge of the surreal pageant. Frost introduced himself, discovering that the master of the revels was Arthur Castagno, detective sergeant with the Greenwich police. The detective seemed puzzled as to who Frost was, so the lawyer tried to explain.

"I'm a friend of Mr. and Mrs. Andersen," Frost said. "And also their lawyer." Frost had wanted to be more precise and say "one of their lawyers" but had decided in time to edit his statement for maximum effect.

"I see," Castagno replied. "We've got a real live mess here, as you've probably figured out."

"That seems a fair statement."

"It looks like some psycho did Mr. Andersen in," the detective said.

"Why do you say it was a psycho?"

"The note. Mrs. Andersen tell you about the note?"

"No, but her daughter did. She didn't tell me what was in it."

"Come here," Castagno said, motioning Frost over to a squad car. "Take a look at this." Castagno showed him a single sheet of what seemed to be normal office typewriting paper, now sheathed in an envelope of transparent polyethylene. Written on the paper in black ink, in block capital letters, was this message:

SUGGESTION BOX x x SUPERBOWL SOUPS ARE GOOD FOR YOU x x HOW ABOUT A NEW FLAVOR CALLED FLEMMING FRIKASEE? JUST MAKE FLEMMING'S OLD BONES THE PRINCIPLE INGREDIENT AND YOU GOT IT x x LOVE x x x

"Where did you find this?" Frost asked.

"Right over there. About ten feet from the hot tub. Folded up under a piece of rock," Castagno answered.

"Who found it?"

"One of the police officers."

"Who found the body, by the way?" Frost asked.

"Mrs. Andersen. Didn't she tell you?"

"Oh yes, I guess she did."

"She said she came down for a swim a little after six, and found her husband floating here then."

"But she didn't see the note?"

"Apparently not. I gather she started screaming and her daughter, Susan, Sissie . . ."

"Sorella . . ."

"Her daughter Sorella came out from her house and then they called us."

"What about her husband?"

"Husband? He's the one that's dead," Castagno said.

"No, no, Sorella's husband. Nathaniel Perkins."

"I dunno. All I know's that he was here when we got here."

"And your man found this crazy note?"

"Yes."

"Did anybody see someone around? Did anybody hear anything?"

"We haven't really pressed 'em yet. They said not, but

I want to run them through everything step by step once they've calmed down a little."

"You got any ideas?"

"None," Castagno said. "But that certainly's a psycho's note."

"Let me see it again," Frost said. "I want to make sure of the wording."

Castagno passed him the plastic folder and Frost carefully read the note through once more, then handed the folder back to Castagno.

"How did he die?" Frost asked.

"The medical examiner can't be sure until he does an autopsy, but it looks like somebody hit the old man, probably knocking him out, and pushed him into the spa, where he drowned."

"No chance of it being an accident?"

"Nobody here thinks so."

"I'm going back to see Mrs. Andersen," Frost said. "I'd appreciate it if you'd keep me posted on developments. Here's my card. I usually can be reached at the number I added there." Frost handed the detective one of his Chase & Ward business cards, but with his home telephone inked in on it.

By the time Frost returned to the library in the main house, Casper Robbins had arrived. A butler offered Frost a drink and, noting that all the others were drinking, he accepted gratefully.

"Sally, I know you'll have to tell your story at least a hundred times to the police," Frost said, "but I'd like to hear your direct account of what happened."

"It's all so weird, Reuben. I went down for a swim about six o'clock, as I often do. . . ." She was unable to go on, but Frost was persistent, though patient, and made her recount her painful story.

"Had you been here all day?" Frost asked.

"Yes, I had. I'd been here since we got back from the Adirondacks on Sunday."

"What about Flemming? When did he arrive?"

"I'm not sure, but I think around five. I was napping, but heard a car pull up and then drive away. I assumed it was a Company car dropping Flemming off. But I didn't get up and go downstairs."

"So you didn't speak to your husband before he died?"

"No," the widow replied, controlling herself with difficulty.

"And before you went down to the pool, did you hear anything? Any shouting? Quarreling? Anything unusual?"

"Nothing. I had no idea anything was wrong until I found Flemming's body floating in the whirlpool."

"How about you, Sorella?" Frost asked. "Did you hear anything?"

"Not a thing. I had been for a swim, actually, about four," she answered.

"And did you see anyone around then?"

"No. I swam for about thirty minutes and I remember thinking at the time how deliciously quiet it was. The first hint of trouble was when I heard Mother screaming."

"And that was about six?"

"Almost six precisely."

"Nate? How about you?"

The bearded writer seemed nervous about being questioned, but then, Frost thought, he was nervous about almost everything.

"I was napping, too," he said. "I finished off some writing up in the attic and then came down to our bedroom. It was just before Sorella went to swim. I must have gone out like a light, because I don't remember another thing until Sorella woke me up to tell me that her mother was screaming for help."

"And none of you saw the note?" Frost asked.

His three listeners all answered that they had not.

"It was the police who found it?"

"Yes."

"As far as you know, who else was here at five or six o'clock or thereabouts?"

"No one, except my cook and butler," Sally said.

"Anyone at your house?" Frost asked the Perkinses.

"Just the two of us," Sorella replied.

"How about Laurance's house? Anyone there?"

"No, Laurance went to California this morning. And Dorothy has gone to stay with her mother," Sorella said.

"I assume he's been notified, by the way. And how about Diana?"

"Diana's on her way now," Sorella explained. "She was in the city. But we haven't got to Laurance yet. We tried to reach him at his hotel, but he wasn't in. We left a message."

"Where's he staying, the Beverly Hills?" Frost asked.

"No, he's changed his hotel. No longer the Beverly Hills or the Beverly Wilshire. He's staying at something called the St. Martin. I think he's an investor in it."

"I hope not too big an investor," Frost said.

"Why?" Sorella asked.

"I was there about three months ago and the place was total confusion. They couldn't keep track of anything— their guests, messages, nothing. In fact, if Laurance doesn't call back soon, I'd call him again."

"Good idea," Sorella said.

"Do any of you have any idea of who might have killed Flemming?" Frost now demanded, sending Sally into tears once more.

"I know it's silly, Reuben, and always said when someone dies in strange circumstances, but I honestly believe Flemming didn't have an enemy in the world," Sally said, once she had regained her composure.

"Casper, you're more familiar with his business dealings than any of the rest of us," Frost said. "Do you have any ideas—do you know of any business enemies he may have had?"

"Well, the Campbell Soup people didn't like the success of SUPERBOWL very much. But it's impossible to think they had anything to do with this. Seriously, to answer your question, I can't think of a single person who had any kind of grudge against Flemming."

Sorella and her husband also had no potential suspects to propose.

The group was still. Then Sally turned to Reuben and fixed him with a steady gaze:

"Reuben, we badly need your help. I don't want to make you sound like a funeral director, my dear, but you *have* been through situations like this before. . . ." she said, then paused, uncertain of how to go on.

"What do you mean?" Frost asked ingenuously.

"You know very well what I mean. That trouble at NatBallet when that choreographer was killed. Or that business in your law firm when your partner was poisoned."

"Oh yes. Disaster seems to have a way of striking when I'm around," Frost said.

"All I'm saying is, the Andersens are going to need your help. Disaster has struck near you again, and we want you around to advise us."

"That's very flattering, Sally. Certainly I'll do everything I can to help. But right now I'm going to have a last word with that policeman, Castagno, and head back to New York. I don't see any point in making plans or decisions tonight, when we're tired and upset."

"I agree," Sally Andersen said. "Let's talk tomorrow."

CONTACTS

9

Cynthia Frost was waiting up for her husband when he arrived back from Connecticut. It was almost one in the morning, but Reuben asked his wife to sit with him while he related the day's events to her. Confused as he was in his own mind about Flemming Andersen's death, he was anxious to see if Cynthia, usually a shrewd analyst of human nature, might offer any helpful insights.

"I'm puzzled," Frost told his wife, after fixing Scotches for them both and then telling her the circumstances of Flemming's death as best he knew them. "Everyone says he didn't have an enemy in the world. Yet here he is, murdered."

"Does it matter whether he had enemies or not if the murder was done by a lunatic?" Cynthia asked. "The lunatic could be anybody, couldn't he? Disgruntled employee, unhappy customer, unrequited lover—though I doubt that, in Flemming's case."

"Yes, I suppose it could have been anybody."

"Of course I guess the note could be bogus and just a way of diverting attention from the real murderer and the real motive," Cynthia said.

"Yes, but then you're back to the truism that Flemming had no enemies."

"He may not have had enemies, but he certainly had family," Cynthia said.

"Family? Do you really think any of the family could be involved? It doesn't make sense, Cynthia."

"Reuben, I know these are your friends. But let's be objective. Coldly objective."

"Very well," Reuben said skeptically.

"Just think back to last weekend," Cynthia said. "Sure, everything was okay on the surface, but I just have an idea there are some family tensions there—probably not made easier by the smell of Jeffrey Gruen's dollars."

"Such as?"

"Such as the relationship with Diana. You told me she's bitter about not having been brought into the Company. And she couldn't have been thrilled at her father's insistence that she keep her stock, since she's already said she wants to sell more of it. Sorella? She seems all right, but I told you how angry she was at being excluded from the *important* flight back to New York on Sunday. And then there's her bitter husband. He's as quiet as a mouse, but deep down, I'm willing to bet that he's unhappy being married into a family that doesn't appreciate his genius.

"And Laurance, what about him?" she went on. "Totally silent, seemingly preoccupied with other thoughts that we're not privy to. Not healthy. And let's not forget Billy O'Neal. He's been mad at Flemming's branch of the family since the day he was born."

"All true, my dear. But that doesn't mean they'd go out and commit the ghoulish murder of the decade to work out their grievances," her husband said.

"I don't know all the ins and outs of this takeover business, but I can't imagine that's helped much, either," Cynthia said, paying no attention to her husband's protestations. "Quite the reverse. My guess is that this fellow Gruen's threatened raid has aggravated whatever tensions were there before—and perhaps aggravated them enough to lead to murder. Take Sally, for instance. When she left the tennis world to marry Flemming, she retired from public notice for good—or so she thought. All she's ever wanted is to have a quiet, respectable—and private—life. Remember how she hated that where-is-she-now piece in *People* a few years ago? Or the publicity about Laurance's third divorce—the *really* messy one?

"Just for argument's sake, look at her situation," Cynthia went on. "Here's Jeffrey Gruen, the infamous raider, about to focus public attention on Andersen Foods. Which attention was bound to increase when Flemming starts fighting him. I know it's a very nasty thought, but don't you think it's just possible that Sally, with her craving for privacy, killed Flemming to prevent the publicity battle? Of course, there would be headlines for a day or two about Flemming's death, and for another day or two after Gruen made his tender offer—but then Gruen would take over the Company and peace and quiet would return."

Frost was silent for a few moments after his wife had spun out her theory about Sally Andersen. "I think that's preposterous, Cynthia," he finally said, a trace of anger in his voice. "Be sensible. A murder as spectacular as Flemming's—can you imagine what the tabloids are going to do with it?—is not exactly the way to protect one's privacy. But now that I think about it, there may be a variation. I'm convinced somebody—and maybe even more than one somebody—is ready to betray the family and sell out to Gruen. Isn't it just possible Sally saw this coming, saw that her husband was about to be defeated, and killed him not only to spare herself the notoriety she hated but to spare him public humiliation—and humiliation caused by a member of his own family?"

"Look, Reuben, we're both very tired, and I'm afraid our imaginations are cooking up some fancy bedtime stories," Cynthia said. "I'm probably wrong, and so are you. Let's go to sleep."

"Maybe the solution will come in our dreams," Reuben concluded.

"God, I hope not," Cynthia said.

Reuben scarcely had time the next morning to drink the orange juice his wife had squeezed for him before the telephone began ringing incessantly. Sally Andersen's secretary called to notify him of the funeral arrangements scheduled for the next day—"Mrs. Andersen wants the funeral to be held as soon as possible"—at eleven at the Madison Avenue Presbyterian Church, to be followed by a luncheon for the family and a few select guests at the Andersen apartment.

Then the widow herself was on the telephone to make two surprising requests: that she herself wished to be elected to AFC's Board of Directors and that Casper Robbins should be elected Chairman as well as President.

"What about Billy O'Neal and Laurance?" Frost asked.

"Nonsense. Laurance is too busy with the high-tech toys he and his friends in California have bought. And Billy just isn't . . . isn't temperamentally suited for the job."

"Billy will be very disappointed," Frost said.

"That may be. But what's he going to do, start a proxy fight?" Sally asked. Out of choice, she had up until now not served on the AFC Board; but she had seen enough and heard enough, and talked with her husband enough, to be both shrewd and clever where the family business was concerned.

The third call of the morning was a conference call with Marvin Yates and Ernest Crowder of Chase & Ward, Fred Stacey of Hughes & Company and Casper Robbins to discuss what the next step with Jeffrey Gruen should be. Frost detested speakerphones and calls to multiple locations; there was no intimacy or privacy, and one could never be sure who was listening to what was being said. Let alone the screaming and shouting often required because of bad connections. But Frost agreed in this case that a short conference call was preferable to attempting to arrange a face-to-face meeting.

"Reuben, are you there?" Casper Robbins asked.

"Yes, I'm here."

"Marvin? Ernest?"

"Good morning, we're here."

"Fred?"

"I'm here."

"Can everybody hear okay?" Robbins asked. All agreed that they could.

"Before we begin, what happened yesterday when Flemming called Jeffrey Gruen?" Frost asked.

"Very puzzling," Robbins said. "I was on the call and when we got through we were told we had to talk to Norman Cobb, Gruen's assistant. You remember how firm Gruen was about getting back to him by noon yesterday? But when we did that, he wasn't there to talk to us."

"That's very strange," Stacey said. "You think it was a deliberate insult?"

"Couldn't tell," Robbins said. "But Flemming gave the message loud and clear to Cobb—no endorsement of Gruen's offer was likely, and the AFC Board was ready to buy back ten percent of the Company's stock."

"What did he say?" Yates asked.

"Not much," Robbins answered. "Thanked us for calling within the deadline and said he would report everything to Gruen."

"And as far as we know, they didn't make an announcement of their tender offer," Yates said. "I find that a little unusual after all Gruen's big talk on Monday about bulling ahead right away."

"You're right, Marvin. There was nothing on the tape yesterday or this morning," Stacey said.

"Maybe he's having trouble raising the money—maybe

that's where he was when Flemming called," Crowder added.

"Or maybe he got cold feet," Frost said.

"I doubt that," Yates commented. "There's nothing Flemming told him that he couldn't have anticipated, if he had any sense at all."

"So what do we do now?" Robbins asked.

"I can't imagine he'll go ahead without waiting some decent interval after Flemming's death," Yates said.

"Probably so," Robbins agreed. "But how do we make sure of that?"

There was silence as the telephone conferees considered the problem. Frost, ignoring George Bannard's implicit stricture to be seen-and-not-heard, spoke up.

"I think I should go and see him," Frost said. "I believe I'm the only one who knows him outside of the context of this deal, or the M&A context anyway. He's a director of NatBallet and maybe I can talk to him in a less adversarial way than the rest of you."

Again the conferees were silent for a moment—an uncomfortably long moment, as far as Reuben was concerned. Then Yates, speaking perhaps too rapidly, said: "I think that's fine. Gruen would have a hard time saying no to a postponement if Reuben asked for it—Reuben being the decent fellow that he is."

Disembodied laughter from the participants came over the line. They all agreed that Frost should approach Gruen and see him as soon as possible, preferably in person, and request a postponement, telling him that AFC's management wanted to think about his proposal for a couple of weeks.

Frost promised to contact Gruen and to report the results as soon as possible. This led to the next call, to Gruen's office, where Frost ended up talking with Norman Cobb, as his colleagues had the day before. The young

man was not at all forthcoming about Gruen's whereabouts. But he did agree that Frost could see Gruen at five
o'clock at Gruen's New York apartment.

No sooner had he completed these arrangements than
Casper Robbins was on the line again.

"Can you come over here, Reuben?" he inquired. "We've
got another goddam note."

"You mean from the killer?"

"Allegedly," Robbins said. "Come to my office."

"I'll be there in twenty minutes."

On his way to AFC headquarters, Frost picked up a
copy of the afternoon *Press*, which had a screaming front-
page headline:

NUT COOKS SOUP KING

Frost hastily read the story. It contained no new information, but made clear that the Greenwich police were
convinced a psychopath had committed the murder,
though the note at the scene was not mentioned.

At AFC, Casper Robbins closed the door to his large
corner office as soon as Frost came in.

"Here, take a look at this," he said, thrusting a sheet of
brown paper at Frost. Frost carefully took out a handker-
chief to cover his right hand, before taking the sheet.

The edges of the paper were uneven, as if cut from a
larger piece of brown wrapping paper. Written with red
crayon, in a script hand quite different from the one in
the note found in Greenwich, was a short message:

*Revenge has come to the Andersens! And high time,
too! Meanness and dishonesty do not go unpunished!
Flemming Andersen died for his!*

"Where did this come from?" Frost asked.

"Somebody left it off at the mail room about an hour
ago."

"How was it addressed?"

"Just to Andersen Foods Corporation. No other name or anything. Here's the envelope." Robbins handed over a kraft envelope.

"Fortunately someone in the mail room had the good sense to bring the thing directly to me," Robbins said.

"It bears no resemblance to the earlier note," Frost said.

"So what does it mean?"

"You've got me," Frost said. "But I do know one thing I'm going to do—and do it right now."

"What's that?"

"Call my old friend Luis Bautista at the New York City Police Department."

Frost excused himself and dialed Bautista's direct-dial office number, where he found the detective desk-bound, working on completing reports. Could he meet Frost in forty-five minutes at his home? Of course; anything would be better than report writing.

"Casper, do you have an office safe of your own?" Frost asked, when he returned to Robbins's office.

"Yes, I do."

"I suggest you put this note in an envelope and keep it in your safe until we decide what to do with it," Frost said. "But first, let me have a Xerox of it and the envelope."

"Whatever you say, Reuben," Robbins replied.

Frost had scarcely gotten home when Bautista arrived. When Frost opened the front door, they greeted each other as the old friends they had become, though Frost at first looked startled.

"What's the matter, Reuben? Never seen a man with a beard before?" Bautista asked.

The Frosts had seen Bautista and his girlfriend, Francisca Ribiero, in late July; the beard was new since then. Reuben had always thought the detective, whom he had first met after the murder of his partner, Graham Donovan, extremely handsome, a nicked front tooth being the only irregularity in Bautista's features. He was not sure the beard did much to enhance his friend's good looks.

"Luis, I've seen plenty of beards, most of them unfortunate," Frost said.

"You don't like it, in other words?"

"The jury's still out," Frost answered. "Why did you do it?"

"I'm working on a couple of real tough cases," Bautista explained. "Murdered drug dealers. I thought it would help if I looked *fierce*."

"I guess you could say you've succeeded. How is Francisca? What does she think of it?"

"She doesn't like it. But she'll get used to it," Bautista said.

"Hmn."

The two men went upstairs and sat down in the living room. Frost offered Bautista a drink, but he declined, saying he was still on duty.

"What's up, Reuben?" the detective asked. "You were rather cryptic on the phone."

"Did you see the headline in the *Press* today?"

"Let's see . . . oh yes, about some guy cooking to death in his hot tub in Connecticut."

"Precisely. His name was Flemming Andersen, he was the Chairman of the Board of Andersen Foods Corporation and he was an old friend and client of mine," Frost explained.

"I'm sorry," the detective said. "Was he a close friend?"

"Fairly."

"Who's got the case?" Bautista inquired.

"The Greenwich police. A fellow named Arthur Castagno seems to be in charge."

"And they think it's a psycho, the paper says? Somebody who wrote a note?"

"Yes. I think Cynthia, by the way, disagrees. She thinks

the 'somebody' involved is using the note as a cover, to create confusion."

"Very possible," Bautista said. "But what can I do for you?"

"Help me with some *real* confusion. There was the note the paper mentioned. Then, today, the Company got another one delivered at its office. Here's a copy of it." Frost showed Bautista the copy. "It doesn't show up on the Xerox, but this one's on brown paper, whereas the first one was on regular white typing paper. The handwriting's different, too. The first one was in block letters."

"So what's the confusion? Whether the same guy wrote both of them?"

"Yes."

"The lab and the handwriting guys can help with that," Bautista said. "Offhand, it seems to me you got three possibilities. One, the killer wrote both notes because he's crazy and the reasons for killing Andersen were crazy. Two, the killer is perfectly sane and wrote both notes to confuse everybody. Third, the killer wrote the first note—either because he was crazy or to throw people off the track—and some screwball who read the newspapers or watched TV tried to get into the act by writing the second. Happens all the time, you know. When you get one note in a case, you may get half a dozen more from nutcakes who had nothing to do with the original."

"Hmn. Shouldn't we tell Castagno up in Greenwich about this?"

"I don't know about the *we*, Reuben. This is brother Castagno's case."

"But don't police departments cooperate in a situation like this?"

"If we have time. Though you've got to understand we're much less interested in a guy killed in Greenwich than somebody bumped off right here under our noses."

"I'm disappointed," Frost said. "But I guess everybody has to have priorities."

"Look, Reuben, I'll try to help any way I can, as a favor to you, but, as I say, I think Castagno is your man right now."

Frost repeated his desire to call Castagno, hinting that he would like Bautista to be in on the call. Bautista caught the hint and said he'd be happy to talk to his Connecticut counterpart. Reuben placed the call, and located Castagno after being directed to two separate numbers.

Frost relayed the news of the second note, read it to Castagno and described it physically. Castagno seemed at a loss as to what to do, so Bautista, on the library extension, suggested that the Greenwich police have the first note brought to the city to be analyzed along with the second.

"Or we can get the second note up to you," Bautista said.

"No, I appreciate your offer of help," Castagno said. "I think having your fellows do it will get things moving faster than trying to get it done in Hartford. How do I go about it?"

Bautista gave Castagno detailed instructions about reaching his office and told him that if he left the office he would leave a message behind.

"Okay, thanks a lot," Castagno said, sounding grateful for the help he was getting. "Anything else?"

"Not here."

"Nor here, either," Castagno said. "Good-bye, gentlemen."

"Luis, thank you," Frost said after the phone conversation ended. "Is this going to cause you a lot of bother?"

"Yes, but that's all right," Bautista answered. "Anything for you, Reuben. Just don't get me involved any deeper."

SHERWOOD FOREST

After Bautista left, Frost was grateful for the chance to rest before his late-afternoon meeting with Jeffrey Gruen. He actually slept for an hour before the alarm he had set woke him at four-thirty. Cynthia, home from an afternoon of grant-committee meetings at the Brigham Foundation, sat on the edge of the bed and talked while her husband changed his shirt.

Once Cynthia found out where Reuben was going, she commanded him to observe carefully what he saw.

"It's supposed to be the most ostentatious apartment in New York," Cynthia said, "which is saying quite a lot. It's always in *W* and the fashion magazines—four floors stuffed with every artifact money can buy. They say that wife of his—you know, Gloria Gruen, the jewelry designer—spends twenty thousand dollars a month on flowers."

"That sounds almost impossible," Reuben said, tying his necktie in front of the mirror.

"Well, you just take a good look and be ready to make a full report."

"Yes, my dear. Maybe I can bring you back one of Gloria Gruen's creations."

"Thank you, no," Cynthia said. "She does terrible designs. Clunky and vulgar gold things with too many stones."

"I agree," Frost said. Shopping for his wife the previous Christmas, he had looked over a selection of Gloria Gruen pieces and had indeed found them clunky and vulgar.

"Wish me luck," he said.

"Of course, my dear," she replied, kissing him good-bye before he left the room.

Frost walked to the building at the southeast corner of Fifth Avenue and Seventy-seventh Street, where the Gruen apartment was located. He was admitted by a maid in uniform and taken through an immense foyer to what he took to be the living room. At once he began to believe his wife's tale about Mrs. Gruen's florist bills—there were flowers, trees and plants everywhere, rivaling the city's Botanical Gardens.

"Mr. Gruen is on the telephone, but he says he will be with you shortly," the maid told him.

"Fine. Thank you." Frost went to one of the windows and looked out at the splendid view of Central Park, twenty-eight floors below. He was about to take a seat when he realized that the walls of the room were covered with paintings, many by eminently recognizable artists at that—Renoir, Cézanne, Monet. He found himself strangely unmoved by the works as he walked around the room. Why should this be so? These were all artists he liked.

Then it came to him: without exception, the paintings on display were decidedly second-rate. The orangey-pinks in the two Renoirs were not pleasing; the pair of Monets, while unquestionably the works of the master, were experimental exercises that did not quite come off. And then there were the oils by minor French artists that filled out the room—thoroughly undistinguished and derivative paintings by Georges d'Espagnat, Henri Martin and Armand Guillaumin.

Did this collection reflect the taste of the Gruens, or had sharp dealers talked them into these purchases? He wondered. It all reminded him of the Getty Museum: lots of money spent for a disappointing result. As he turned from the walls, his eye caught sight of an enormous coffee table with a recessed top covered by glass. Inside was a sampling of the jewelry designed by Gloria Gruen. Frost sat down and looked at the pieces through the glass, concluding that he saw no reason to change his earlier assessment of her work. He also thought it slightly queer that the living room had been turned into a sales annex.

Gruen entered and shook hands with Reuben, addressing him as "Mr. Frost." He apologized profusely, both for being unavailable to Flemming Andersen and Robbins the day before and now for being late.

"It turned out I had to be out of town yesterday, but I got the message from AFC through Norman Cobb," Gruen explained, as the two men stood facing each other next to one of the Renoirs.

Gruen then expressed great sympathy over Flemming's death. "It's a great tragedy, Mr. Frost. He was an eminent businessman. Are there any clues to identify the madman who did it?"

"Nothing very promising, I'm afraid," Frost replied.

"Let's go into the library, where I think we'll be more comfortable." He led Frost back to the wood-paneled foyer, turning off the lights in the living room as he did so.

"Have you been here before, Mr. Frost?" he asked.

"No, I haven't."

"We had a party for the NatBallet benefactors last year, but I guess you didn't come."

"No, I'm sorry we didn't. We had a conflict, I forget just what. I think something to do with my wife's Foundation work."

"You didn't miss much. One hundred twenty-five sitting down for dinner," Gruen said. "We practically had tables on the ceiling."

"Good heavens," Frost said, scarcely able to comprehend a party of such a size in a New York apartment.

"Before we talk, let me show you the dining room," he said, guiding Frost toward double doors across the foyer. Gruen went inside and turned up the rheostats on one wall.

Frost had trouble believing what he saw, although he vaguely recalled Cynthia showing him, with some amusement, a magazine picture of the room. The floor was blue, gray and white marble—blue squares surrounded by white borders on a gray background. Towering over the long dining table were three portraits of truly heroic proportions, each considerably larger than life-size.

"That's Sir Walter Scott," Gruen explained, pointing to a seated young man looking out into the landscape. "Sir Henry Raeburn did that about 1810."

"Very interesting."

"Scott has always been a hero of mine, ever since I read *Ivanhoe* in school."

"Really?"

"And over there is Lady Lucy Fox-Strangeways, daughter of the first Earl of Ilchester and niece of the first Lord Holland. Done by Allan Ramsay about 1763."

"Is that so?"

"She's quite attractive, don't you think?" Gruen asked.

"Oh yes. Yes, indeed."

"And finally, that's the Duke of Atholl over there."

"Who?"

"The Duke of Atholl. Oh, ha, ha. It's spelled A-T-H-O-L-L."

"Of course."

"Painted by Johann Zoffany in 1766."

Frost was as close to being speechless as he had ever

been in his life. What could one say to this boy from
Brooklyn babbling on about the Earl of Ilchester and the
Duke of Atholl?

"Is your wife from England?" Frost asked, trying both
to get at the root of this Anglophilia and to say something.

"Oh no. Pittsburgh. We just like these old portraits,
that's all. We find them expressive. And it's fascinating to
study the lives of the sitters."

"Hmn. I see. Very impressive."

"Come on, let's get down to business in the library."

"Fine."

Gruen turned off the dining room lights and led the way
across to the library, which turned out to be only slightly
more believable than the dining room. It looked like an
uptown annex of the American Craft Museum; in addition
to the plants and the flowers, there was an anonymous
panoramic oil of the Erie Canal at Schenectady on one
wall; an Ammi Phillips portrait of a lady on the facing
wall; and a Shaker wardrobe taking up a third. On one
large table at the side of the room, there was a crowded
and large collection of small scrimshaw pieces. And on
two other large tables, and in bookcases next to the wardrobe, were bound leather volumes of Currier & Ives and
Audubon prints. Not to mention a proliferation of duck
decoys, weather vanes and other assorted folk objects in,
on and under the room's furniture. The total effect was to
create the impression that everything in the room had
been purchased at once as a preassembled package.

Is it possible to buy taste? Frost wondered to himself.
On the evidence he was viewing this afternoon, the answer was no. Though it clearly was possible to spend a
fortune on "art."

"Who should go first?" Gruen asked, once they were
seated in facing chairs in front of the room's large fire-
place.

Frost said he would be happy to, and started by confirming that Gruen had gotten AFC's position straight from his assistant.

"Yes, unfortunately, I think I understand what the AFC Board decided," Gruen said. "No to my proposed purchase and yes to a self-tender for something like ten percent."

"Yes, that was the decision," Frost said. "Of course, you must appreciate that now everything is in turmoil after Flemming's death. As I'm sure you can imagine, the Company and the family have quite enough to consider just now without dealing with a tender offer from you."

"So what are you proposing?"

"Basically, that you give the Company some breathing space by postponing your offer for, say, two weeks."

"I don't think I can do that," Gruen said. "I've already started to pay a commitment fee to my banks for the money I'll borrow to do the deal. So I want it over and done with just as soon as possible. Besides," he went on, "the 13D I filed Monday said I was contemplating an offer. If I don't make one, people will wonder why. I can get along without a lot of wise-ass comments in the financial press—'Has Jeffrey Gruen stretched himself too thin at last?'—that kind of thing."

"Mr. Gruen, I'm obviously not in a position to advise you," Frost said, leaning forward and rubbing, perhaps unconsciously, the head of a carved duck decoy on the coffee table in front of him. "I'm in fact your adversary, or a representative of your adversary. But may I give some unsolicited advice—public relations advice—just the same? My own opinion is that it would be disastrous for you to pursue a hostile tender offer against a Company that has just lost its chief executive and a major stockholder—and lost him through a bizarre murder, at that. I don't think such a move would do your long-term reputation much good."

"I don't see that the two things are related," Gruen answered.

"Also, Mr. Gruen," Frost went on, cutting off further

comment, "it seems clear to me that you must be assuming that some part of the Andersen edifice is going to crumble. Otherwise your offer doesn't make any sense. If the holders of forty-seven percent of AFC's stock hold firm—and that's what management, the Foundation and the family have—there's no way, realistically, that you can get control of the Company. You *have* to be betting that someone's going to defect. I can't say you're wrong about that. I don't know the innermost thoughts of those involved. But I think the likelihood of the family façade giving way is a good bit more likely two weeks from now than it is within hours of Flemming Andersen's death.

"Two weeks from now management and the Board may feel exactly as they did yesterday morning," Frost continued. "But they may not. I submit to you, sir, that you have nothing to lose and perhaps something to gain by holding back on your offer."

"What about the Company's buyback proposal?" Gruen asked.

"I assure you AFC won't get out in front of you on that," Frost answered.

"Maybe you'd just like to buy me out and have me go away," Gruen volunteered.

This was a possibility Frost knew the AFC Board would never accept—paying Jeffrey Gruen "greenmail" to keep him from making his takeover bid.

"That's out of the question," Frost said. "There is absolutely no point in discussing it."

"Just thought I'd ask," Gruen replied. Then he paused and appeared to be thinking.

"I'll give you a week," he finally said. "A week from today. Wednesday."

"All right."

"That means if there's any change in the Board's position you'll have to get back to me by the close of business next Tuesday, sooner if you can," Gruen said.

114

"That's not really a week, is it?" Frost said.

"Okay, okay, close of business Wednesday," Gruen shot back, slightly irritated. "You want a standstill agreement?"

"That won't be necessary, Mr. Gruen," Frost said. "I think your word will suffice." Frost, a lifelong believer that a man's word was his bond, tried to keep any hint of scorn or disdain out of his voice. If such a hint was there, Gruen ignored it.

"I don't know how much influence you have with your client," Gruen said, "but I suggest you try to persuade them that the way to go is a friendly takeover. Much easier for them, even if it's more expensive for me. Shall we drink to that?" He pushed a button on the wall and a uniformed butler appeared.

"I can't say I'll drink to your proposal but, yes, I'll have a drink. An extra-dry martini with a twist, please. On the rocks." Frost was usually leery of ordering a martini in strange territory, but the sight of the butler in uniform gave him confidence it would be prepared correctly.

"A Lillet mist," Gruen ordered, and the butler disappeared.

Once the two men had drinks in hand, Gruen proposed a toast to a "friendly outcome." Frost smiled but remained silent.

"Who's going to be AFC's new Chairman, can you say?" Gruen asked.

"The Board hasn't met yet, but I'm almost certain it will be Casper Robbins. He's the President already, as you know."

"He's not family, is he? Won't that be the first time AFC has gone outside?"

"Yes."

"What about the son? Or the nephew, O'Neal?"

"I don't think either one will be picked."

"I'm not surprised. I'd never met them before last Monday, but they both seemed like backseat types at our meeting, though I guess O'Neal has been quite a go-getter in the beer business."

Gruen then changed the subject and he and his guest had a reasonably amiable time discussing National Ballet affairs until Frost rose and announced that he had to leave.

"When's the NatBallet fall board meeting?" Gruen asked.

Frost consulted his pocket diary and told him that it was on September 28.

"I hope I'll be able to make it," Gruen said. "I'm going to September on the twentieth of London."

"Excuse me?"

"Sorry, I'm going to *London* on the *twentieth*."

The pair continued chatting as Gruen led Frost though the flora to the door.

Walking home, Frost thought about the little oddities of the interview. That unlikely slip of the tongue at the end, for example. Did a small glass of Lillet disorient the man? Or was he nervous for some reason about meeting with Frost? Very strange. And what about switching the lights on and off? Here was a paper billionaire obsessively turning off lights like an economizing Lyndon Johnson. Also strange. But nothing, Frost concluded, was nearly so odd as the Sherwood Forest where this modern Robin Hood lived.

11

The next morning, the Frosts had a leisurely breakfast and then got ready for Flemming Andersen's memorial service at the Madison Avenue Presbyterian Church. Reuben put on what he chose to call his "funeral uniform," a gray, almost black, flannel suit, with a white shirt and dark blue-and-gray striped tie.

"I'm getting to wear my uniform more and more these days," he told his wife. "But I guess that's part of the price of getting old."

Cynthia replied noncommittally.

"This is a memorial service, isn't it?" she asked.

"Yes."

"When was the funeral? Flemming is scarcely dead."

"It was yesterday in Connecticut. Just the immediate family. Sally had the body cremated. Of course, that didn't take much. The poor devil was already half cooked."

"Reuben, really."

The service itself was mercifully brief. Casper Robbins gave a short eulogy that all agreed was both felicitous and apt. The crowd at the church was relatively small, though Reuben noticed substantial representation from all the service organizations that did business with Andersen Foods: Chase & Ward, of course, but also AFC's trademark lawyers and Washington counsel; the Company advertising agency; its accounting firm; the leading banks in the syndicate from which AFC traditionally borrowed; even the insurance agency through which the Company placed its insurance. How comforting to be remembered by one's friends, Frost thought.

Frost had spoken with Sally Andersen at the church, but did so again at her apartment, where she had invited close friends to come by for lunch. The Andersen residence was only two blocks up Fifth Avenue from Jeffrey Gruen's quadruplex, but the difference between the two apartments was profound. The Andersens had only two floors, not four, and while the works of art on view were not as plentiful as those at Gruen's, they were uniformly of better quality, among them an early Braque assemblage, two blue-period Picassos and two large, dramatically ravishing Jasper Johns oils from the 1950s. No heroic portraits of total strangers and no hand-carved ducks.

Two waiters, not regular staff but hired for the occasion, moved among the guests with trays of glasses of orange juice and white wine. Given the early hour, surprisingly little of the orange juice was taken up, and several requested even stronger spirits than the white wine being proffered. Indeed, there seemed to be a move toward Bloody Marys that kept the waiters busily running to and from the kitchen.

"Reuben, dear, can you stay for lunch? It's important to me that you be here," Sally Andersen said, as he expressed his condolences once again.

"Of course."

"And will you have some time after? I want to get the family together for a few minutes once lunch is over, just to evaluate what's going on," she said. The widow was already greeting another guest before Frost could reply, so he moved on into the large living room.

"How are you, Reuben?" a voice behind him asked. He turned to find Laurance Andersen facing him.

"How are *you?*" Frost said. "You must have been spending most of your time on airplanes the last couple of days."

"Yes, it seems that way. No time to finish up my business in L.A."

"I'm very sorry about your father," Frost said.

"Thank you. I just hope they catch the wacko who killed him soon, so the publicity will stop."

"You don't have any ideas, I take it?" Frost asked.

"None. I don't think Dad had an enemy in the world."

"It's certainly puzzling," Frost said and then, changing the subject, asked about the St. Martin.

"St. Martin?"

"The hotel in L.A. I understood the other night that you were staying there."

"Oh yes. It's not great."

"That's my impression. I was stuck there once last spring. It's that fancy British outfit that runs it—high prices and all that—but an absolute minimum of service."

"Yeah, I agree," Laurance said, before flagging a waiter to get a second Bloody Mary. As he did so, a signal was given that lunch was being served, and the group moved toward a buffet in the dining room.

Frost, carrying a full plate, was about to join his wife and Sorella Perkins in the living room when Billy O'Neal slipped into the chair next to Sorella. Reconnoitering, Frost could only see a seat next to Diana; he sighed and went toward it.

"Here we are again," Frost said, trying to be jaunty.

"Yes, well, if you can stand it I guess I can," Diana replied.

They ate in silence for a bit, and then Diana asked what Frost thought Jeffrey Gruen would do.

"Unless he keeps going and raises his price sky-high, the Board will still turn him down," Frost guessed. "And I think it's more than likely that the directors will make a self-tender. That's what they were going to do before your father died, and I haven't seen anything that would change that."

"Let me ask you a question. I think I know the answer, but let me ask you anyway," Diana said.

"Go ahead."

"Is there any reason I can't sell my stock to Gruen, if his price is right?"

"No legal reason that I know of," Frost said. "But I think your mother and the rest of your family would be pretty annoyed."

"There may be more important things than the annoyance of my family."

"Such as?"

"Such as the group I do a lot of work with. Concerned Women. Have you heard of it?"

"Yes, indeed."

"And I suppose you don't approve."

"You want an honest answer?" Frost asked.

"Of course. I'm a big girl."

"I suspect I approve of almost all of Concerned Women's goals. But I'm not sure I always approve of their methods, or their rhetoric."

"Your answer doesn't surprise me, though I'm grateful you support our goals—even if you'd deny us the means to achieve them," Diana said.

Frost had said no such thing, but he held both his tongue and his temper. What he really wanted to do was to shout out his *bona fides* on the subject of women's rights: his pioneering insistence on fairness to women in hiring and promotions at Chase & Ward, especially during the years when he had been the firm's Executive Partner; his consistent support of his wife's career as ballerina, as ballet mistress and now as an officer of the Brigham Foundation. He also thought darkly to himself that a martini at his all-male club, the Gotham, would not be an entirely bad thing at precisely this moment.

"I take it you're suggesting you'd like to liquidate your holdings in AFC and make a donation to Concerned Women," Frost said.

"That's about it. My sisters in Concerned Women and I have lots of projects that desperately need funding."

"I'm sure that's true," Frost replied. "But before you make up your mind between your family's feelings and Concerned Women, can I tell you a story? Do you know about the AFC processing plant in Parkersville, California?"

"No, I don't believe I do."

"Let me tell you about it," Frost said. "AFC has a tomato-canning factory in Parkersville that employs about eight hundred people. It's an old factory, been around since the thirties. It's also the principal industry in Parkersville. Many of the workers are the grandsons—grandchildren—of retired AFC workers.

"The Parkersville plant is inefficient. Canning techniques have changed so much in recent years that a new plant, with lasers and robots and all the rest, would pay for itself in no time. But a new plant would be run with about fifty employees.

"Every new M.B.A. that joins AFC, every management consultant the Company has ever hired, says get rid of Parkersville. Your father never did so. He felt an obligation to the workers there, felt an obligation not to wreck the economy of that tiny California town. I heard him say many times, 'I know it's inefficient to keep Parkersville, but we're going to do it just the same. People can criticize if they like, can accuse me of not squeezing out every dime of profit that I can. But as far as I'm concerned, those people can sell out anytime and go ride on someone else's railroad.'

"Now, why do I tell you this?" Frost went on. "I tell you because Jeffrey Gruen, if he took over AFC, would close Parkersville as soon as a new plant could be built. And his bankers would applaud him for doing it. And if he did, I ask you how much closing the plant would do for women's rights in Parkersville?"

"I can't comment, Mr. Frost, I don't know all the facts," Diana Andersen said sullenly.

"What I'm suggesting is that some of these questions may be more complicated than they seem at first."

One of the waiters appeared and announced that dessert and coffee were available in the dining room. Frost often did not eat dessert, but he knew he was going to have some this day, and the sooner the better. He excused himself and left Diana's company with what he hoped was not undue haste.

But not before making a mental note to have either Castagno or Bautista check on the whereabouts of Diana Andersen on the previous Tuesday afternoon.

MOTHER AND DAUGHTER

12 As lunch ended, Sally Andersen moved discreetly among those gathered in her living room, asking members of the family to stay behind and meet in the library. Frost watched her in action, and noted that she had also asked Casper Robbins.

When all the other guests had left, the widow came into the library and sat down behind the desk, facing her family. Frost liked the symbolism of the desk, which showed that she was now in charge of events.

"I just wanted to have a few words with you about three things," she began, speaking deliberately. "The first is the transition at AFC and who's going to be in charge. The second is the police investigation of Flemming's death. And the third is Jeffrey Gruen, and what we're going to do about him. Right now, we can talk about the first two. As for Mr. Gruen, I think we should wait for Randolph Hedley, who called me this morning and said that before we did anything it was urgent that he talk to us about the Foundation."

"Mother, I'm sorry to interrupt, but what did Hedley have to say?" Sorella Perkins asked.

"Nothing, my dear. I have no idea what he wants," Mrs. Andersen said.

"He's probably going to tell you, sis, that the Foundation has to sell to Gruen. He was hinting about that on the plane on Sunday," Laurance Andersen said.

"Mr. Hedley seems to have broadcast his thoughts about the Foundation to everyone except me," Sorella observed. "He hasn't talked to me at all."

Frost silently agreed with Sorella. New York law required a minimum of three directors; she had been one of them, serving with her father and Randolph Hedley (who did not share Frost's compunction about board service for clients). Sorella and Hedley, and any director to replace Flemming, if they could agree on one, would have to decide whether or not to sell the AFC stock owned by the Foundation if Gruen—or the Company, for that matter— made an offer. Hedley, as her fellow director and the Foundation's counsel, should be consulting her, not her mother.

Sally Andersen tried to get the discussion back to the agenda she had outlined. "I understand the Board is scheduled to meet tomorrow morning. Isn't that right, Casper?" she asked the Company President.

"That's correct," Robbins answered.

"I have talked to all the outside directors by telephone and have let them know that I want to go on the Board," Mrs. Andersen said. "When Flemming was alive, it wouldn't have made any sense. But now that he's dead, I feel I must protect what he started.

"I've also made it known that I want Casper to be the new Chairman and Chief Executive Officer, in addition to being President. Down the road, I hope we'll be able to identify someone for the President's job, but until we do, I think it best if Casper holds both positions."

Frost listened intently to Sally Andersen's unquestioned assertion of control over the affairs of Andersen Foods. He also noted the glum looks with which Laurance Andersen and Billy O'Neal, sitting on opposite sides of the living room, greeted her pronouncement about Casper.

Sally Andersen's determination did not surprise Frost at all. While her husband was alive, the woman had always appeared to defer to him. But from many conversations with the late Chairman, Frost knew that Sally followed events within the Company intently and that she was not at all afraid to express her views to her husband, or to lobby him until her objectives were achieved. With Flemming dead, there was no longer any need for modesty or deference.

"Now. Flemming's murder," the widow continued. "I talked with the detective in Greenwich early this morning. There aren't any new developments. No clues. Except that he heard from Reuben Frost's policeman friend in New York that the two notes—the one left in Connecticut and the one delivered to Casper—were definitely not written by the same person. So it appears we have two lunatics on the loose, not just one.

"Detective Castagno did say that he wants to talk to the members of the family he hasn't seen already, which means those that weren't in Connecticut Tuesday night. That would be you, Laurance, and Diana. And you, Billy."

"What in the name of heaven does he want with us?" Diana asked.

"He said it's just routine," Mrs. Andersen replied. "He wants to make sure no one has any information that might offer a clue."

"It seems pretty unlikely we would, if we weren't even there," Laurance said.

"Let's not quarrel about it," Sally said. "All I ask is that you give Mr. Castagno your help. And as I said in Greenwich Tuesday night, I've asked Reuben to coordinate with the police to make things as smooth as possible."

"I still think it's a waste of time," Laurance muttered petulantly.

"Laurance, I don't understand your attitude," his mother said. "There's a psychopath loose out there, maybe two.

One of them murdered your father and I don't know how you can be confident that he doesn't want more victims— like you or any of the rest of us."

"Okay, Mother, okay," Laurance grumbled.

"On to our final problem—Mr. Gruen," Sally Andersen said. "Reuben, tell the others about your conversation with him yesterday—and the slight breathing room he's given us."

Frost did so, and then reviewed the current antitake-over strategy.

"As you all know," he explained, "the Board decided two days ago to turn down Jeffrey Gruen's bear hug. The Board also decided, if Gruen persisted, to make a counteroffer for ten percent of the outstanding stock, but of course excluding the shares owned by all of you, by management and by the Andersen Foundation.

"That was Flemming Andersen's grand design to thwart a raid, subject to being able to raise the money to do it. Since there is every indication the money can be borrowed, it seems to me that Flemming's strategy should be followed. If there is any feeling to the contrary among those of you here, the Company should know it now. The fight with Gruen is going to be fought in a very public way, and the press is going to follow every move—the story has all the elements the press loves. So, if there are any surprises, if there is any dissent from the position Flemming took, management should know it right here and now."

While Frost spoke, Randolph Hedley came into the room and tried to sneak quietly into a chair near the door. Looking over at the new arrival, Frost thought that he was agitated, his face appearing white at one instant, slightly red the next. He was also sweating, possibly from hurrying uptown to this appointment, but possibly also because of the message he was going to convey.

"Does anyone else want to speak?" Sally Andersen

asked. "If not, I assume it is agreed that we proceed the way Flemming wanted—that we continue to say no to Mr. Gruen and, if and when he makes an actual offer, to have AFC make the counteroffer that's been discussed. Laurance? Bill? Sorella? Diana?" She looked at each of the principals in turn; all were silent and none offered any disagreement.

"I think we're agreed," Sally Andersen concluded. "Are we ready to listen to Mr. Hedley?"

Randolph Hedley was unquestionably uncomfortable, as evidenced by his violent sweating and the almost startling changes in his skin coloration. He was trying to project New England take-charge gravity, instead of the fear arising from the inexorable conclusion that he might lose an esteemed and valued client because of the legal conclusions he was about to express.

"Sally, I wonder if we might have a few minutes' recess," Hedley said. "I know what I have to say is probably of interest to all of you, but I'd like to talk to Sorella privately for a few minutes. Now that Flemming's dead, we are the two surviving directors of the Foundation. Will you excuse us?"

Sally Andersen looked at Hedley with impatience, silently expressing her thought that whatever Hedley had to say could perfectly well be said to the entire group. But, having no real choice, she acquiesced. "How much time do you need?" she asked. "Ten minutes? Twenty? You tell us, Randolph."

"Let's compromise on fifteen," Hedley said, laughing weakly at what he thought was a joke. "We'll be back just as soon as we can."

Sorella, behind Hedley's back, shrugged her shoulders and rolled her eyes at the gathering. But despite this subversion, she dutifully followed Hedley out of the library and into the adjoining living room.

When they were comfortably seated, facing each other, Hedley again apologized. "I'm afraid what I've got to say is not going to be very popular in there," he said, nodding toward the library. "And probably not very popular with you.

"I've been talking with some of my partners," he went on. "And I've even had a couple of our young associates do some *actual legal research*." He looked at Sorella and smiled when he finished speaking, the reference to the rarity of legal research apparently being intended as another jest.

"The long and the short of it, Sorella, is that the Foundation may have to sell out to the highest bidder for its AFC stock—either Jeffrey Gruen or the Company itself, depending on how things develop," Hedley said.

"How can that be?" the woman bristled. "Isn't it a decision for the Foundation's directors—that is, you and me, and whoever we elect to replace my father?"

"Yes, yes, that's right, that's right, the directors decide, no question about that. But the directors have a duty to do what's best for the Foundation—not what's best for themselves, or Andersen Foods, or anyone else. And it may just be that the best thing—the prudent thing—would be to take the most money offered and run."

"But Father specifically said the Company's tender was conditioned on the Foundation staying out and not tendering its stock," Sorella pointed out.

"I know that, Sorella, but your father couldn't override the law."

"I must be dense, Randolph, but I really don't understand. Leave aside my loyalty to the family. Are you telling me that I can't decide—can't objectively decide—that AFC is going to be a better investment for the Foundation than anything we might buy with the money we would get from selling?"

"Yes, you could decide that—if the facts warranted that decision. But you'd have to get an investment banking firm to back that up."

"Why?"

"Prudence. You would certainly need an independent valuation of the Company to support your decision not to sell."

"I still don't see why. I'm the Foundation director, not some investment banker. Why isn't it my decision how I vote?"

"It *is*, Sorella," Hedley replied. He began speaking more slowly, as if talking to one slightly retarded, an exasperated tone to his voice. "But you have to be *prudent,* and the way you demonstrate your prudence is to have your conclusion backed up by a banker."

"What if I *wanted* to vote to sell? Would I need an investment banker to back up that decision?"

"It certainly would be the wise thing," Hedley said.

"What if I decided today to sell and then changed my mind next week? Could I use the same investment banker to back me up?"

"Sorella, this is a very complicated matter. Please don't try to make it even more difficult."

"I have heard, Randolph, that there are investment bankers around that will tell you whatever you want to hear. 'Is the tender offer price fair?' 'If that's what you want, we conclude that it is.' 'Is the tender price too low?' 'If that's the way you want to go, we agree.' Is that what your 'independent' bankers do, Mr. Hedley?"

"I'm sure there are some like that, yes. But there are plenty of firms around with integrity."

"You'd never know it, to read the papers."

"Besides, the issue I raise may well be moot. When a final price is established—either by the Company or by Gruen—it may be a proper conclusion that it does not reflect the real prospects of the Company. If the investment bankers tell us that, then I'll be right there with you voting against accepting a tender."

"And if they're not?"

"Then I will have to vote on the basis of all the facts presented to me," Hedley said.

"Let me say just one thing. There are no circumstances under which I will agree that the Foundation's stock will be sold. None. We won't sell to Gruen and we won't accept the Company's tender. I don't care what any investment banker says and, quite frankly, I really don't care what you say. I intend to respect my father's wishes and do everything I can to keep AFC out of Jeffrey Gruen's hands. Shall we go back in? I don't think there's anything more to discuss."

Hedley, who had turned white listening to his obstinate client, rose to follow her back to the library. "I . . . I don't know what to say. . . . I . . . I . . ." he burbled at her back. Incoherently, he spoke about personal liability, the role of the state's attorney general as the guardian of private foundations and other matters to which Sorella paid absolutely no attention whatsoever.

Back in the library, the group became quiet when Sorella and her lawyer returned.

"I think you all may be interested in what Mr. Hedley has to say about the Foundation," Sorella said. "I'll let him tell you in his own words, and then I'll tell you what *I* think."

As Hedley launched into a tortured explanation of his position, Frost, sitting off in the corner, felt that he had seldom seen or heard a more uncomfortable lawyer. The man tried to qualify what he was sure would be unpopular advice, but each new qualification obscured the clarity of what he was saying. Finally, Sorella interrupted.

"I believe what Randolph is trying to say is that the directors of the Andersen Foundation may have to vote to sell its AFC stock, either to Jeffrey Gruen or back to the Company. That would be the case, as I understand it, unless we think the Foundation would be better off keeping the stock as a long-term investment.

"While the trustees apparently make the final decision, Mr. Hedley seems to think they must be guided by an investment banking firm willing to back up the decision they make. I have told Mr. Hedley that I am not interested in any investment banker's opinion and that my mind is made up: the Andersen Foundation will not sell. To do so would disgrace my father and I won't hear of it.

"If Mr. Hedley persists in telling me otherwise, or persists in that position as a Foundation director, I will fight him every way I can. If needs be, I'll get a new lawyer for the Foundation who will help me preserve AFC's integrity."

Frost saw some astonished faces in the room. Not, he thought, because of what Sorella Andersen was saying, but because of the conviction and feeling with which she said it. He himself was not surprised, having always suspected a steely determination underneath the woman's soft demeanor.

"And I, for one, don't need any investment bankers to tell me the decision I have made is right—or wrong."

"Sorella, all I said was that retaining an investment banker as an adviser would be prudent," Hedley interrupted.

"Prudence be damned," the woman countered. "There's such a thing as honoring the memory of the man who made Andersen Foods worth raiding. Selling out the Company that he built—and against almost the last wishes he expressed—is not my idea of honor. And no lawyer is going to tell me differently."

"May I ask a question?" Sally Andersen said. "What happens if the Board of the Foundation has to make a decision? It now has two directors, Sorella and you, Randolph. What if you disagree?"

"We would have to go to court to resolve the deadlock," Hedley said.

"And what would the court do?"

"Probably liquidate the Foundation because of the deadlock."

"Good God, Randolph," Sally said. "You mean not only might we lose the Company, but the Foundation would disappear as well? I suggest, sir, that you and my daughter elect a third director—me—just as soon as possible. What do you say to that?"

"If you want to serve, Mrs. Andersen, I'll be happy to vote for you," Hedley answered. "Without even knowing for sure how you feel about selling the Foundation's stock."

"Precisely," Sally Andersen said. "The important thing is to have a full board if there are decisions to be made. Sorella, do you agree?"

"Absolutely, Mother," the younger woman replied, confident that her mother was on her side.

"Will you draw up the papers and get it done right away?" Sally Andersen asked.

"I'll get up a directors' consent as soon as I get back to the office," Hedley replied.

"Good," Sally Andersen said. "Now, leave me alone. I'm exhausted." She got up from behind the desk and walked toward the doorway. The others dutifully followed, and soon the widow was alone, except for Casper Robbins, who did not leave with the others.

13

Reuben Frost walked home to Seventieth Street after leaving the Andersen apartment. He reflected on Randolph Hedley's advice to the Andersen Foundation as he went along. Wasn't Randolph being a bit conservative? he asked himself. Why shouldn't the directors be entitled to decide that the Foundation would be better off in the long run holding stock in AFC? Why must the Foundation, unlike any other stockholder, be forced to sell out? His instinct was that Hedley was off base, reading the cases far too cautiously. But he wasn't sure—trusts and estates was not his field, and he had not had any research on the question done at Chase & Ward.

When he got home, he called one of the senior trusts and estates partners in his old firm. His colleague's initial reaction mirrored his own, but both agreed that the matter should be well researched.

"You do that just by poking a button these days, don't you?" Frost asked, referring to the LEXIS computer system that all the office's young lawyers seemed enamored of. "No heavy books to haul around, no dust, no missing volumes—it's wonderful!"

"Yes, wonderful if you want your desk covered with computer printouts," his former partner grumbled. "These

young ones can serve up copies of all the cases ever decided on a subject, retrieved and reproduced at the client's
expense. But don't ask whether your associate thinks the
cases are right or wrong, or distinguishable from your
own. Don't ask him—or her—to think, in other words."

"Oh, the modern world," Frost lamented. "But whatever
the system, I'm afraid we need the work done. If Hedley
continues to be obstinate, I'm sure the family will ask our
opinion, and we'd better be ready."

Frost did not relish a confrontation with Hedley. He
was no special friend, but it was never easy publicly to
disagree with another lawyer over the exercise of the most
basic professional skill—reading and interpreting the decided cases relevant to a question. Maybe Frost and his colleagues would ultimately come to agree with Hedley. But if
they didn't, he could foresee both embarrassment and un-
pleasantness.

Waking up from a nap an hour later, Frost picked up
the copy of *New York Newsday* that he had purchased on
the way home. It contained a long profile of Jeffrey Gruen
and his wife, Gloria, describing in glowing terms the apartment Frost had found so appalling two days earlier. It also
mentioned Gruen's interest in AFC. Frost read with interest the article's speculation on Gruen's strategy:

"Wall Street observers are intrigued by Gruen's threatened tender offer for Andersen Foods. More than 47 percent of AFC's stock is owned by the Andersen family, management and the Andersen Foundation. On the face of it,
securing a majority position in Andersen Foods would appear nearly impossible for Gruen. Flemming Andersen,
before his death, certainly said as much, indicating that
the insider group would stand firm and never sell to 'a
cheap raider like Gruen.'

"Is the barrier not quite as thick as the family patriarch
believed? Does Gruen think he can crack the united front
arrayed against him? These questions are intriguing Street

analysts—even more so than usual, since there is no information, no gossip and no rumors to support Jeffrey Gruen's confident assertion that he can buy control of AFC."

No light shed there, Frost thought. After the afternoon's events, he could only think that Gruen was betting that the Foundation would sell to him. Or did he know something that Frost did not about the Andersen heirs?

Frost's reflections, which yielded no guesses and certainly no conclusions, were brought to an end by the arrival of his wife.

"Hello, dear," she said, entering the bedroom and kissing her husband on the forehead. "Can you use a grant? We've got plenty of money to give away. Remember the line from that old Irving Berlin musical, where Ethel Merman played the ambassador, 'Money, money, money—can you use any money today?' That's about the way I feel after reviewing grant applications all afternoon," she said, referring to her current activity at the Brigham Foundation. "Sometimes I think there are more performance groups than people in this country."

"So you spent the afternoon shoveling out the money," Frost said, as his wife sat down on the edge of the bed. "I hope none to any group that would give offense to the memory of Martin Brigham."

"No more so than usual, my dear," she replied.

"Or the Mayor," her husband added.

"The Mayor! Please, Reuben. We did our best to preserve hearthside values, but a little of that goes a long way," she said, referring to a recent television interview in which the Mayor had bemoaned the lack of "hearthside values" in the New York theater.

"All right, all right," Frost said. "I just don't want Norman running around accusing you of corrupting the young and demoralizing the old."

"Let me handle Norman, dear. You just don't understand how friendly and close the Mayor and I are."

"Mmn."

"By the way, changing the subject, I had a very peculiar call from Sorella Andersen this afternoon," Cynthia said.

"Sorella?"

"Yes. She was calling from Connecticut and seemed very upset. Said she was being pushed every which way and didn't know where to turn."

"Pushed how? What was she talking about?"

"As best I could gather—she really was too upset to be completely understandable—she feels threatened by the conflicting advice she's getting about the Andersen Foundation. She says she wants to do right by her father and not have the Foundation sell its AFC stock. But then she said there was pressure for the Foundation to sell."

"What did she mean by that, I wonder?" Reuben said.

"She didn't elaborate," Cynthia answered, "except to say that Randolph Hedley was being very difficult."

"Why was she calling you, by the way?" Reuben asked.

"Because of my generally sympathetic nature," Cynthia answered.

"Yes, yes, but leaving that aside, why was she coming to you?"

"She said she had to talk with someone. She didn't want to talk to you or another lawyer, because that would look as if she were going behind Hedley's back. And she said she thought I could help because of my experience at the Brigham Foundation."

"Very interesting."

"She wants to have lunch with me first thing next week."

That lunch would not take place. Within the hour, as Reuben and Cynthia Frost sat in their living room having a drink before dinner, Sally Andersen called to relay more appalling news from Connecticut.

"Sorella's been taken to the hospital," she fairly shouted into the telephone. "Her dogs turned on her and bit her all over her body. . . . They don't expect her to live." The woman's voice dropped as she spoke.

"How on earth did it happen?" Frost asked, devastated and even a little frightened at what he was being told.

"God knows, Reuben. I was coming down for my evening swim—just as I had the day Flemming was killed—when Nate Perkins came running from his house, screaming that the dogs had turned on Sorella.

"He had heard the dogs—you know, those awful Dobermans that Sorella kept—yowling in the dog run outside their kennel. He went down to investigate and saw Sorella unconscious by the kennel and the dogs in a frenzy, licking the blood off Sorella's wounds. Reuben, I can't take much more of this," she said, sobbing into the telephone.

"Why would the dogs turn on her? Had they ever done that before?"

"Not that I know of. I don't understand it. All I know is that my husband is dead, and now probably my daughter."

"Sally, I'll be up there just as soon as I can."

"Oh, Reuben, I hate to put you out, but it would be a great comfort to me if you were here."

"Don't say another word. I'll leave immediately," Frost said.

Frost was unable to think clearly on the ride to Greenwich. This new and horrible turn of events left him both depressed and confused. Was Sorella wounded by accident? He remembered reading of cases where dogs—Dobermans at that—had turned on their owners. Perhaps that was all there was to the attack on her. But couldn't someone have provoked it? The same person who had killed Flemming perhaps? Maybe it was Randolph Hedley, Frost mused, repressing a sour laugh. Anything to keep business! No, it certainly would not have been Randolph, upright and straitlaced Randolph.

Frost was greeted at the Andersens with the news that Sorella was dead. He did his best to comfort her relatives— her mother, crying profusely; her husband, Nate, pathetically quiet and so shaken it was not clear that it had fully registered on him yet that he was a widower; and her brother, Laurance, also silent and also apparently stunned.

Sally Andersen, amid sobs, also told Frost the other ugly news. Another note had been found, again held down with a rock and placed behind the dog kennel.

"Where is it?" Frost demanded.

"On the desk in the library. We've all tried not to touch it."

Frost went to the library immediately. What he saw was sickeningly familiar—a sheet of white typewriter paper with a message in block capital letters written in black ink. It read:

HEART O GOLD IS THE FINEST PET FOOD x x BUT DOGS LIKE IT WITH A LITTLE ZIP x x LIKE CHUNKS OF SORELLA ANDERSEN x x LOVE x x x

Reading the ghoulish note made Frost slightly dizzy. He steadied himself by leaning against the desk, then rejoined the family in the living room.

"Have you called the policeman, Castagno?" he asked.

"Yes," Nate Perkins answered. "He's on his way. In fact, here he is now."

The Greenwich detective came into the room, and Sally Andersen again reviewed the afternoon's tragic events. Nathaniel Perkins took him, two other police officers and Frost back to the kennel. When Castagno, Perkins and Frost returned, and after the detective had examined the latest note, he began asking questions.

"Mrs. Andersen, about what time was it when you came down to swim?"

"Just about six. When I'm here, I always try to swim at six."

"And you said you heard barking from the Perkinses' kennel?"

"Yes."

"But no screams, no cries for help?"

"No," the woman replied, looking puzzled. "No, I don't remember anything like that."

"And you, Mr. Perkins. You heard the dogs barking, but you didn't hear any cries for help either. Is that right?"

"That's right," Perkins answered, the cigarette in his hand shaking badly. "I had never heard the dogs barking so intensely."

"What were you doing when you heard them?"

"I was just finishing up some writing in the attic. I've got a room tucked away up there where I write."

"When was the last time you saw the deceased?"

"When we got back from New York. We'd been to her father's funeral and then a luncheon at Mrs. Andersen's."

"What time was that?"

"About four-thirty. I left Sorella in our bedroom and told her I was heading upstairs to write. She said she was going to take a nap and then would go shopping for dinner."

"How did she seem to you?"

"Perfectly normal. She was a bit upset about some business having to do with the family Foundation, but no, she was really normal."

"What did you do when you found her?"

"I shouted at the dogs and somehow got them to calm down and go inside the kennel."

"Which is where they are now?"

"Yes."

"I'm going to call a vet and have them locked up. Okay?"

"Yes," Perkins said. "I never want to see those dogs again."

"I can understand that," the detective replied. "Mr. Frost? Would you come with me for a second? I'd like to talk to you after I phone the vet."

The two men went to the library, where Castagno made his call. When he had finished, he and Frost stood facing each other inches from the latest murder note.

"Any bright ideas, Mr. Frost?" Castagno asked.

"Afraid not."

"What was this Foundation business Perkins was talking about?"

Frost explained in some detail the Gruen raid and the possible role the Foundation's AFC shares might play in it.

"What you're telling me, Mr. Frost, is that there's a pretty high-stakes poker game going on, is that right?"

"Yes. The whole matter of the Andersens controlling AFC has been called into question."

The detective sighed. "I don't understand any of that financial stuff. It's all beyond me."

Frost took in the man's despairing answer, wondering if other things—such as the two Andersen murders—might be beyond him as well. Thinking quickly, he ventured a suggestion.

"You know, Officer Castagno, I was wondering whether it might not be a good idea for you and me and Detective Bautista from New York to sit down and go over what we know and what we don't know."

"I'd go for that. Do you know where to reach him?" Castagno said.

"I do during the day, but I might have some trouble finding him at this time of night. But I'll try," Frost said. "Shall we meet tomorrow morning, if that can be arranged?"

140

"Sure."

"Here or in New York?"

"Here would be better, don't you think? All the physical evidence is here."

"Fine."

Frost made the first of what turned out to be a series of telephone calls. But he ultimately located Bautista, who consented—with some reluctance—to come to Greenwich the next morning. Frost told Castagno that he would expect Bautista about ten o'clock and would give him a call when he arrived.

He then informed Sally Andersen of his plan, and asked if he could stay overnight.

"Reuben, it would be both a relief and a pleasure," she said. "We've got to track down this killer before he's murdered the whole family."

Frost called Cynthia to tell her he would not be returning until the next day. He and Sally and Laurance had a quiet dinner, interrupted by the arrival of Diana—dry-eyed but demanding to know all the details of her sister's death. Frost, feeling overpoweringly tired, excused himself before Sally began a new rendition of the afternoon's bloody event.

Ensconced in the Andersen guest room, Frost lay awake trying to put together the disparate pieces of the puzzle. But the pieces blurred unintelligibly, not fitting into a clear, logical pattern. Frustrated, he rolled onto his side and was asleep almost at once.

THE POLICE

14 Frost woke early on Friday morning and watched the local news on the small television set in the guest room. Sorella's murder was the lead story. He watched intently as a camera panned in on a Tudor brick house, then realized with a start that it was the very house he was in.

The TV commentator reported that no member of the Andersen family would talk about the previous day's events. Detective Castagno and the local chief of police appeared, but refused to confirm or deny whether they thought a psychopathic killer was loose in Fairfield County. The commentator fed this speculation, however, and several bystanders in the streets of Greenwich expressed suitable degrees of apprehension and fright for the cameras.

After the broadcast, Frost shaved with the razor he had borrowed the night before, got dressed and went downstairs. He found Sally Andersen eating breakfast alone in the dining room.

"Good morning, Reuben. Did you see the TV?"

"Yes. I watched it upstairs. I'm sorry, Sally, to see you subjected to this, on top of everything else."

"There was a camera crew calling here at six o'clock. Wouldn't you think they'd have some sense of decency?"

"I doubt that word's in their vocabulary," Reuben answered.

"Well, as you saw, they didn't get anything out of us. And they won't either," Sally said. "And do you believe the business that there's a maniac behind the killings?"

"I don't know. Those notes aren't exactly sane."

"Yes. But they could be a put-on."

"True enough," Frost said. "Maybe my detective friends will have a nice, lucid theory."

"I hope so. What time are they coming?"

"Around ten."

"You make yourself at home and order some breakfast. I'm going over to see Nate. He's in an awful state, and we have to make the funeral arrangements."

"Where is Diana?"

"She's staying at Laurance's. I haven't seen her yet this morning."

"How did she take the news last night?"

"Coolly," Sally said. "But then, she's cool about everything."

When Mrs. Andersen had left, Reuben picked up the morning *Times* and read its account of the murder. There were no new facts, but the focus was less on an anonymous crazed killer that the telecast's had been.

Bautista arrived almost precisely at ten.

"It's a good thing I'm a friend of yours," he said to Frost, almost before saying good morning. "Do you know what I had to go through to get authorization to come up here?"

"No, but I can imagine," Frost said. "I'm thankful that you did, though. Unless I can get both you and Officer Castagno in the same room, and knock your heads together, I don't think we'll ever solve anything."

"Can you show me the scene of the crime?"

"Certainly. Come with me."

Frost took the detective to the kennel, explaining the

circumstances of Sorella's death as best he could. They returned to the main house just as Castagno arrived.

"Shall we talk here?" he asked.

"Mmn," Frost said. "Maybe not. There're quite a few people around."

"You want to go to headquarters?" Castagno asked.

"That might be better," Frost said. He went off to tell one of the staff that he was leaving and would call Sally Andersen later. The three men then set out, Frost in Bautista's car, Castagno driving alone, for the sand-colored granite fortress on Havemeyer Place that was police headquarters.

Once there, Castagno found a vacant conference room where the three of them could sit comfortably, and managed also to produce coffee.

"How shall we proceed?" Castagno asked.

Frost subtly but firmly took charge.

"Did either of you see the TV news this morning?" he asked. Castagno said he had—his wife was most excited to see her husband on television—but Bautista had not.

"They speculated, Luis, that there's a maniac on the prowl up here who's killed both Sorella and her father," Frost said. "What do you think of that theory?"

"I dunno," Bautista replied. "I take it the note they found last night is in the same lettering as the one left when the father died?"

"It appears to be the same, yes," Castagno said.

"Of course, that doesn't help us with the second note left the last time," Bautista said.

"Oh my God," Frost said. "Do you think we should alert them in New York to be on the lookout for a new note?"

"Yes," both of the police officers said, almost in unison.

"Can I call from here?" Frost asked.

"Sure," Castagno said. "Dial nine."

The two watched as Frost called and reached Robbins, admonishing him to alert properly the people in the AFC

mail room, where the first "follow-up" note had been delivered.

"Luis, you feel the note AFC got in New York the last
time was from somebody unrelated to the crime, is that
right?" Frost asked, when he had finished his call to
Robbins.

"Yes, I do," Bautista said. "It was different paper, different ink, different handwriting and even a different
tone. Some screwball probably wrote it, but I don't think
it's the one we want."

"I agree with that," Castagno said.

"All right. What about the notes that were left here in
Connecticut," Frost asked. "Are they the work of a psychotic, or not?"

"Who can say at this point in time?" Castagno replied.
"Either we've got somebody with a grievance against the
Andersens or it's a blind to throw us off the track."

"If you ask me, I think it's the latter," Bautista said.
"But we've got to comb everything to make sure it isn't
a nut."

"I plan to sit down with everyone in the family to see
if they can remember anyone with a grievance," Castagno
said, as Bautista nodded approvingly.

"And I think we've got to put people on AFC's personnel
records. See if that turns up anything," Bautista said.

"You have guys to do that?" Castagno asked.

"It'll be hard," Bautista said. "But I think I can get a
couple people to start on the records in New York."

"Luis, I think you and Art—may I call you that?—agree
that the notes are probably a cover. Isn't that correct?"
Frost asked.

The two police officers nodded.

"So don't you have to investigate on that theory as
well?" Frost asked.

His listeners agreed that such was the case and asked

him if he had any theories, if he knew of anyone who had it in for Flemming Andersen and his daughter.

"I can think of one or two people who may have had a quarrel with one or the other, but not both."

"Like who?" Bautista asked.

"Randolph Hedley, the lawyer for the Andersen Foundation. Sorella hinted very strongly yesterday afternoon that she might fire him. I know the Foundation account is a big thing for his firm. But I can't imagine him murdering anybody. And he certainly wouldn't have had any motive to kill Flemming."

Bautista nonetheless wrote down the name in his notebook. "Who else?" he asked.

"Well, Casper Robbins, the President of AFC, may have felt under Flemming's thumb. Could he have killed Flemming to increase his own power? Pretty unlikely, but it's at least theoretically possible. But even if you accepted this far-out theory, he had no reason to kill Sorella.

"Then there's Nate Perkins. I'm sure Sorella's will left everything to him and their children. So he had a motive to kill Sorella—but not his father-in-law.

"Or take Billy O'Neal, resenting for his whole life the position of Flemming and his family in the Company."

"What do you mean?" Castagno asked. Frost told them the story of the first Laurance Andersen's will, and its sexist shortchanging of O'Neal's branch of the family. Both policemen found the tale interesting and both were now writing in their notebooks.

"But again," Frost concluded, "even if O'Neal's hatred got the better of him and he did in Flemming, he had no reason to follow that up with a second murder."

"Do you have *any* theory, Reuben?" Bautista asked, with some exasperation. "What about this fellow Gruen and his takeover? Could that have any bearing?"

"Yes, it could. There's one thing Flemming and his

daughter had in common—they both refused to knuckle under to Jeffrey Gruen."

"So Gruen could be a suspect?" Castagno asked.

"I suppose so," Frost answered. "Though I don't quite see how he'd know his way around well enough to push Flemming into the hot tub and to let Sorella's dogs out of their kennels."

"Who else might have wanted Gruen's offer to go through?" Bautista asked.

"You mean, who might have wanted to end Flemming's and Sorella's opposition?" Frost asked. "Hard to say," he said, after a pause. "Diana, the other daughter, is the obvious one. It's been an open secret—she told me so herself yesterday—that she wants to sell the rest of her stock so she can support this organization she's tied up with."

"What organization?" Castagno asked.

"Something called Concerned Women. A very militant, very politicized female group."

"What about this O'Neal fellow? Couldn't he and Gruen have teamed up to carry off the takeover?" Bautista asked.

"Perhaps," Frost said. "But I just don't see it."

"But you don't rule it out, either," Bautista pressed.

"No . . . no, I don't, at least not entirely."

"How about Robbins? Could he have been Gruen's teammate?"

"Maybe. But he had a golden parachute, so he had no need to team up with Gruen."

"I'm sorry, Mr. Frost, but what's a 'golden parachute'?" Castagno asked.

"It's a sweetheart deal," Frost replied, and then, thinking he might have to explain "sweetheart deal," he went on. "It's an extremely favorable set of arrangements for an executive that only comes into play if his corporation's taken over and he's fired by the new management."

"Sounds like a good idea to me," Bautista said. "They

got anything like that in the Greenwich police force, Art?"

"Christ, the Silver Shield Association can't even get them to pay overtime," Castagno answered.

"Sounds like the N.Y.P.D."

"Anyway," Frost continued, "Robbins has always seemed loyal to me."

"Is anybody getting hungry?" Castagno interrupted. "There's a diner down the street. Maybe we ought to continue this conversation there. Usually you can get a back booth where other people can't hear you."

"Sounds good," Bautista said.

Once they were at the diner, the conversation turned quickly to small talk or, more precisely, shoptalk between Bautista and Castagno. Frost had very little to add, but was fascinated by the workaday grievances the two police officers had.

As the three sat drinking their coffee after lunch, Frost spoke to his colleagues. "You know, I've been trying to think through the takeover angle. If Flemming and Sorella were killed because they would oppose Gruen's offer—and assuming they were killed by the same person—that points to somebody who knew what Sorella's position was. As far as I know, she didn't tell anyone that position until yesterday afternoon, when she announced it at the informal meeting her mother had after the funeral."

"So what do you conclude?" Castagno asked.

"I conclude that it must have been someone at that meeting, or someone close to a person at that meeting."

"What exactly was this meeting, and what happened there?" Castagno asked. Frost explained, and summarized what had been said.

Bautista looked through the pages he had written on in his notebook. "Reuben, it seems to me that everyone you mentioned was at Mrs. Andersen's powwow except Jeffrey Gruen himself. But O'Neal, the lawyer Hedley, Diana Andersen and Robbins were all there. Now, Reuben, who else was present?" he asked.

Frost paused to think. "Let's see. Laurance, the son. Nate Perkins, Sorella's husband. And of course Sally Andersen. That's all, I'm pretty sure."

"Any reason to think that any of the people we've been talking about have been cozy with Jeffrey Gruen?" Bautista asked.

"It seems utterly improbable to me," Frost said.

The waitress brought the check for lunch and the three men divided it equally. They did not show any signs of leaving, however, Castagno asking for more coffee for the group after the check was paid.

The two detectives agreed that the people on the list they had developed should be questioned closely about their whereabouts on both Tuesday afternoon and Thursday afternoon, and their alibis carefully checked. Castagno and Bautista divided the names between them, and Bautista and Frost headed back to New York. Not having had a chance to talk in some time, they soon left the problems of the Andersens in favor of personal conversation.

Bautista, who would soon finish his night law school course, was uncertain what to do—should he leave the Police Department or not? Frost wanted to be helpful, but his vantage point in the legal profession, from the summit occupied by his eminent Wall Street firm, was so different from Bautista's, situated somewhere in the maze that was called the "criminal justice system," that he simply could not make concrete suggestions. All he could do was talk his companion through his choices, probing for weaknesses and uncertainties in his reasoning and analysis.

"What about the District Attorney's office? Or the U.S. Attorney? He should be a good, lively fellow to work for," Frost said.

"Yeah. But I'm not sure they'd have me. They want real hotshots, you know."

"Surely your police experience ought to be worth a great deal to them."

"I guess."

"And let's face it, your ethnic background should count for something, too."

"But Reuben, I don't want to get a job just because I'm Puerto Rican."

"I didn't say that," Frost said. "I didn't say you should get a job *because* you're Puerto Rican. I said that it was one factor that should work in your favor—one out of many."

"We'll see. Maybe I'll go into practice for myself. Did you ever think of doing that?"

"I can truthfully say I never did," Frost replied.

"Any reason?"

"Well, I got interested in corporate law pretty early. And you really can't do that by yourself."

"Got to have a *giant* firm to beat up on people, right?"

"That's not really the reason," Frost explained. "It's just that a corporation of any size requires a lot of lawyers expert in different things—tax, real estate, securities law, antitrust, you name it. One person simply can't keep up with developments in all those fields."

"I don't know what's right," Bautista said. "All I want is a decent, clean life with a little more certainty—and a little more money—than I've got in the Police Department. Odd as you might think it sounds, that's probably criminal law for me."

"I'll refer all my criminal cases to you, Luis," Frost said.

"And I'll send you all the takeovers that come my way," Bautista replied.

"Except I might have to re-refer some of that business to you, if you're going to be the criminal lawyer."

Frost's joke brought both of them back to the serious business at hand.

"Reuben, assuming there's no nut on the loose—which

will disappoint the TV crews, but I really think it's unlikely—aren't the murders somehow linked to the takeover? I know you said it was improbable that there might be a link between this guy Gruen and anybody on our list, but isn't it just possible there *was* such a link? That there *was* some funny business between Gruen and someone hooked up with the family?"

"I still don't think so. Or maybe it's just that I'd *like* not to think so," Frost replied. "But look, Luis, after one Andersen has been found boiling in a hot tub and another's been chewed up by dogs, I'd have to say that almost *anything* is possible."

"Any advice?" Bautista asked.

"Yes. It's a fine thing to say to a policeman, but let me say it anyway: overlook nothing, let no detail go unnoticed. This whole puzzle is so grotesque, so absurd, that its solution will probably depend on some minute scrap of information that is triviality itself."

CRAZIES

Bautista dropped Frost off at the Gotham Club, where the old lawyer wanted nothing more than a quiet hour reading magazines, but he was interrupted soon after his arrival by a telephone call. He went to a private booth off the great hall of the club to find an agitated Casper Robbins on the other end of the line.

"Goddammit, Reuben, where have you been? There's another note," Robbins shouted into the telephone. "Delivered to the AFC mail room at lunchtime."

"Did they catch the person who brought it?" Frost asked.

"No, they didn't," Robbins answered. "The mail-room supervisor was out to lunch when someone simply dropped an envelope on the receiving counter. Whoever left it didn't have it logged in or didn't get a receipt. No one has the faintest idea who it was."

"Damn," Frost said, almost adding, "I thought you were supposed to set up an effective watch for just this occurrence," but did not.

"I'm sorry, Reuben. My instructions were apparently just too complicated for the geniuses in our mail room."

"Is the note like the other one?"

"Yes. It's on brown paper and written in red crayon, the same as before."

"What does it say?"

"I'll read it:

"Revenge again—and so soon, too! The wickedness of the Andersens is being punished. First Flemming, now Sorella. Justice is done!"

"Good Lord," Frost said. "Have you called the police?"

"No, they just brought the thing up here a few minutes ago. What's the name of your cop friend?"

"Luis Bautista," Frost replied, giving Robbins Bautista's direct telephone number as well.

"Nothing's simple, is it, Reuben?" Robbins said.

"It certainly isn't. It certainly isn't."

Frost felt slightly weak as he left the Club; Robbins's announcement undid whatever contentment his brief stint of magazine reading had induced. Normally he would have walked home, but he now felt it wiser to take the bus.

At Madison Avenue the buses were, as usual, traveling in packs, like circus elephants. He boarded one that was practically empty, the lead motorized pachyderm having already picked up most of the customers at Fifty-fifth Street.

Sitting on the bus, and reflecting on the latest news Robbins had conveyed, Frost was suddenly aware of a loud cacophony coming from the front. It was the middle-aged black driver, in all other respects a seemingly model citizen, tooting on the horn, manipulating the warning light that went with the STAND BEHIND THE WHITE LINE sign, squeezing the air out of the brakes and performing at least three other procedures Frost could not identify. The result of this multifarious activity was a rhythmic, surrealistic, Spike Jones rhapsody. The sparse collection of passengers reacted in typical New York fashion—impassivity on the faces of some, an occasional smile, here a look of resignation at being in the living asylum that called itself a city.

Frost himself looked around and caught the eye of a well-dressed matron sitting across from him.

"Only in New York," he said.

"Yes," the good-looking woman replied, "how true."

By the time the bus reached Seventieth Street, the driver was playing and humming *The Blue Danube,* tooting the bus's horn on the afterbeats.

"I hope you're not going too much farther," Frost said to his fellow passenger. "He'll be doing Ravel's *Bolero* soon."

"You think before Eighty-fourth Street?" the woman asked.

"Maybe not," Frost answered. "Good luck." He left the bus by the middle door as the driver launched into the repeat of the *Danube*'s first theme.

Frost's involvement that day with the city's crazies was not yet over. Back home, he received a call from his old friend and Princeton classmate Homer Matthewson, saying that it was "urgent" that he see Frost right away on a matter of "great delicacy."

He was amused at the melodramatics of his caller. From long experience, he knew that Matthewson operated in a semihysterical state much of the time; he led his life as if it were being conducted on the stage of Princeton's Theatre Intime, where he had earned a certain notoriety as an undergraduate for his plummy—not to say hammy—performances.

Frost of course agreed to see Matthewson; his old friend's somber tone gave him little choice. As he waited for his classmate's arrival—Matthewson was coming to the

Frost brownstone from his bachelor digs in the Village—
Frost reflected upon his fifty-five-year friendship with him.
The two men had been in an English precept together at
Princeton—Frost the naïve and rather guarded orphan
from upstate New York, Matthewson the theatrically ur-
bane (at least in Chicago terms) sophomore from the
Midwest. Both were admirers of the works of their fellow
Princetonian F. Scott Fitzgerald, an enthusiasm not
shared at the time by the English Department faculty.

Matthewson and Frost had become friends, although
not especially close ones. They enjoyed each other's company, Matthewson's flamboyant outrageousness serving
as a useful tonic to Frost's more serious career path: history major at Princeton, Harvard Law School, association
with Chase & Ward. Their encounters after college had
been infrequent, although Frost usually found them of
interest because of the surprising quirks and turns of
Matthewson's life.

Despite his fluty—one less charitable might have said
effeminate—voice, Matthewson had been married for a
long stretch in his early career and had sired, if Frost remembered correctly, seven children. A wealthy heir to a
Chicago heavy-machinery fortune, he had been able, after
an amicable divorce, to provide very comfortably for his
ex-wife and children. And before, during and after his
marriage, he had been able to indulge his ideological in-
fatuation of the moment. Successively, he had given a
tight, emotional embrace to moral rearmament, one
world-ism, proletarian off-Broadway theater, the Sri Meher
Baba, Eugene McCarthy and the return of the Dalai Lama.
Most recently, with even his youngest children maturing,
he had begun to feel intimations of mortality and, when
he looked fate squarely in the eye, had apparently seen reflected there the image of the Archbishop of Canterbury.
The result had been countless charitable undertakings for

Episcopal churches around New York City, involving not so much Matthewson's money as his considerable energy.

At their last meeting, some four months earlier, Frost had gotten the impression that Matthewson's current projects were not at all quixotic, as they had often been in the past, but were practical, and almost saintly, good works involving the city's poor and homeless.

Minutes later, when the bell rang, Frost pushed the buzzer that unlocked the front door; instantly Matthewson, a mountain of a man, was bounding up the stairs with a speed that belied both his age and his size. Despite the mild weather, he was wearing a wool lumberjack shirt under a sport coat Frost swore he remembered from undergraduate days. Snow-white hair accentuated his healthily ruddy face, or perhaps it was the other way round.

"Reuben!" he fairly shouted in his melodious voice. "Thank you so much for seeing me!"

"Homer, it's a pleasure, as always," Frost replied. "What can I do for you?" He motioned Matthewson to the sofa in the living room as he spoke, sitting down himself in the chair beside it.

"You're still the lawyer for the Andersen family, aren't you?" his guest asked.

"In a manner of speaking, Homer. I'm pretty much retired from practice, as you know, but I still do some work for them. Why?"

"I don't quite know how to explain this, but I'll do the best I can," Matthewson said. "You remember the last time we talked, I told you I was working with homeless and unemployed men at St. Timothy's Shelter?"

"Yes, I do. I remember your description very well."

"I'm sort of a counselor for the men there, which means I get to know a lot about them—often more than I want to," Matthewson said. "One of them is a fellow named Oscar Brothers—he's about forty-five, but he's had a

rough enough life for someone twice as old. He's functioning pretty normally now, but there was a lot of craziness
and violence in his past.

"He used to be a cook, then alcohol got the better of him
and he lost the last job he ever had, twenty years ago,
probably. After that, he wandered the streets and got so
violent he was finally committed to one of the state mental hospitals up the Hudson. But then 'deinstitutionaliza-
tion' came along and he was released, along with just
about every other psychotic under the state's care."

"Ah yes," Frost said. "That great humane program that
put the demented back on the streets, to their great dis-
comfort—and everyone else's."

"Exactly. It was a misguided disgrace, thought up by
some bureaucratic psychiatrists without a particle of common sense among them," Matthewson said. "But I'm getting off the track."

"That's all right," Frost interjected.

"One of my jobs is to listen to the men who come to St.
Timothy's when they want to talk. Brothers is one of my
best customers. He doesn't live at the Shelter—he's got a
single room at a hotel downtown paid for by the City—but
he does come there to work part-time. And to talk to me.

"Everything had been going pretty well with Brothers
until very recently," Matthewson continued. "He's no
longer drinking and is almost off medication."

"What does he do all day?" Frost asked.

"Nothing very exciting. He goes to the local branch library near his hotel and reads the magazines. Or, if the
weather is nice, he just sits around on the street outside.
And he works at the Shelter as a cook three nights a week.
But let me get to the point—I'm sorry, Reuben, I simply
can't tell a story in a hurry."

"You never could, Homer. That's part of your charm."

"At any rate, Brothers got all excited when he read
about Flemming Andersen's murder. He brought the pa-

per to show me. Said he knew Andersen well and used to work for him. But there was no remorse—boy, was there no remorse. Brothers hated Andersen with a vehemence that came right through his Thorazine."

"Any reason given?" Frost asked.

"Oh yes. Andersen is the man who fired him from the last real job he ever had. He didn't tell me the reasons at first, but he obviously thought a terrible wrong had been done."

"Mmn."

"Anyway, he couldn't stop talking about the dead man. Every time he saw me he recalled new tales to tell. He was determined to convince me that Flemming Andersen deserved what he got. Then, this morning, he got even more frenzied when the papers reported the daughter's death."

"I suppose he'd had problems with her, too?"

"Yes, he did. The girl, Sorella, was the one who complained to her father that Brothers had made a pass at her. It was her complaint that led to his being fired."

"Quite a coincidence."

"I'd like to think that's all it is," Matthewson said. "But this morning, when Brothers came to see me, he was in a manic mood, bragging that justice had been done—*and he had done it!*"

"You mean *he* murdered Flemming and his daughter?"

"I don't know, Reuben. All he would say was that justice had been done, and that he had told the world about the wrongs that had been righted, in notes to the Andersens."

"What did he tell you about notes?" Frost asked sharply.

"Nothing. He just kept saying he had delivered them. A fact that seemed to please him immensely, by the way."

"Do you think he could have done the killings?"

"I don't think so. But who knows?"

"Let me ask you a couple of questions," Frost said. "Where was your Mr. Brothers Tuesday night?"

"I don't know, now that you mention it."

"Was he at St. Timothy's? Was he cooking there?"

"No. He cooks on Mondays, Wednesdays and Fridays. I don't think I saw him at all on Tuesday."

"Or Thursday?" Frost pressed.

"No, I didn't see him on Thursday, either," Matthewson answered, taken aback.

"Homer, when this man says he worked for Andersen, where was that?"

"In Connecticut."

"So he knew the house—or I should say the compound—in Greenwich?"

"Yes, he did."

"Now," Frost went on, "what did he say about the notes? Where did he leave them?"

"He didn't tell me. All he talked about was delivering them."

Frost did not let on that there were four notes in all. Nor did he discuss their contents.

"Homer, it's obvious that your Mr. Brothers is at least slightly crazy," Frost said, looking straight at his former classmate. "But is he crazy enough to have killed Flemming and Sorella?"

"I honestly don't think so," Matthewson answered. "And that's really why I'm here."

"What do you mean?"

"Just this: Brothers has either committed murder or he's written some silly notes. If it's the former, that's easy. The quicker we get him locked up the better. But if it's the latter, that's more complicated. He'll be thrown right back into the street if the City finds out about it. Human Services will cut off his support so fast it will make your head spin.

"Now you may say that's exactly what they ought to do," Matthewson went on. "Writing hate mail to the family of murder victims isn't very nice. But if Brothers goes back to the street, that means the end of medical care, psychiatric care, stabilizing medicine, everything."

"What am I supposed to do, Homer?"

"I figured you might know the inside situation, or at least could find out about it," Matthewson said. "The papers said there were notes left by the killer. I need to know whether those were the ones Brothers wrote."

"As it happens, you may have come to the right place," Frost said. "I *do* know about the notes, and I even know what they said."

"Would you be willing to talk to Brothers?" Matthewson asked.

"The prospect does not fill me with delight," Frost said. "What if he is the killer and wants to make me victim number three?"

"Don't worry about that. You can talk to Brothers at St. Timothy's, where I can keep an eye on what's going on. And I'll have a couple of others watching, too. So you'll be perfectly safe."

"For you, Homer, I'll do it," Frost said, with a deep sigh. "When?"

"Could you come to St. Timothy's at five-thirty? Brothers will have started work by then."

Frost looked at his watch. Four o'clock. Just time enough for a short rest. "Fine, I'll be there at five-thirty. What's the address?"

Matthewson gave his old friend the street address in Chelsea, shook hands warmly and departed.

Frost took a taxi to Ninth Avenue and Twentieth Street shortly after five o'clock. Both he and the taxi driver had difficulty making out the house numbers, so Frost dismissed the taxi and sought out St. Timothy's Shelter on foot. Soon he found the somber gray former school building that had become (on the ground floor and in the basement) St. Timothy's Shelter and (upstairs) a communal art gallery and performance space.

The entrance doors, originally designed to accommodate an onslaught of students, were all locked except one. Frost opened it gingerly and entered a dimly lighted corridor. There was sound coming from a room beyond, so Frost went toward it, finding a lounge with a beat-up television set, several wooden funeral-parlor chairs and some upholstered furniture with the stuffing coming out.

There were half a dozen men sitting in the room, impassively watching a cookbook author being interviewed on "Live at Five." The Surgeon General had not been to visit recently or, if he had, it had been to no effect; the space was the haziest smoke-filled room Frost had been in since the national antismoking crusade had begun in earnest.

Frost hesitated to interrupt, but finally did so, whereupon he was told that Homer Matthewson could be found in an office down the stairs in the basement. He was indeed there, attending to paperwork.

"Oh, Reuben, you're wonderful to do this," he said. "Let me tell you what I'm going to do. Brothers is here. He's working upstairs in the kitchen. We'll go up to the dining room and then I'll call him out and introduce you."

"What on earth are you going to say?" Frost asked.

"Just that you're a friend of Sally Andersen. I'm going to use her name because Brothers doesn't seem to have anything against her. Then you can ask him about the notes."

"Thanks," Frost said. But he was ready; after a lifetime of legal-strategy sessions he knew that it was invariably the lawyer who was tagged with asking the unspeakable, or at least the embarrassing.

"You wait here a minute. I want to position my two 'bodyguards,'" Matthewson said.

Soon he returned and took Frost up to the dining room, a grim affair with institutional green walls, long tables covered with shabby cream-colored oilcloth and uncomfortable-looking metal chairs.

"There's your protection," Matthewson whispered, nodding at two young—and strong-looking—men sitting at a corner table drinking coffee. "Wait here."

Matthewson returned with a stocky man—pretty strong-looking, too, Frost thought—dressed in a cook's white pants, shirt and paper hat and black army combat boots. The man had an even tan, and did not at first glance look the derelict Frost had expected to find. As soon as he was introduced and began talking, however, Frost noticed that most of his upper front teeth were missing. And, when he removed his paper hat, there was an ugly scar along his forehead, a vivid reminder of some past violence.

Frost guessed that Brothers had been handsome when younger, but the absence of teeth, the scar and the deep lines in his face certainly indicated that life had not been very kind to him. He seemed uncertain as to why Matthewson, hovering nervously between them, had brought him together with Frost.

"Haven't I seen you before?" he asked.

"It's possible," Frost answered, though he had no memory of the man.

"Connecticut? The Andersens?"

"Yes, that's very possible. They are friends of mine."

"Dinner. You came to dinner with your wife."

"How do you remember that?" Frost asked.

"The fish. Laurance Andersen flew in with a fish. Big goddam striped bass he'd caught off Long Island. We had to stop everything and cook his goddam fish. You were a guest."

Frost could not recall the event. He and Cynthia had been guests in Greenwich so many times that the occasion the man recalled did not stand out.

162

"Striped bass. Boiled potatoes. Asparagus soup to start—
just regular, this was before SUPERBOWL—and peach
cobbler for dessert."

Who was this idiot savant, Frost thought, able to recall
a menu from a generation ago? He probably could remember the date and the day of the week, too.

"Well, sir, I've no reason to doubt you," Frost said. "But
I don't remember the dinner you describe."

"Too bad. It was a nice meal," Brothers said. "Now,
what can I do for you?"

Frost plunged ahead to the matter of overriding interest.

"Mr. Brothers, I'm sure you've read about the deaths of
Flemming Andersen and his daughter Sorella," Frost said.

"Sure. He fell in his hot tub and her dogs ate her."

"Yes. But that's not quite the way the police see it, as
the newspapers have said. They think he was pushed and
that someone let her dogs loose and egged them on to kill
her."

"Can they prove it?"

"By the time they get through, I'm sure they'll be able
to."

"It's justice," Brothers said. "No question about it."

"That's quite a strong statement, sir," Frost said.

"I meant it to be. Twenty years ago that woman and her
father did a terrible wrong to me."

"Do you want to talk about it?" Frost asked.

"Sure. I'll tell anybody who'll listen."

"Then please do," Frost said.

"I never wanted to work for the Andersens in the first
place," Brothers began. "I was very happy working in the
test kitchens at Andersen Foods. Then Mrs. Andersen—
Flemming's wife—suddenly needed a cook in a hurry and
I was sent off to Connecticut.

"Everything went okay at first," he went on. "Mrs. Andersen was a fine woman and very considerate. But her

daughter was something else again. Sorella. She wouldn't leave me alone. She'd taken it into her head she was going to get me into bed, and she tried everything to do it. I was no angel, mind you, and she *was* a pretty girl back then. But I wasn't going to put my job in danger for a horny teenager.

"She got more and more obnoxious, bothering me all the time. Finally, I told her to lay off, or I was going to tell her mother. Well, the next thing I knew I was called into the library by Mr. Andersen and fired—for 'molesting' his daughter."

"That was not true?" Frost asked.

"Absolutely not true!" Brothers replied, with some heat. "I never touched her. But her lie, and her father's believing that lie—he never even asked me if his daughter was telling the truth—meant that I never could get a job again. I say good riddance to both of them."

"Did you kill them?" Frost asked, his voice slow, even and deliberate.

"Did *I* kill them? Maybe I did!" Brothers replied, seemingly pleased with the attention he was getting and especially the discomfiture this last statement created.

"What about the notes you sent?" Frost asked. "What was that all about?"

"Notes? What notes?" Brothers asked innocently.

"Come, come, Mr. Brothers. Mr. Matthewson has told me that you sent notes to the Andersens about the two deaths."

"Matthy, do you tell everyone my business?" Brothers asked, turning to Matthewson, who had been listening silently, but nervously, to Frost's interrogation.

"Never mind," Brothers went on before Matthewson could answer. "Yes, Mr. Frost, I sent notes. I wanted the world to know what Flemming and Sorella Andersen had done to me."

"Your plan hasn't been a great success so far, has it?"

Frost asked. "The police haven't said a word about them."

"I know. But I'm sure they will eventually."

"Where did you leave them, by the way?" Frost asked.

"You know so much, you tell me," Brothers shot back.

"Why did you risk getting caught? Why didn't you mail them?"

"Mail them? They were too important to trust to the mails!" Brothers looked at Frost as if *he* were mentally unstable. "I wanted to make sure they got out and became public."

"Let me ask you another thing, Mr. Brothers. Have you ever heard of HEART O' GOLD pet food?"

Brothers' incredulous stare at Frost continued, but he did answer the question. "Pet food? Nah, I deal in human food, not pet food."

"You've never seen it advertised on TV?"

"Oh yeah, I guess I have. That ad with the cats in skirts. But I tune all that crap out."

"Do you know who makes it?"

"I'm not sure. Is it Andersen Foods?"

"Yes, it is."

"Why do you want to know, by the way?" Brothers asked.

"Just asking," Frost said. He looked at his watch and then told Matthewson he had to leave.

"Before I go, Mr. Brothers, can I offer you one bit of advice?" Frost said. "From talking to you, I now understand how strongly you feel about what happened up in Connecticut twenty years ago. But my advice to you is to forget it. Or at least not to write any more notes about it. What you've done up till now is probably not a crime. But getting involved in murder investigations—even around the edges—is not a good idea."

"And you want my advice to you?" Brothers asked. "Bug off!" He rose quickly and both Matthewson and Frost—as well as the two "bodyguards"—tensed. But the threat was over as soon as it arose, with Brothers walking quickly toward the kitchen without saying anything more.

Back in Matthewson's subterranean office, he asked Frost if he thought the police should be notified.

"No, I don't think so," he said. "Brothers is not the man they're looking for. But he may be if he keeps on sending love letters to the Andersens."

"So you don't think he killed them?"

"No."

"Can I ask why?"

"You can ask, but I'm not going to tell you," Frost said, thinking it imprudent to tell his old friend about the four notes.

"I'd keep an eye on him, and let me or the police know if anything queer develops. But I don't think your cook is a murderer."

"I'm mystified, but I'll abide by what you say, Reuben," Matthewson said.

"Good. Let's get together soon."

On his way back uptown, Frost reviewed his encounter with Brothers. He was *sure* he was right, that Brothers was the peddler of the second set of notes, designed to take revenge for a festering old grievance, not to explain the double homicide. It was true that he knew of SUPER-BOWL—but then, what red-blooded American didn't?— but his lack of familiarity with HEART O' GOLD seemed genuine. On the other hand, Brothers had had a violent enough past to arouse suspicion. But Frost was sure— *almost* sure—that Brothers was not the murderer.

Encounters

Reaching home, Frost called Luis Bautista to report what he had learned about Brothers. Bautista himself had nothing new to report, nor did anyone else during the Labor Day weekend.

The Frosts stayed in town over the holiday. They obsessively discussed the murders, but did not achieve any new insights or reach any new conclusions. When they still had heard nothing from Bautista, Castagno and Sally Andersen on Tuesday, Reuben called them. The calls produced neither revelations nor evidence of progress; the only thing Frost learned, from Sally Andersen, was that Casper Robbins had somehow negotiated another week's breathing time with Gruen before his tender offer would be made.

"The hell with it," Frost muttered to himself, after hanging up on the last inconclusive call. He had to get ready for a busy evening to start the fall season that, he thought gratefully, would have nothing to do with the Andersens: an off-the-record speech at the Foreign Affairs Forum by the new French Ambassador to the United States, followed by the monthly black-tie dinner of the members of the Gotham Club.

The black-tie feature of the Gotham event put Frost in the ridiculous position of hailing a cab on Park Avenue in a tuxedo at four-fifteen in the afternoon. But there was really no alternative, since the Foreign Affairs program did not end until six, and the predinner festivities at the Gotham began at six-fifteen. There was simply no realistic chance of getting back home in the rush hour, changing and reaching the Gotham at a reasonable time.

He probably thinks I'm an off-duty waiter, Frost thought to himself as his driver eyed him fishily after picking him up at the corner of Seventieth Street. Or I guess a prosperous headwaiter, Frost reasoned, after realizing that most waiters do not go to work by taxi.

Headquarters—or "world headquarters" as some said—of the Foreign Affairs Forum were at Fifty-ninth Street and Park Avenue. Known as "FAF," the Forum consisted of two thousand members, one thousand in New York and the balance scattered judiciously around the country, most of whom fancied themselves as leaders of the American foreign-policy establishment. (The small minority that did not have such a fancy were more than happy to aspire to such leadership.) Formed to combat the isolationism and anti-internationalism of the 1930s, the Forum had a distinguished record of supporting beleaguered Presidents and Secretaries of State in their efforts to conduct sound international relations. (Its record in dissenting from Presidential decisions was much less impressive; in the Forum's deliberations there was almost observable deference to those occupying positions of national power.)

Membership was by invitation only, and those already members by and large did a cautious job of adding to their ranks. This had led to a large amount of inbreeding, which had the same disastrous effect on organizational reproduction that it did on human: it produced idiots far too often.

Reuben Frost had been asked to join as a young man (that is, when he was in his early forties, which was young by FAF standards) by one of his seniors at Chase & Ward. At the time Frost was engaged heavily in the firm's international financial practice, so it seemed logical that he should occupy one of the Chase & Ward "seats" at the Forum.

Participating in the Forum supposedly marked one as a person of influence; Frost had been flattered when he was invited to join and had accepted eagerly. Only then was he to discover that its avowed purpose—to provide an assembly for the discussion of important foreign policy issues—was secondary to at least two others.

One was its discreet use as an employment agency for diplomats about to leave the foreign service, exhausted college presidents looking for peaceful foundation havens and businessmen being pushed or falling into early retirement. (Over the years, Frost had come to recognize the telltale sign of an FAF member about to lose or leave a job—frequent and ubiquitous appearances at Forum meetings, wearing a figurative "I'm Available" button.)

The other extraneous purpose the Forum served was what one might call its nursing-home function, providing a place for the old and retired to go in the late afternoon to socialize and meet acquaintances. The age and state of decrepitude of some of the members were truly awesome—there were three members within comfortable striking distance of one hundred, and all showed up regularly for meetings.

The quality of the meetings had been a major disappointment to Frost. Every important foreign statesman was invited to talk to the group when passing through New York. Most accepted, at least the first time they were invited. Frost's own theory was that they only came back for subsequent appearances reluctantly, after having addressed a congregation of septuagenarians nodding off to sleep the first time. (He also speculated about the national security implications of the Forum. Was it not possible that a foreign adventurist, after seeing its heavyweight mem-

bership snoozing away, might conclude that he had nothing to fear from the United States?)

By tradition, the meetings were off-the-record, though
Frost could never understand why; in all his years as a
Forum member he had never once heard anything remotely resembling a secret or an indiscretion. And as for
the soft-pitch questions to the guest speakers, one could
find more trenchancy on "Sesame Street." (Frost, relax-
ing in the late afternoon as he often did, was a sometime
television watcher and knew this for a fact; Ernie's questions to Bert were invariably sharper than those of the
Forum's members to their distinguished guests.)

Despite the years' accumulated reservations about the
Forum, Frost had never bothered to resign. And now that
he was retired himself, he had to admit that there perhaps
was some selfish merit to the group's pro-geriatric tilt. One
did meet there old acquaintances seldom seen otherwise
and, as the result of a recent "youth" policy that brought
in junior members under thirty-five for short terms, the
place was not as stodgy as formerly.

Frost did not come to the meetings often. He rarely attended speeches by ambassadors; as a general proposition
ambassadors were the most disappointing, speaking almost always of the warm personal and institutional
bonds between their countries and the United States. Ex-
ceptions (and ones Frost made in the meetings he attended) usually were the French and British ambassadors,
who handled their speaking assignments with wit (and
the barely concealed knowledge that their Forum appearances had no practical significance whatsoever).

The Forum's hour-long programs were always preceded
by tea (an ironic British touch for an American foreign
policy group, Frost thought). Today Frost stood, in his
tuxedo, at the side of the room talking with Harry Knight.
They were soon joined by Knight's successor as Chairman

at First Fiduciary, an athletic, fiftyish man named Frederick Dawson.

Frost had met Dawson before, but Knight reintroduced them.

"Looks like you're going out on the town, Mr. Frost," Dawson said.

"Just a fancy dinner," Frost replied, wishing to high heaven that there had been time to change his clothes after, and not before, the Forum meeting.

"I'm relieved, Reuben. I thought maybe you'd joined the Philharmonic," Knight declared.

The three laughed and Reuben took a long sip of his weak tea. As he did so, Knight got sidetracked and Frost found himself talking to Dawson alone.

"Mr. Frost, I remember meeting you when I was a young bank officer negotiating a loan with Andersen Foods. You were their lawyer and you were plenty tough."

"Well, you seem to have survived all right," Frost answered, with a laugh.

"Those murders are a tragedy," Dawson said, looking appropriately grave.

"Mmn," Frost said.

"What about Gruen? Is he really going to make a tender offer?"

"That's what he says," Frost replied.

"I assume all the stuff in the press about hostility is a cover and it will be a perfectly friendly offer," Dawson said.

"Why do you say that?" Frost said. "That certainly isn't my reading."

"I just thought it was all arranged on a friendly basis."

"How did you get that idea?"

"I was just putting two and two together. Last winter my wife and I were at Gstaad skiing. The great Gruen was there, too. And spending most of his time with Casper Robbins."

"I beg your pardon?"

"I was saying that Jeffrey Gruen and Casper Robbins were inseparable at Gstaad last winter."

"Are you sure about that?" Frost asked.

"Absolutely. That's why I thought Gruen's offer would be a cinch."

"When was this?"

"Let's see. February. No, first week in March. Shall we go in? They seem to be ringing the bell."

Frost did not concentrate much on what the new French Ambassador, one Robert Dujarric, was saying. Could Dawson be right? He mentally went over the conversations that had taken place the previous week when Robbins was present. Hadn't he denied knowing Gruen? Frost was almost sure he had; certainly he had never come right out and said that he *did* know him.

Could Robbins and Gruen be conspiring together? Frost tried to shut off his train of thought and concentrate on the words of the Frenchman speaking. But he could not stop the train, leading to the next question: did Robbins kill Flemming and Sorella to advance Gruen's takeover scheme?

As soon as the Forum meeting ended, Frost jumped up and left without speaking to anyone. Was it really possible that Casper Robbins was betraying his own employer? Or worse, *killing* his own employer? He tried to put the thought out of his mind as he walked down Fifth Avenue toward the Gotham Club. Thank God for the distraction of a Gotham evening, he thought.

As he approached the Beaux Arts façade of the Club and entered the front door, he was greeted by Jasper Darmes, the new black doorman. Jasper was a mere twenty-five years old and therefore did not convey the comfortable, settled feeling of most of the Gotham's older employees. But he had inherited the job from his father,

John Darmes, who had greeted Gothamites for more than fifty years until his retirement to devote himself to the affairs of his evangelical church in Queens and (a fact known only to his closest confidants at the Club) to perfect his not inconsiderable skills as a ragtime piano player. Most members, respectful of his antecedent, gave young Darmes the benefit of the doubt. (Some found him a bit too pudgy for his role as the first person one saw on entering the Gotham, but that was a quibble, and most were delighted by the Darmes succession.)

Jasper Darmes and Stanley, Darmes's assistant, stood at a table inside and handed out blue-and-white ribands that signified membership in the Gotham and which the members solemnly wore around their necks at the monthly dinners.

The cocktail hour preceding dinner at the Gotham was quite different from tea at the Foreign Affairs Forum. Alcohol was available, for one thing (including the famed double-sized Gotham martinis and a lethal rum drink called the F.D.R., named for an enthusiastic, and perhaps its most distinguished, member). And the tone of the party was one of self-satisfaction, of successful arrival, unlike the striving, job-seeking *angst* that so often pervaded Forum gatherings.

At the Forum, tea was served beneath four walls of undistinguished portraits of (presumably) distinguished past leaders of the group; at the Gotham, cocktails were served in the opulent club library, surrounded by shelf after shelf of books, many by Gotham authors.

Frost loved the club's diversity. He now took delight, once he had donned his riband, in joining a small group standing in the middle of the room, the members of which he knew only through previous meetings at the Gotham: Leslie Grubert, an assistant to the Mayor (and slightly embarrassed about being a member of an all-male society); Raymond Sheldon, a boisterous and amusing

American history professor at an upstate college (not at all embarrassed about the club's male status and pleased to be there, away from the mean, bucolic and petty atmosphere of the institution of higher education that employed him); and Warner Kilbourne, a popular, solid and (to his credit) nontrendy New York City artist.

"Hello, Leslie, gentlemen," Frost said, calling Grubert, whom he knew best, by name. "What are you fellows discussing so vigorously?"

"Machu Picchu," Kilbourne replied. "Ever been there?"

"No, I haven't," Frost said. "I assume all of you have?"

"Good heavens, no," Sheldon answered. "We're all expressing strong views from positions of invincible ignorance."

Sheldon had nicely described many conversations at the Gotham, Frost thought.

"The whole subject came up because my wife and I are going to Peru later this fall," Kilbourne explained. "So I was simply asking if anyone had been to Machu Picchu. I was getting all kinds of responses—mostly ill-informed—when you joined us."

"I was saying," Grubert said, "that some friends of mine once told me that one should stay overnight there, and not be rushed through on the day trip."

"I've heard that, too," Frost said, adding to the store of secondary wisdom. "The little hotel at the ruins is supposed to be quite nice."

"Well, I certainly thank you gentlemen for all your good advice," Kilbourne said, laughing. "Oh, oh, there's young Darmes. He's about to ring the bell for dinner, so I'm going to get another drink."

The stout doorman did indeed begin sounding the gong that meant dinner was about to begin. Frost had accepted the invitation of an old friend, Vincent Kendall, a curator at the Modern Museum, to sit at his table, so he now scouted the dining room for him. He located Kendall without much effort, and found himself with what promised to be a congenial group, Kendall flanking him on one side and Christopher Terry, a New York book editor, on the other.

The group of eight, seated at a round table, began at once discussing one of the three most frequently addressed topics at the Gotham—the quality of the food; the quality of the wine; and the quality of the members. This time the subject was the quality of the wine, which Gothamites generally assumed (not quite correctly) was below that in other clubs around the city. The Gotham's mistake had been leaving the decisions about wine purchases to the club manager. For many years, this had been perfectly satisfactory, but the manager a decade ago had turned out to be woefully ignorant of the subject—a fact now coming to light as his misguided selections reached what should have been the proper age for drinking.

When the deficiencies of the club's cellar were discovered, a committee of Gotham oenophiles had been hastily assembled to supervise future purchases, but it would unfortunately be some time before their efforts would be evident to the club's drinkers.

The conversation quickly switched to topic number two—the food—when the main course arrived.

"Wouldn't you think they could cook a simple lamb chop?" a member across the table from Frost said, eyeing contemptuously the partially cooked pieces of meat on the plate in front of him.

"My boy, the attraction here is the *conversation*, not the food," Vincent Kendall declared.

"That's what Toots Shor said, and his restaurant went bankrupt, remember," the complaining Gothamite said.

As often happened at these gatherings, dinner conversation started rather stagily, with each person speaking to the whole table. Only later did the general conversation split into smaller segments. By the time dessert was served, Frost was engaged in a serious and private conversation with Christopher Terry about the future of American publishing.

"Back in the seventies, everyone was worried that the conglomerates would kill publishing," Terry was saying. "That didn't happen. But now, we've got an absolute invasion by foreigners, and nobody seems to care."

"Will it make any difference, do you think?" Frost asked.

"Not politically or ideologically, if that's what you mean," the editor responded. "But it's going to affect quality. Those absentee owners in Germany or London or Milan are going to want profits. Big profits. That means you've got to concentrate on the bodice-rippers and the beds-in-Hollywood stuff."

"You really think this will happen?" Frost asked.

"It's started already."

"At your house?"

"At Miller's? No. We're still independent. Nobody's bought us yet."

"What have you got going at the moment?"

"Oh, the usual. A couple of novels by old reliable hands. A nice history of opera in the United States. They'll be out this fall. And right now I'm working on a manuscript that might interest you. A real feminist book about business— about a daughter whose family screws her out of her rightful place in the family business."

"A corporate *Mommie Dearest*?"

"Not quite. Not as vulgar as that. But damned outspoken stuff. A woman named Diana Andersen, whose family owns most of Andersen Foods."

Frost could scarcely believe what he was hearing.

"Did you say Diana Andersen?" he asked.

"That's right."

"The daughter of the man who was murdered last week?"

"That's the one."

"This is the first I've heard of it," Frost said.

"That's not surprising. There hasn't been any publicity—yet."

"No, it *is* a little surprising. You see, I'm rather close to the Andersen family. My firm's been counsel to the Company for many years. So I *might* have heard about it."

"I do see," Terry said. "Diana doesn't have much use for lawyers."

"When will this book be coming out?" Frost asked.

"Oh, it will be a while. I'm still working on the manuscript with her," Terry said. "And I expect she'll want to do some rewriting after the events of last week."

"But you have a manuscript now?" Frost asked.

"Yes, yes. I worked on it all day today, as a matter of fact."

The waiter interrupted, taking orders for the Gotham's special Port and other after-dinner drinks. Frost ordered a Port, as did Christopher Terry.

"You staying for the speech?" Terry asked, their orders completed.

"Yes," Frost answered. "And you?"

"I can't decide. Should I go play bridge downstairs or listen to the speech?"

"Try the speech. Never heard of the fellow giving it. Some classics professor from Chicago. But a most intriguing subject—'The Contract as Promise on the Bay of Naples.'"

"Yes. An extraordinary topic," Terry said. "Do you suppose it's about the ancient Romans or the Mafia?"

"I don't know," Frost answered. "But they certainly can cook up some good titles in academia."

"Shall we go down to the library?" Terry asked. Port

glasses in hand, both he and Frost got up from the table.

"Yes, let's go," Frost said. Then, taking his dinner partner by the arm, Frost asked if he would be in his office the following day.

"As far as I know," Terry said. "But why do you ask?"

"I may want to come to see you," Frost answered.

Terry, realizing the possible implications of Frost's statement, looked stricken.

"I hope I haven't been indiscreet," Terry said.

"Not at all," Frost replied, silently grateful for the editor's enormous indiscretion.

In the library of the club, Professor Clyde Anthony Fleese of the University of Chicago gave a witty talk on the commercial legal system in Naples at the time of the Roman Republic. He avoided the pitfalls unsuccessfully negotiated by many a Gotham monthly speaker: he was brief and did not, in his brief moment in the spotlight, try to tell his fellow Gothamites everything he knew and everything he had ever learned. Instead, he did just what a speaker at the monthly meeting was supposed to do—inform his audience, in a sprightly manner, about some topic on which he was expert and they were not. The result was far fewer listeners off in slumberland than had been the case at the earlier speech by the French Ambassador at the Forum.

Frost tried to concentrate on Fleese's diverting talk, but his mind kept coming back to Diana Andersen's manuscript. He had never heard so much as a hint about it, nor did he think any of the Andersen family had. What could the woman be saying at book length that an experienced New York editor found so compelling?

The thought of what lay ahead made Frost tired. He must, one way or another, get a look at Diana's manuscript. And he must get to the bottom of Casper Robbins's involvement with Jeffrey Gruen.

But tired or not, Frost found that his night was not yet over. Stanley, the assistant doorman, was standing outside the library when the speech ended and signaled to Frost as he left his seat.

"You have a message, sir. He said it was very important."

"Who called?" Frost asked.

"Man by the name of William O'Neal. Said it was important that he meet you."

"And where am I to meet him?"

"At the Red Rose Bar."

"Did he say where that is?"

"Avenue D and Ninth Street."

"Oh my God," Frost mumbled, groaning. He knew that O'Neal must be on one of his low-life bar rampages and needed a sounding board. But tired as he was, Frost had no choice. With two unsolved murders outstanding, O'Neal might, in his condition, have something of interest to say about them. *In vino veritas*, or so one could hope.

17

Frost left his blue-and-white riband at the table by the door and went outside the Gotham to look for a taxi. It was just eleven o'clock, when the Broadway theaters were breaking; a most inconvenient time to find a cab, leaving aside the annoyance of meeting what would probably be a nearly incoherent drunk in a dark and smelly bar in the East Village.

Frost had been down this path before, always the "friend" summoned in the middle of O'Neal's monumental binges—or, given the difference in their ages, perhaps O'Neal's uncle (Dutch or otherwise). Out of loyalty to the Andersens, Frost had responded over the years when at all possible, going to O'Neal's side and gradually talking him back in avuncular fashion to his wife and family and polite society. Whether the stray alcoholic was in Baja California, or Fairbanks, Alaska, or Hoboken or Coney Island, or Times Square at three in the morning or (as now) the East Village, Frost had dutifully gone to fetch the stray Executive Vice President of Andersen Foods, keeping him from being found sleeping in the gutter or otherwise disgracing family and corporation.

Frost had to admit that in his younger days acting as O'Neal's keeper had not been entirely unpleasant. Even when tight as a tick, O'Neal was usually amusing (though

he often repeated a good line or a joke several times over).
There had been the five-day *fiesta* in Acapulco, when Frost
had been sent south of the border to retrieve O'Neal after
a particularly long absence. Or the three-day binge in
Wilmington, Delaware, of all places, where O'Neal had
been determined to drink absolutely dry the aptly named
Brandywine Room of the Hotel DuPont.

Disagreeing with Flemming Andersen, Frost had always felt that O'Neal, if he ever pulled himself together,
would be an effective executive and a perfectly logical heir
to Flemming.

O'Neal's adolescent escapades had long since ceased to
amuse Frost, but he still, as this evening, was pressed into
service. When drinking in the city, O'Neal usually sought
out the lowest dives imaginable. The degree of cleanliness,
the sexual orientation of the customers, a threat of violence, none of these things mattered to O'Neal when he
was drinking; indeed, the seedier the better seemed to be
his aesthetic premise at such times. (A psychiatrist friend
had once explained to Frost that this preference for
squalor often went along with the desire to go on a
bender.)

Frost dreaded what he would find at Avenue D and
Ninth Street. In his younger days, the "alphabet avenues"
had always seemed provincial and ethnic and not worth a
visit, and later, when the East Village achieved a sordid
reputation as a drug center, there was even less reason to
go there. In fact, he had been in the area for the first time
only recently, visiting a chi-chi art gallery in one of the
gentrified parts of the East Village.

When the taxi got to the appointed intersection, there
was nothing that Frost saw that reassured him—the
wreckage of a burned-out and vacant tenement on one
corner, a crowd of teenagers on another. And no sign of
the Red Rose Bar. Not exactly the place, at midnight, for
a solitary seventy-five-year-old in a dinner jacket.

Looking out the taxi window, he finally spotted a red neon Max Beer sign in a window down the street.

"I think it's down there," he said, pointing toward the sign. "Would you mind waiting for me? I want to check and see if my friend is here," Frost asked.

"Are you kidding? I'm not staying around here any longer than it takes you to open that door and get out," the driver said, doing nothing to reassure Frost.

"Look. Let me pay you what's on the meter," Frost said. "And a tip, and ten dollars besides. When I get out, you can lock the doors. And if anything happens that you don't like, you can take off. If my friend's here, I'll come and tell you in one minute. If he's not, I'll come back and you can take me home. All right?"

The driver paused and then grudgingly accepted the offer. "But I'm not going to stay here and wait very long," he said.

"Fine," Frost said, paying him and then heading toward the gray, small-windowed façade of the bar, which indeed had a beaten-up tin sign across the front reading "Red Rose Bar & Grill."

Entering the narrow front door, Frost found himself in a public room than confirmed all his worst forebodings. In the corner was a food steam table, now closed, but still emitting fetid and rancid odors from the day's overcooked "specials."

The stale cooking odors were not the only reminders of the past: here, in the beginning of September, were Christmas tinsel and ornaments from the previous Christmas, or perhaps several Christmases ago. And dead center, fastened to the mirror behind the long wooden bar, was a badly colored lithograph of General Douglas MacArthur.

There was only one customer in the dimly lighted room—Billy O'Neal, seated at the last stool at the bar, slumped against the wall, a drink and a pile of change and bills in front of him. He had loosened his tie, which hung at a rakish angle outside the vest of his three-piece suit.

"Reuben, ol' buddy!" O'Neal called out, when he spotted Frost entering.

"Hello, Billy," Frost called across to him. "I'll be with you in a minute." He went back outside to dismiss the waiting taxi driver, then returned and joined O'Neal.

"Glad you could make it, Reuben, my friend," O'Neal said, putting an unsteady arm around Frost. "Have a drink."

The bartender seemed relieved that he had company in dealing with O'Neal. He brought Frost the Scotch and soda he ordered and then retreated to the other end of the bar, as if to avoid being drawn into any confrontation or conversation with the two customers. He had barely gotten away when O'Neal demanded another drink.

"The same?" the bartender said.

"Yup."

The bartender brought a bourbon and soda. O'Neal took a sip and then complained that the order was wrong.

"Bourbon and *water*," he said. The bartender took the offending drink and replaced it. "Damn soda tickles my nose," O'Neal explained to Frost.

"Thanks for coming," O'Neal said. "Nobody will drink with me anymore. Not my wife, not my son, not anybody. Just you, good ol' Reuben. *Uncle* Reuben." O'Neal nodded slightly and took a deep sip from his new drink. "You like this place?" he asked.

"Well, Billy, it's a little off the beaten path," Frost said.

"Damn right," O'Neal replied, "I suppose you'd rather be at '21.' Or that damn club of yours."

O'Neal was at least partly correct, but Frost did not admit as much.

"No, no, Billy. I'm perfectly happy to drink at Ninth Street and Avenue D."

"I like it here. People leave you alone. And nobody's tongue's thwacking the next day about how they saw you drunk, blah, blah, blah."

"You may have a point," Frost said. "But why are we here, Billy? What are we celebrating?"

"What are we celebrating? Reuben, sometimes you're dense. And a wizard Wall Street lawyer like you! We're celebrating my taking over Andersen Foods, that's what we're celebrating!"

Frost was used to the irrational thoughts O'Neal expressed when drunk. But this one seemed particularly off base.

"What do you mean, Billy?" Frost asked.

"I mean I'm going to be the new CEO of Andersen Foods," O'Neal answered. "Now that my old friend Flemming's gone, God rest his soul, I can take over."

"I thought Casper Robbins was going to have the job," Frost said.

"Robbins, schmobbins. Casper Robbins is a little toady. As long as there's somebody to suck up to, he can do that just fine. But he can't be number one. He hasn't got it in him."

"Billy, I hate to say this, but where is your support going to come from? Sally will never vote for you."

"Sally, schmally. She should stick to playing tennis. Playing tennis with ol' Casper, probably." O'Neal poked Frost in the ribs and winked at him. Frost ignored both gestures.

"Besides, she's not the whole Board," O'Neal added.

"No, she's not. But do you think the Board is going to support you, when you go off drinking like this?"

"Drinking and screwing, Reuben," O'Neal said.

"Yes, I suppose you're still up to your old habits in that department, too."

"None of your business. But look at that Company. In all honesty, Reuben, who's going to run it? Who've they got left? Nobody. Nobody but their star salesman, Billy O'Neal. The man who made Max Beer a household name." O'Neal was now speaking with some effort, nodding in his drink between sentences. "Besides, I can always go out to that hospital in California and get dried out, if that would make people happy.

"What hospital?"

"Oh, you know. The President's wife."

"Mrs. Reagan?"

"No. No. No. No. The other one."

"Oh yes. Mrs. Ford."

"Right—righto, Reuben. Betty Ford. I'll go out and get all tidied up and then I'll be President of Andersen Foods! Whadyya think—should we change the name? O'Neal Foods, maybe?"

"What about Laurance?" Frost asked.

"Not a chance. He's too busy with his new California bunch. He's not interested in AFC. Besides, he's a nasty turkey just like his father. His *late* father," O'Neal said. "Here's to Flemming, good ol' Flemming." He lifted his glass, drained it and beckoned for another drink. Frost, seeing that he was not about to get O'Neal to go home, ordered another one too.

The two men drank in silence for some moments, Frost expecting his companion to continue his screed against Flemming Andersen and his branch of the family. But he did not do so. Taking advantage of the silence, Frost decided to feel him out.

"I know Flemming was not exactly your favorite person," Frost said. "But who do you think killed him?"

"Some nut," O'Neal replied.

"Do you really think that?"

"You saw the note the guy wrote. And the one he wrote after Sorella got it. Certainly sounds like a nut to me."

"But couldn't the notes be a red herring? A false lead to put people off the trail?" Frost asked.

"Maybe. But who do you think did it, then? Who's the big smarty-pants?"

"I wish I knew," Frost answered.

"Maybe it was me," O'Neal said slyly, then shooting Frost a defiant look. "Maybe I killed my dear uncle."

"No, I don't think so," Frost said.

"Why the hell not?" O'Neal answered, as if hurt that he was being ruled out.

"If it wasn't a nut, it was somebody that wanted Jeffrey Gruen's tender offer to succeed. That's the only way you can explain both Flemming's death and Sorella's. They were both stubbornly against the offer and had to be gotten rid of."

"Frosty, I'm ashamed of you," O'Neal said, using a nickname for Reuben he had made up years before and which he used only when extremely drunk. (Frost, it goes without saying, hated it.) "You're jumping to conclusions. I still say I could be the killer."

"I don't think so."

"Frosty, lookit. I want to be the head of Andersen Foods. How do I get there? Number one, I got to get rid of the guy who's sitting in the seat right now. Flemming. Flemming but not Robbins. Robbins will take care of himself. Robbins will shoot *himself*. In the foot, but he'll shoot himself."

"But how about Sorella?"

"Easy. The best chance I've got of taking over is if there's one helluva lot of confusion. A real mess. And what better way to start a mess than to screw up the Foundation? Get that hand-wringing jerk that advises the Foundation—what's his name? Hedley. Randy baby. Get him all hot and bothered and you'll have a real circus. Giving me my chance to come in and be the ringmaster."

"Hmn," Frost muttered.

"A ding-a-ling idea, you say? Well, you think about it. Don't sell ol' Billy O'Neal short."

To Frost's relief, the bartender announced the last call for drinks. O'Neal ordered one, Frost did not.

"Where we going next, Frosty?" O'Neal asked.

"I don't know about you, but I'm going home," Frost replied. "Drink up and I'll give you a ride."

"No more bars? What's the matter?"

"Old age, Billy."

"You're prob'ly right. Home it is."

Frost was again relieved; it seemed that he would be able to deliver O'Neal uptown without a struggle. Leaving the Red Rose, they were lucky enough to get a taxi without much of a wait. At Fifth Avenue and Sixty-fourth Street, where O'Neal lived, Frost guided his charge to the door, rang the night bell and almost literally dumped O'Neal into the arms of the night porter who answered the ring. By this time O'Neal was mumbling incoherently. Frost said good night but did not expect, and did not get, a reply.

Frost got back into the taxi for the short ride to his town house. O'Neal was gone, but one line from the evening's conversation—"Maybe I killed my dear uncle"—lingered in Frost's mind. Could it be true? Had O'Neal just now been so uncontrollably drunk that he had confessed to Reuben, his drinking companion? Frost did not think so, but there was an uneasy doubt; tired as he was, he stayed awake for a good hour wrestling with it.

Purple Prose

18

The next morning, Reuben Frost sat in his library. Cynthia had gone off to an early meeting, leaving him to read the morning papers at his leisure.

Sprawled out on the library sofa, wearing the red silk paisley bathrobe his wife had given him the previous Christmas, Frost tried to get ready to face the day. But the reality was that he was extremely hung over. He had behaved relatively abstemiously at the Gotham dinner, but the drinks with which he had topped off the evening at the Red Rose Bar had been enough to cloud his head right through to the morning.

Looking about the library, he spotted Edmund Wilson's *American Earthquake*, part of a large, admiring collection of the works of a Princetonian of an earlier generation. (All the books in the Frost library were relentlessly shelved alphabetically by author. No matter that this juxtaposed Aristotle with Renata Adler, Chekhov with Julia Child or Proust with Mario Puzo, the point was that a book, regardless of its subject, could be readily found, as Reuben ceaselessly pointed out to those who found his subjectless regime eccentric.) Frost rapidly leafed through the Wilson work, finding with satisfaction what he was looking for—an essay detailing the almost endless number of slang words used in the twenties for being drunk: *"lit, squiffy, oiled, lubricated, owled . . . canned, corked, corned, potted . . . full as a tick, loaded for bear, loaded to the muzzle . . . to burn with a low blue flame."*

As he read the short essay, Frost gradually came fully awake, realizing to his great surprise that it was almost ten o'clock. Painfully reconstructing the previous evening, he decided that the most immediate task was to get in touch with Christopher Terry, the editor of Diana Andersen's "memoirs."

Ordinarily, he couldn't imagine that Diana's writing would attract much attention. That book by Joan Crawford's daughter was one thing; Joan Crawford was a household name. But no one would really care about Diana Andersen's views of her parents. Except now that Flemming had been murdered, there would be a macabre interest in it; the splattering of blood would rally the public round.

It was essential that he have a chance to look at Diana's manuscript; the family must be warned about it, and what it said. And besides, could there possibly be a clue to the family murders buried in its pages?

Frost had no idea whether there was some sort of publishers' code of ethics that would prevent Terry from showing him the work. From what little he knew about the industry, he assumed there was not; from what he had ever been told by some of his literary friends, the relationship between author and editor was more like that of prisoner to jailer than penitent to priest or client to lawyer. It was his best guess that he would get to see the manuscript.

He looked up the number of Terry's publishing house and placed a call. Eventually he got through to the editor and asked if he might come and see him. Terry agreed, out of deference to their Gotham friendship.

The offices of Miller's were located in a tower on the lower edges of midtown Manhattan and one that had been recently renovated in a cheap and ugly manner that made the building less attractive than it had been before. The building was owned by a consortium headed by a young realtor with enormous intellectual pretensions. Frost had met the fellow, Dennis Flachman, on a number of occasions. The developer had always been accompanied by a woman novelist, professor or playwright, acting as an offset to his less than sparkling presence. Flachman was a name-dropper and a climber eager for public recognition not of his money but his intellect. Unfortunately, despite his recently acquired ownership of a highbrow movie company and enthusiastic backing for difficult off-Broadway plays, his intellect *was* generally recognized: it was pedestrian and unexciting. And, try as he might to conceal his real estate connections, everyone who mattered to him knew exactly the source of his fortune— buildings as monumentally bland as he was.

Miller's, one of the oldest and most prestigious publishing houses in New York, had offices that belied the vulgar modern exterior of Flachman's building. They were narrow, cramped and paper-strewn; the only cheerful note in the reception room of the offices, on the eighteenth floor of Flachman's revamped steel-and-glass sheath, was provided by framed dust jackets from the firm's books currently on the market.

Christopher Terry came out to meet Frost once his arrival had been announced. The office area was surprisingly dim; Miller's seemed to be exacting a small saving on lighting—an odd position for a publisher to take, Frost thought—and the walls were paneled in dark wood.

Terry's office was minuscule, though Frost noted the lettering on his door included the title "Deputy Editor." The piles of manuscripts, galley proofs and actual bound books left very little room to accommodate a guest. Terry hastily removed a pile of detritus from the only extra chair in the office and invited Frost to sit down.

"Sorry about the mess," he said.

"Don't worry, my office used to be almost as bad," Frost answered with a smile.

"I always like to say I have a *very* orderly mind and a *very* disorderly office," Terry noted. Frost did not reply, and the young editor continued:

"I suppose you're here about Diana Andersen's book. I should have been more discreet and not been blabbing about it last night."

"Yes, you're right. I mean, yes, it's the manuscript I'm here about," Frost said.

"I'm afraid I can't let you see it. You're the lawyer for the Andersen family, isn't that what you said?"

"In a manner of speaking. My firm has been counsel for Andersen Foods for many, many years and, while I was in active practice, I handled AFC's affairs for the firm. As AFC's counsel, I inevitably got to know members of the family and have advised some of them on occasion. But I'm not the regular personal lawyer for any of them."

"After you called, I talked to *our* attorney—Ed Dunning, our house lawyer—and he advised me against showing you the manuscript. I'm sorry, but I'm afraid that's our answer."

"Is there any appeal?" Frost asked. "Could I talk to Mr. Dunning myself?"

"I don't know. Let me call him." Terry did so and, judging by the expression on his face as he talked, was not getting a positive response. He looked pained as he put down the telephone. "I'm afraid Ed feels there's nothing to talk about."

"So he won't see me?" Frost asked.

"That's right."

"Christopher, I don't want to put you in an awkward

position, but could you call Mr. Dunning back and ask him whether he would rather deal with me or the police in this matter?"

"Police? I don't get it," Terry said.

"My friend, there have been two murders—your author's father and your author's sister. Both are unsolved, and I think the police, at this point, would be interested in any evidence that might be even remotely relevant to the killings—including the manuscript in your possession."

"Will you wait here a minute?" Terry said. "Dunning's office is just down the hall. Let me talk to him."

Terry disappeared, leaving Frost alone and awash in the editor's sea of paper. Presumably the disputed manuscript was readily at hand, but Frost decided not to snoop.

"Reuben?" Terry said, returning and poking his head in the door. "Come with me. Ed will be glad to talk to you."

"Certainly," Frost said, following his host down the hall. They went into an office no bigger, but considerably neater, than Terry's.

Edwin P. Dunning, Jr., General Counsel of Miller's, stood up to greet Frost. As if to compensate for a baby face that made him look exceedingly young, Dunning wore a severe, dark three-piece suit, in contrast to the shirtsleeve and even open-shirt informality Frost had observed about the office.

Dunning's tone was not especially friendly, and Frost soon pigeonholed him with those pompous, self-important house lawyers who give their branch of the profession a bad name.

"Mr. Frost, I know Christopher has explained our position to you. I'm sure it can't surprise you terribly. But if it will help, I'll explain the position again. Though I think it's a waste of everyone's valuable time to do so."

"Mr. Dunning, I don't think that will be necessary,"

Frost said. "I understand your position. Undoubtedly you feel I stand on the other side from you and would have an interest in stopping Diana Andersen's book from being published. Not having read it, I cannot comment—though I suspect that might well be the case.

"But let me assure you that stopping publication is not what I'm interested in. What I *am* interested in is whether there is anything—*anything*—in her book that could shed light on the murders. I give you my personal word that I will not take, or advise anyone to take, any action to stop publication, no matter what's in that manuscript.

"If that's not enough to satisfy you, so be it. Don't show me the manuscript. But I can assure you that if you don't you'll have half the detectives in Manhattan South Homicide up here turning your offices into a reading room."

"You sound very knowledgeable about what the police might do," Dunning said.

"I've worked with them before, and I'm working with them now on the Andersen murders. I think I know what I'm talking about," Frost replied crisply.

"How do we know you won't change your mind about trying to stop the book?" Dunning asked. "Terry tells me it's pretty negative about your friends and clients."

"You have two assurances," Frost replied. "First, I have given you my word. And second, the Andersens would have to be idiots to try and stop publication. As I need not tell you, Mr. Dunning, it is nearly impossible to enjoin publication of a book. There's very little chance a legal action could ever succeed. All litigation would do is call more attention to what she's written."

"You really think the police would be interested in the manuscript?" Dunning asked.

"Yes I do," Frost said. "It's an unfortunate fact that members of the family cannot be excluded as suspects. That being so, any clues that can be gathered from any source will be of interest to the police."

"Mr. Frost, I want you to realize that your request is most unorthodox," Dunning said.

"I do. But the circumstances are also pretty unorthodox."

"Granted," Dunning said. "I'm going to take you at your word. That you won't do anything to try and stop the publication of Diana's book. I know of your reputation and that of your fine firm's. So here's what we'll do. We'll make an office available where you can read the manuscript, for the rest of the day if you like. We can't go beyond that, because Christopher's working on it. Are you free to start now?"

"Yes."

"There's one other thing. There'll be no photocopies of any of it. And we'll ask you not to take any notes. Agreed?"

"If you insist," Frost said, angry at the pompous lawyer's inconvenient conditions.

"Yes, I'm afraid we do," Dunning answered. "Can you see if there's an empty room for Mr. Frost?" he said, turning to Terry.

"Sure."

"Good. It was a pleasure to meet you, Mr. Frost," Dunning said. Frost shook his hand without comment.

Frost and Terry went back to Terry's office. Just as Frost had guessed, the Andersen manuscript had been almost under his nose when he had been sitting in the office before.

"Here it is," Terry said, handing Frost four or five pounds of typewritten pages. "You're not going to like what you read, but if it's any help in solving the murders—I really don't see how it can be, by the way—I guess it's worthwhile."

"I'm grateful," Frost said. "As I said, I have no ulterior motive in wanting to read—"

"Reuben, I know that," Terry interrupted. "Ed Dunning likes to show off a little. And I think dealing with a high-powered attorney like you probably made him nervous." Terry did not apologize for his colleague, but he came close.

"Let me show you to a vacant office down the hall," Terry went on. "We're keeping right up with the fashion here at Miller's and having a cost-cutting party. We're trying to turn success into demoralizing failure, just like every other successful communications company in America. This office belonged to the other deputy editor. She left last week."

The office was probably the same size as Terry's but empty, and without piled-up papers, it looked bigger. Frost sat down at the desk and placed his day's work before him.

"Take your time with this, Reuben," Terry said. "Frankly you've given me an excuse to spend a day away from Diana's output. There's something to be said for that, as you will see. If there's anything you need, just ask my secretary."

"Thanks," Frost said. "I'll try to finish just as soon as I can."

He got his first jolt when he removed the blank sheet atop the manuscript pile. Beneath it was a page bearing the title *Women's War: The Struggle to the Top*.

The page where the first chapter started contained a handwritten note, *"Introduction?"* presumably by Christopher Terry. Realizing that he would not be spoon-fed with any sort of summary of the author's arguments, he plunged ahead into the initial chapters. Diana's thesis, or at least one of them, soon became evident: there was a male conspiracy against women in business, keeping them in a subordinate role, despite money or brains or both.

Even when a woman achieved economic control of an

enterprise, Diana argued, she was still made to feel dependent by a web of male lawyers, accountants and bankers. Women were traditionally the "underclass," whether in the executive suite, at the stockholders' meeting, on the assembly line or—just for good measure—in bed. ("The missionary position is still another example of male domination of the female underclass.") Frost had thought "underclass," as used by his young friend Ken Auletta and others, referred to the poorest members of the society; the only qualification for membership Diana set was that the subject be female.

The confrontational prose made Reuben Frost uneasy. Married to a woman who was, professionally, one of the most successful in America, he found it difficult to sympathize with a millionairess who regarded herself as part of an underclass. And when, as the Executive Partner of Chase & Ward, he had insisted that greater efforts be made to recruit more women lawyers, he had really not cared what positions they had assumed, or were expected to assume, in bed.

But if Frost was appalled at the canons of the author's "Postmodern Feminism," he was even more appalled, as he read on, at Diana's diatribe against her family, which occurred in the middle chapters of *Women's War*.

The original Laurance Andersen was, of course, excoriated for the unfair, sexist manner in which he willed his property. And Flemming—Reuben's friend Flemming, a patient, wise and occasionally brilliant businessman— was found wanting both as father and executive. His daughter considered him conventional and plodding, a pillar of exploitative capitalism, indifferent to workers', and especially women's, rights. (Frost was glad that the manuscript, when attacking Flemming's antifeminism, was out-and-out polemic, unsupported with facts. Flemming, like Reuben, had pioneered in encouraging equal employment rights for women; his mistake had been in overlooking his daughter when it came to the governance of AFC.)

But however purple the prose, Flemming Andersen came off infinitely better than Diana's brother, Laurance. Laurance and cousin Billy O'Neal were characterized as the male successors to power at AFC, and their shortcomings were detailed at considerable length.

Her view of Laurance was scathing, and violative of the standard of privacy that Sally Andersen had always tried to impose on the family. Most of her revelations were new to Frost, close as he had always been to the Andersens. There was, for example, the matter of Laurance's bad checks at St. Paul's and Yale (scandal being averted by Flemming's willingness to make his son's rubber checks good); the forced marriage to a pregnant secretary at the AFC offices averted by an abortion, illegal at the time, allegedly arranged by the Andersen family doctor; his three divorces; his near-bankruptcy—but for another rescue by Flemming—in the ski-resort escapade he had become embroiled in before his recent plunge with the Californians. All in all an unflattering portrait—to say the least—and one designed to show his unworthiness as an heir to the AFC business.

Billy O'Neal fared little better at the pen of his cousin, although the section on him was devoted principally to his alcoholic escapades and sexual peccadilloes. The author seemed to resent the fact that O'Neal had not gotten into more trouble, the reason he had not being "the ambitious rescue efforts of members of the family or, more often, the efforts of a faithful and highly paid family legal retainer." As he read, Frost breathed a sigh of relief that he had not been described in harsher terms (and a second sigh for not being mentioned by name).

As he finished the description of Billy O'Neal, Frost realized that it was midafternoon. He did not feel especially hungry—his unappetizing reading matter helping in this regard—but knew that he must eat something if he were to plow through the rest of the manuscript by the end of office hours at Miller's. Rather than attempt to get food sent in, he went down to the lobby of the building and had a quick sandwich at the lunch counter there. He also bought a cup of coffee to go and took it back with him.

Returning to the manuscript, Reuben found that the women had their turn in the next chapters. Sally, Diana's mother, came under the fiercest barrage. In Diana's version, Sally Andersen viewed her years as a tennis pro as somehow disreputable and, as a result, had desired respectability above all else from the time she gave up tennis and married Flemming. She had looked on her daughters purely as "narcissistic extensions" of herself; her only concern was that the two girls behave in a manner consistent with their mother's notions of "respectability." This of course provoked a rebellion—Sorella married Nate Perkins, the first man who had ever showed a real interest in her, while Diana openly avoided marriage and spoke out against it.

"I was determined to shape my life in a way that would differentiate me from my mother and free me from the confining expectations she had for me. Avoiding marriage and refusing to have children were the most dramatic statements I could make to the cold, loveless and manipulating woman who was and is, as far as I am concerned, my birth mother and nothing else," Diana wrote. Sally received no affection from her daughter, that affection being reserved for the "consummate social activists" of Concerned Women.

Frost was both weary and dispirited as he read on, reaching Diana's fiery conclusion. The struggle of women, in "an indifferent post-feminist generation," was a class struggle, Diana wrote, calling it "Women's War I." Women were a class unto themselves, to which men were neither welcome nor wanted; as a class, women must work to destroy both the family and the capitalist institutions of the society.

"In my own case, I am going to sell my stake in American free enterprise, my stock in the Andersen Foods Corporation, as expeditiously as possible, consistent with getting a fair price. The money I receive can be better spent helping to secure victory for the female underclass in Women's War I."

When he had finished, Frost took the manuscript back to Christopher Terry. He wanted to ask the editor what he thought he was accomplishing by publishing such gibberish, but did not. Terry had, after all, cooperated and let him see the work.

Frost was relieved to be rid of the splenetic manuscript and left the ugly Flachman building as quickly as possible.

19

Despite the distance, Reuben Frost decided to walk home. The city's air, polluted as it might be, seemed to him fresh after he had been confined for a full workday in an airless, windowless office with only Diana Andersen's militant prose for succor. As he walked up Lexington Avenue, he kept trying to put unpleasant thoughts out of his mind. No, he told himself, his opinion of Diana Andersen's lifestyle had nothing to do with his newly developed conclusion that her hatred might have become homicidal. And neither did her venom against his old friends Flemming and Sally have anything to do with it. The truth was that Diana, in her own words in her own manuscript, had displayed an anger so ferocious that one could not exclude murder as a logical extension of her rage.

Frost was pleased to find his wife at home. He needed to talk to someone about the day's painful reading and she, as always, would be a shrewd and sympathetic audience of one. He knew that she had spent the day at the Brigham Foundation and was undoubtedly tired; dinner out was in order. He proposed that they go to Orso, a modest but chic Italian restaurant in the heart of the theater district. It was not especially convenient from the

Frost's house, but they both liked it, so the trek west was worthwhile.

Orso was an odd spot. Its decor could have been done by Michael Graves (or a spaced-out Philip Johnson), relying as it did on curved archways and columns, all painted in odd shades of blue, pink and green. Yet for all the post-modernist suggestions, it was basically a comfortable trattoria. The menu was relentlessly Italian, though the pizzas were of the thin, austere, weightwatching variety and the pasta sauces tended less to the customary tomatoes than to salmon, shrimp and other seafood.

"They've done their best to turn pasta into sushi," Reuben had once remarked to Cynthia. But the reality was that the seafood sauces, often made with odd combinations of vodka and cream, were usually good, often startlingly so.

Dinner at Orso had a predictable rhythm: a hectic sitting for playgoers that ended just before eight, a leisurely two-hour hiatus when the restaurant was only partially filled, often with agents and producers making deals, or play doctors making whispered suggestions to despondent playwrights and directors, followed by a crowded after-theater phase when an often amusing mix of actors and spectators formed the crowd.

The Frosts arrived shortly after eight, as the mide-vening downtime was starting. They were greeted warmly by the staff, mostly attractive out-of-work actors and actresses, but not the sort—for which the Frosts were grateful—who behaved histrionically when reciting the menu or serving the food. Reuben found them all appealing and, from regular visits, knew much about them. (The young women all called him "Mr. Frost," which was all right, while to the male employees he was "Reuben." This matter-of-fact approach, not at all intended as disrespectful, was all right, too; it was not often that a lawyer of his age and eminence could escape being called "Mr.

Frost," except by equally aged contemporaries. He liked being called by his first name by these youths roughly one-third his age; their camaraderie, while certainly not making him one of the boys, did give him the pleasant illusion that he was younger than he really was. And the young women, when they called him "Mr. Frost," did so in a way that was not condescending or designed to make him feel like a superannuated fossil.)

The Frosts ordered quickly and began drinking the excellent house Bardolino. Reuben told his wife about his day with Diana Andersen's manuscript. Cynthia listened with horrified fascination.

"Do you think she'll withdraw it, now that her father and sister are dead?" Cynthia asked.

"I don't think there's a chance of it," Reuben said. "If she was willing to write the vile things she's written while her father was alive, why should his death change anything?"

"Poor Sally," Cynthia said, shaking her head. "It's bad enough having an ungrateful daughter without having her advertising it all over the country."

"I know," Reuben answered, starting to eat his pasta.

"I met one of her friends from Concerned Women yesterday," Cynthia said.

"You did? Why didn't you tell me about it?"

"My dear, you may not recall—and you probably don't—that you didn't come home last night. I haven't had a chance to talk to you in days."

"You exaggerate," Reuben said. "Though I was up much too late."

"Having fun with Billy O'Neal."

"Listening to Billy O'Neal," Frost corrected.

"Anyway, there was a forum yesterday afternoon, sponsored by Philip Morris of all companies, on women in the arts—silly, fuzzy topic, but there it was. My friend Lucille Margetts was running it, so I felt I had to go."

"Where was it?"

"The Whitney Museum. Anyway, one of the panelists was one Molly Cayman, who's a national vice president of Concerned Women. She was all antiman talk. Men keep women down, put women down, shout women down—and so on."

"Sounds just like Diana's book to me," Reuben said.

"Yes. Well, I'm afraid I got angry. I was going to be quiet, but she really got to me. So I finally stood up and said I didn't think her antimale approach was either constructive or particularly accurate. I said straight out that her point of view is rubbish when you consider the performing arts. Or the visual arts, for that matter."

"How did she react?"

"She said she pitied me. That my consciousness had not been raised. I don't think she knew who she was talking to.

"Anyway," Cynthia went on, "at the cocktail party afterward, she came up to me and began her harangue all over again. I told her rather firmly that I had spent more than a quarter century in the performing arts—and long before the enlightened eighties, too—and that I simply couldn't agree with her view of men."

"How did she react?"

"Violently! She was a big woman, and I really thought she was going to get physical. She leaned into me and practically spat in my face. I was a traitor to my sex, a manipulator of men—I liked that the best—and an elitist who felt that the struggle of women was for others and not oneself."

"What did you do, pull her hair?" Reuben asked, a tease in his voice.

"Reuben, really. No, I said—and it was *very* arrogant of me—that I thought I had done more for the women's movement by example than a lot of others were doing by their speechmaking. *That's* when I really thought she was going to haul off and hit me. But, my dear, I just couldn't help but point out to her that there was a difference between hating men and hating the *attitude* of some men— like those old cronies of yours at the Gotham."

Frost did not dispute his wife's characterization of at least some of his clubmates. He finished the last glass of wine and began eating his dish of homemade *gelato*—an Orso specialty that always made Frost break his resolve to pass up dessert—as he beheld in his imagination a vision of his wife's encounter with the Concerned Women's vice president.

"I wonder, is that whole bunch like this Cayman person?" Frost asked.

"I hate to think."

"Certainly she sounds like Diana. Do you suppose . . . No, no, it's too absurd," Reuben said, his voice trailing off.

"What were you going to say, Reuben?" his wife asked.

"It's too silly."

"Tell me anyway."

"Do you think Diana's friends in Concerned Women could have pushed her into the murders? Could they have reinforced her anger until it bubbled out of control?"

Cynthia paused for a long time. "I'm afraid it's just possible," she finally said. Both were quiet for a long interval while they absorbed Cynthia's conclusion. Then Cynthia spoke again:

"You realize, Reuben, this is the second time now we've linked one of the possible suspects with someone else."

"You mean the way we think Casper Robbins and Gruen are linked?"

"Yes," Cynthia answered. "And if you're going to play detective, you should think of all the other possibilities, too, however distasteful they may be."

"Such as?"

"Such as Billy O'Neal and Gruen, or Laurance and Gruen. Or Robbins and Sally, or Robbins and Sally and Gruen."

"Whoa, wait a minute. One at a time. Why Billy or Laurance and Gruen?"

"They're weak characters, Reuben. And probably pliable ones, too. Oh, I know they're willful, stubborn and selfish. But I'll just bet either one could be taken in by the power of suggestion."

"Maybe. But Billy just seems so weak, so pathetic, it seems unlikely. And Laurance, well, he wasn't even in the East when his father was killed."

"True enough."

"And as for Sally and Casper . . . I'm afraid you're imagining things because of the old rumors about the two of them. The family that plays tennis together plots together, is that it?"

"Look, I don't know whether the rumors about Sally and Casper are true—I never have known, and neither have you. What I do know is that Sally was worried about Flemming continuing on, and certainly Casper has always been ambitious for the top job at AFC. I was just linking those two things together. And if they should happen to be lovers, that makes their joint scheming even more plausible."

"What about Sorella? Her murder certainly had nothing to do with Casper succeeding Flemming," Reuben said.

"That's why I say perhaps it was a trio—Casper, Sally and Gruen."

"*That* one I'll have to sleep on," Frost said, announcing that it was time to go.

"You're right. We've both had a long day and our nice little inconclusive conversation has made me very tired," Cynthia said.

The couple left the restaurant with some haste. Their

dinner conversation may have been inconclusive, as Cynthia had said, but it had managed to upset them both.

Frost spent another restless night, during which he decided that he must call Sally Andersen the next day and arrange a meeting. He must tell her about his newly acquired information that Casper Robbins and Jeffrey Gruen were friends (and, also, after hearing his wife's hypotheses, study Sally's reactions). She was also entitled to know about her daughter's poisonous book. He was not especially eager for the encounter, but Cynthia urged him on and he knew that she was right.

When he called Sally the next morning, she invited him to tea that afternoon. Frost had hoped to see her earlier—with her permission, he planned to challenge Robbins outright about why the AFC President had lied about knowing Gruen. But she said she was busy until five and there seemed no way of expediting their meeting.

He was at Sally Andersen's front door at the dot of five. When tea had been requested—Frost loathed both tea and the custom of it, but suffered in silence out of deference to his hostess—he began his business gently, telling the widow about the demented Oscar Brothers, author of at least two of the murder notes. Once reminded, she remembered both Brothers and his unpleasant departure vividly. But she also agreed, while conceding that he would have been completely familiar with the Andersen estate in Connecticut, that it was just too unlikely that he would have committed the crimes.

Frost then ventured into more treacherous territory and told Mrs. Andersen what he had learned about Robbins and Gruen.

"I don't believe that, Reuben!" the woman said, with obvious, flaring anger. "That son of a bitch! That slippery, nasty man! My friend! My tennis partner!" The pitch of

Sally Andersen's voice rose as she talked, ending in a near-scream. "The man *I* picked to run the Company! A traitor! A bastard!"

"I can't argue with you," Frost said. "Though his disloyalty completely baffles me. Unless you object, I'm going to confront him squarely with what I've found out."

"By all means. Just so long as I don't have to be present."

"Could he have killed your husband?" Frost asked.

"Casper Robbins a killer?" Sally asked rhetorically. "I don't think so. Casper may have taken risks over the years, but being sneaky is different from killing. That's too risky."

"I hope you're right," Frost replied.

"What about the great Jeffrey Gruen himself?" Sally asked. "Why couldn't he have killed Flemming and Sorella?"

"I'm afraid that doesn't make sense," Frost answered. "He's never been at the Connecticut place, has he?"

"Not that I know of."

"Then how could he possibly have committed the two murders?"

"Maybe someone told him what to do and where to go."

"Most unlikely. Jeffrey Gruen is much too wily to get his hands dirty directly. If he were involved at all, it would be behind the scenes. *He* would be the one giving directions."

"With all that money of his, maybe he hired somebody," she said.

"Possible, but there's not a shred of evidence of it," Frost said.

"It's just a thought. Don't you have any good news for me?" Sally asked.

"I'm afraid not. And I'm also afraid I have some more bad news," Frost replied. Hesitating no longer, he outlined the gist of her daughter's forthcoming book. As he talked, the straight and upright Sally Andersen seemed to melt. By the time he had finished his synopsis, the tanned, determined and leathery woman sitting across from him seemed much more vulnerable.

"Did you know about the book?" Frost asked, as he concluded his account.

"Absolutely not. She's never mentioned it," Sally told Frost. "But I'm not surprised. Over the last few years, I've very often learned what my daughter's thinking by reading the newspapers or the magazines. So, finding out what a wretched mother I was from a book wouldn't be out of the ordinary."

"I'm sure it can't be very pleasant."

"No, it isn't. It hasn't been."

"So the degree of her hatred doesn't surprise you?"

"Good heavens, no. Diana has been a horrible girl since she was eight years old. Not the Bad Seed exactly, murdering pet cats and stray relatives, but very nasty just the same."

"I'm sorry, Sally," Frost said, trying to be comforting. "But to come right to the point—could she have killed her father and her sister?"

Sally Andersen did not answer immediately. She rubbed her tan face, as if to convince herself she was awake and not dreaming.

"Not alone," she finally replied. "Diana could never have done such a thing alone, however demented her views or however bitter her attitude. No, Reuben, it's just not possible that my daughter would do such a thing. But . . ."

"But what?"

"But working together with some of the monsters in that group of hers, yes, yes, it's possible—letting them fire her hatred. Yes, Reuben, I'm afraid that would be possible." The woman began crying as she reached her painful conclusion. "You know, Reuben, I'm afraid I've failed in my most important role in the Andersen family," she said after she had pulled herself together.

"What's that?"

"I've always tried to preserve the family's privacy. Yes, and Diana's right, I've tried to preserve its respectability and its reputation, too. We've never been what used to be called café society. And our wealth has been too old to interest W and the other parvenu magazines. Flemming and I never made public fools of ourselves. We were probably stodgy, Scandinavian and square, but we never swam in the Plaza fountain, or got thrown out of Harry's Bar, or partied all night on the *Île de France*. And our children weren't weaned at the Stork Club or El Morocco.

"But all our efforts were doomed to failure. My husband and daughter have been murdered, and the minutest detail of our lives is available for every subway rider to read about. And now, this afternoon, you've told me that one of my dearest and oldest friends is a lying traitor and that my surviving daughter is about to burst forth as the new prophet of the female sex! God help me, Reuben, this is not what I had in mind, not what I had in mind at all! I knew that Jeffrey Gruen would get us a little publicity, but I thought it would be temporary. And when the dust settled, we could go back to leading normal lives."

" 'When the dust settled'?" Frost asked. "What do you mean by that?"

"I mean, either Gruen would have been beaten, or he would have taken over the Company."

"Did you ever think that was possible?"

"Of course. And—God rest my husband—would it have been entirely bad? If Gruen bought AFC out, Flemming could have retired gracefully, and all my ne'er-do-well relatives—son, daughters, son-in-law, drunken nephew—could have been happy with their new bank balances. And so could Casper Robbins."

"Did you ever say that to Flemming?"

"Oh no. It was a very, very private thought, Reuben. I only tell it to you now because Flemming is dead. Even so, can't you hear him whirring around—right there, up above your head?" Sally laughed, almost out of control, at her afterlife joke.

"Reuben, dear Reuben," she continued, "I've always done whatever was necessary to keep the Andersens together, to keep trouble at bay. Some of the things I've done I wouldn't dare tell you now, even years after they happened. But what good has it done? I've failed. We've been conquered, or are about to be, by the Jeffrey Gruens, the tabloids and God knows who and what else. Probably even the *National Enquirer*. Well, so be it. Which means, dear Reuben, that I have only one request of you."

"What's that?"

"That you find the murderer of my husband and my daughter and bring him—or, I suppose, her—to justice."

Frost left Sally Andersen's tea with a craving for something stronger. He stopped at the Mayfair on Sixty-fifth Street and peremptorily commanded one of the long-skirted waitresses in the frumpy lobby to bring him an extra-dry Beefeater martini. Straight up, thank you, with a twist of lemon.

As he drank, he reflected on his confrontation with Sally. She had confirmed his conjecture that Diana Andersen was capable of murder. And Cynthia's intuition that Sally wanted her husband to step down as head of AFC.

Was her rage and anger an act? Or was it real rage? And if real, was it directed at Casper for what he did or for being found out?

Answers to these questions were ambiguous. But there was the undeniable fact that Sally Andersen had been present in Connecticut on both the fatal evenings. And that she certainly was fit and strong enough to overpower her frail husband, or to manipulate Sorella's dogs.

Reuben Frost was in a foul mood as he finished his martini and headed home.

A Smooth One

20

Frost's frustration level was high as the week came to an end. He had been in frequent touch with both Bautista and Castagno, but neither of them was making any progress at all. He was particularly angry with his old friend Bautista. He realized that the detective was very much involved with a series of drug murders, but still he was sorry that Bautista didn't have more time to spare for him.

Over and over again he had emphasized to the two policemen the importance of pinning down where the acknowledged suspects had been during the hours on Tuesday and Thursday the week before when the murders had occurred.

Friday morning, he exhorted Bautista and Castagno once again, and then turned to the business of cornering and confronting Casper Robbins. Frost thought it would be most advantageous to meet him on neutral ground, outside the confines of the imperial office he occupied as the President of AFC. But he could not think of a fitting way of doing that. He didn't want him for lunch at home—and Robbins would not at all have liked one of Reuben's homemade tuna-fish sandwiches—and he didn't want to challenge him at lunch at the Gotham. (Though such a lunch would presumably not have violated the club's rules against doing business within its confines; surely accusing someone of murder was social, not business.)

Frost called Robbins at AFC. He held his temper through a substitute secretary's screening inquiries, though he was tempted to answer her question "Will Mr. Robbins know what this is in reference to?" with the response "The double homicide he committed last week." But he finally reached the President before insulting anyone.

"Casper, do you have some time this afternoon?" Frost asked. "I'd like very much to come by and see you."

"Oh, goodness, Reuben, this afternoon's very bad," Robbins answered. "Can't we talk over the phone?"

"I much prefer not to," Frost said. "I'll be happy to come to you, and I won't take long."

"What time?" Robbins said, trying without much success to conceal his annoyance. "I have a rather full plate this afternoon."

"Two-thirty?"

"Fine. But I have to leave for the country at four."

Truth will out. What Robbins really wanted was to get away to Katonah for the weekend.

Casper Robbins had calmed down by the time Frost was shown in to see him. As he traversed the enormous distance between the entry door and the chairs set in front of the President's desk, Frost wondered anew what possessed executives to have such offices.

In his palmy days, as the Executive Partner of Chase & Ward, Frost had had what he at least considered magnificent quarters, with a splendid downtown view of New York harbor. But its size was tiny compared with the fascist proportions of the office he was now in. And the furnishings were as expensive and elaborate as the jewelry bedecking the poitrine of the East Side's latest popsy—an imposing antique desk, a large ship model in a bottle, sporting prints on the walls. The overall effect made no sense whatsoever, other than to convey the message that the room had been decorated at great cost.

"What can I do for you, Reuben?" Robbins asked, as he came from behind the fortresslike desk to greet his visitor. "Let's sit over here." He guided Frost to two parallel sofas at the side of the room, sitting down in one himself and motioning Frost to the other.

"I'm here about the murders," Frost said. "It's now been over a week and the police have yet to find the killer."

"So what are you doing, playing amateur detective?"

"In a very modest way, I suppose I am. I happen to be a friend of the detective handling the case here in the city."

"Well, I can't help you. The killer is obviously a lunatic. Probably saw too many AFC ads on television and wrote those crazy notes. Don't you think?"

"Not for a minute," Frost said. "Whoever killed Flemming and Sorella knew the Greenwich estate intimately—knew about the hot tub and how it worked, and knew about the dogs and their kennel, too."

"You could be crazy and still know such things," Robbins said.

"Yes. But not very likely."

"To each his own. I say it was a nut. And the police will never find him. Too bad, but it looks to me like that's the way it's going to be."

"That would be the most convenient, you mean."

"I don't understand."

"If it's an unknown psychopath, there's no embarrassment, just uncertainty. Whereas if it's a relative, or an employee, or somebody else close to the Andersens, it all becomes rather unpleasant."

"What are you getting at?"

"Nothing. I just wondered if you had any opinions. You know the family pretty well, after all."

"Sure. But I don't think there's a one of them capable of murder."

"I must have a dirty mind," Frost said. "I'm not saying it's true, or that I suspect anybody, but with a little imagination, I can make a plausible case for any one of them doing it. And I say that even knowing them all as old friends."

"Sure, they all *could* have. But why *would* they? Where's the motive?"

"I see the murders being related to Gruen's takeover bid," Frost said. "Flemming was determined to defeat it. So perhaps someone who wanted it to succeed got him out of the way. Then Sorella took up the battle where her father left off, so she had to be gotten rid of as well."

"Interesting theory. But I still say it was some stranger who's mentally ill."

"Well, Casper, you're not much help."

"What do you want me to say? That feckless old Nate Perkins finally got his act together and did in his wife and his father-in-law? I'm sorry, I just don't have any plausible theories that can help your gumshoe efforts." Robbins's fabled charm seemed to be wearing thin as he looked pointedly at his watch; the country was beckoning.

"Just one more question, Casper. I know you're eager to get away. What do you think will happen if Gruen makes a tender offer?"

"It's hard to say. I hear that Diana Andersen is ready to sell. And now that Randolph Hedley is in total charge of the Foundation—he never did get around to appointing Sally to Flemming's seat on the Board—I'd be surprised if the Foundation didn't sell also. Hedley would be too scared to be as defiant as Sorella. That means the Company will have to buy a helluva lot more stock to defeat a tender than was originally thought. I don't know what the directors will decide. I don't know what I'll do, for that matter."

"You don't?" Frost asked.

"No. I don't know whether it's the best thing to keep going independently if the price is saddling AFC with a lot of debt. Besides, would Gruen be so bad? I don't know him. But he's on your ballet board, isn't he? What do you think?"

"I don't know Gruen very well. You don't know him at all?"

"The only time I ever met him was at our meeting last week," Robbins said.

"For what it's worth, I think the man would milk the Company for everything in the till," Frost said. "And AFC certainly wouldn't continue to be the benevolent enterprise that Flemming was so proud of."

"I know, but Flemming's dead. We've got to look out for those who're still here."

"Including yourself?" Frost asked.

"I don't have to worry, as you may recall."

"Your golden parachute, you mean?"

"Yes."

"No, Casper, your parachute is rather hard to forget. It's made of the finest silk. Two million dollars a year for ten years, isn't that right? Plus a limousine and driver for that long and an apartment in New York paid for by AFC. And, if I remember correctly, even Blue Cross insurance for those ten years."

"That's about it, Reuben. But it's all contingent on someone firing me. Like Gruen, for instance. Since I don't even know him, I have no idea whether he'd keep me or not."

"I don't think it's very likely he'd fire you," Frost said. "First off, getting rid of you and paying you out wouldn't be very profitable for him. And second, while Gruen fancies himself as being a managerial genius, your expertise in the food business ought to be of great value to him."

"Maybe you're right. Maybe once we got to know each other things would be fine. But I can't predict that."

Frost noted that Robbins, in a very biblical way, had now denied Gruen thrice. He was furious, but kept his temper under control, even though it was time, he thought, to confront Robbins with his basic lie.

"Casper, let me ask you a very frank question, to which I would like an equally frank answer," Frost said, leaning forward on the sofa to face AFC's President straight on. "Are you sure you never discussed your future at AFC with Jeffrey Gruen?"

Robbins's body visibly jerked back, as if he had been hit in the face. But he recovered at once, a slight flush the only lingering evidence that Frost's question had disturbed him.

"Reuben, as my young son would say, what are you smoking? I've never heard such an absurd question in my life."

"Absurd it may be, but would you be good enough to answer it?"

"I told you, the only time I met the man was at that meeting a week ago Monday. You were there, you know what was discussed."

"What did he offer you—even more than two million a year? Blue Shield as well as Blue Cross?"

"You're not making any sense. And since I'm late for the country, I'm leaving now. Right now."

"Why do you persist in lying to me, Casper?" Frost asked, as Robbins got up to leave. "I *know* that you met Jeffrey Gruen before last week."

"I suppose I may have been introduced to him somewhere, but I can't say as I remember it."

"Your memory's like that of President Reagan," Frost said. "What about last winter in Gstaad?"

Robbins stopped at the door and turned around. He looked straight at Frost, but did not speak for a moment. "Yes, I probably did meet him there," he finally said, in a quiet but markedly angry voice. "I met Bill Buckley and John Kenneth Galbraith there, too. I met a lot of people there. So what? And how did you find out about it anyway?"

"Casper, I may be old, I may be over the hill, I may be out of it in the eyes of many. But I have a large network of friends who get around, and who tell me things. Such as the juicy little nugget that you and Jeffrey Gruen seemed inseparable in Gstaad last winter. The first week in March, I believe." Frost had deliberately used his informant's word—"inseparable"—and added the specific reference to early March.

"I guess you do get around," Robbins said, still speaking quietly. "Yes, I did meet Jeffrey Gruen at Gstaad. A mutual friend was there and introduced us. Gruen pursued me the whole time—he was already interested in AFC—wanting to know everything I would tell him about it. It was some vacation, being hounded day and night about the Company I was trying to get a rest from."

"To go back to my question," Frost said, "did he discuss your future at AFC?"

"Not really. He told me that if he ever made an offer, he hoped I'd be on his side. And that he would make it worth my while for any help I could give him."

"Did you tell Flemming about this?"

"No, no, it was far too 'iffy.' "

"When it became less 'iffy,' two weeks ago, did you tell him then?"

"I didn't see any reason to. There was nothing I could do for Gruen anyway."

Except murder the strongest opponents of the offer, Frost thought. But he was not about to pursue that possibility.

"Let's just say you were going to play it safe," Frost said. "If the offer didn't go through, you'd carry on without anyone being the wiser. And if it did, you could cash in your parachute, or stay on if Gruen made you a better deal. Very clever, if I do say so."

"That's a harsh way of putting it, but, yes, I was pretty well protected."

"The nineteen-eighties version of corporate loyalty," Frost said scornfully.

"Now look here, don't start lecturing me about that," Robbins shot back, all traces of his charming façade gone. "You remember when I came to AFC, from HAG Communications? I'd been done out of the top job there after twenty years of day-and-night, round-the-clock loyalty. Which got me approximately nothing. I had learned my lesson by the time I came to AFC. From then on, I was going to look after me, myself and I. Period. Full stop. I did and I have and right now I'm going to the country."

"Don't let me stop you," Frost said.

"I wouldn't if I were you," the AFC President replied ambiguously as he got up and left, neither pausing to shake hands nor to say good-bye.

A Surprise

 Leaving AFC's offices at 272 Park
Avenue, Frost hailed a cab heading
uptown.

"Two-seven-two Park Avenue, driver," he said, as he
settled into the narrow backseat.

"Huh? You kidding, mister? That's two-seven-two right
there," the driver said, pointing toward the skyscraper
Frost had just left.

"My mistake, sorry," Frost mumbled, giving his home
address on Seventieth Street.

"Jeeze, for a minute there I didn't think you was all
put together," the driver said helpfully.

Frost grunted, but he had not thought much of his own
performance. Was this another sign, more dramatic than
most, that he was aging and, God forbid, perhaps getting
senile? He chose not to believe so, attributing his lapse
to his distasteful meeting with Casper Robbins. He leaned
back in the seat, closed his eyes and tried not to think
either of Robbins or his own mental acuity as the driver
crept very slowly northward in the late-afternoon traffic.

At the end of the arduous trip uptown, he found Cynthia at home.

"You're early," he said.

"I know. But it's an Indian summer Friday afternoon,

so everyone was leaving early. I decided to do the same."

"I'm not surprised," Reuben said. "I practically had to tie Casper Robbins up with a rope to keep him in his office."

"How did it go?"

"Depends how you look at it. He's an appalling, greedy, sneaky man. But I got him to admit that he knew Gruen and, for all practical purposes, that he'd been scheming to run AFC for Gruen."

"Didn't you tell me once that he had a very sweet arrangement with AFC?"

"Yes, I'm sure I did. He was protected three ways to Sunday if the Company ever got taken over."

"But that wasn't good enough for him?"

"No, it seems not."

"But wasn't it something like two million dollars a year he was supposed to get?"

"Yes it was."

"Is *anyone* worth that amount?" Cynthia asked incredulously.

"Of course not," her husband replied. "But consider the very sensitive situation he was in, with twenty-five-year-olds on Wall Street making more than a million. It just wouldn't have been *right* to give Casper less than double that if he were kicked out."

"You *are* kidding, aren't you?"

"Yes," Reuben answered. "I was dead set against it, but Flemming thought it was worthwhile to insure Robbins's loyalty. Even if the payments were two million."

"That's an awful lot of cans of SUPERBOWL," Cynthia observed.

"One can only hope that Gruen's tender offer fails. If it does, I think the Board will rip Casper Robbins's parachute to shreds when they find out about his double-dealing. Fortunately I managed to get some rather explicit fine print into his contract to the effect that he doesn't get paid off if he's fired for misconduct."

"How about getting arrested for his misconduct?" Cynthia asked. "Do you think there's any chance he committed the murders?"

"I'm now convinced that's a real possibility. Robbins has shown he was unscrupulous and devious. How big is the distance from his lies and his double-dealing to murder? Maybe a long way, but then again maybe not so far. I've asked Luis and that fellow up in Greenwich to check pretty closely on his movements at the time of the murders.

"But I'm discouraged," Reuben went on. "The more time goes by, the longer the list of suspects. It's supposed to work the other way around."

"What about Laurance, by the way? I haven't heard much about him."

"How do you mean?"

"Well, look at the business about Diana's bitter manuscript. Or the tough conversation you had with her mother. Or my run-in with Diana's friend from Concerned Women. Every conversation seems to create more suspicion. But never about Laurance."

"They've checked him out pretty thoroughly. He said he was in California when his father was murdered, and they confirmed that he was staying at the St. Martin Hotel in Los Angeles. I haven't heard yet about Thursday, at the time of Sorella's death, but he certainly seems in the clear on the first one."

"I was just curious. But cheer up, dear. Something is bound to break loose," Cynthia said.

"I'm sorry I seem down," her husband responded. "It's the stalemate over the murders, of course, but also the unprincipled greed of Casper Robbins."

"He does seem a charmer," Cynthia said.

"You know, I've been involved with businessmen for, what, fifty years? I've seen dedicated and smart ones and I've seen oafs. And I've seen many who were more interested in feathering their nests than doing a good job. But the kind of outright greed you see today is appalling. Money is the only measure of success with too many of them—and far too many of the young ones, especially. I'm glad I'm retired."

"I think what you need is a martini—and a break in the case," Cynthia said. As usual, she was right.

The weekend was quiet—too quiet for Frost's taste. There was no news from the police, which annoyed him. He was exasperated further when he found that his friend Bautista and Francisca Ribiero had left town for three days—exasperated because it meant Bautista was not working on the Andersen case and also because he and Cynthia could not ask them to dinner.

His enforced tranquillity was broken only once, by a telephone call from an irate Billy O'Neal. The police had visited for a second time, pressing him about his whereabouts at the two murder times.

"They act as if they don't believe me," O'Neal fairly shouted on the phone. "I was at the New York Athletic Club both afternoons. They say there's no record of me having been there."

"Is that true?"

"There probably isn't any record," O'Neal said. "All I did was sit in the library and read magazines."

Frost tried to calm O'Neal down. But he couldn't help thinking that his caller's story was inherently improbable. Not a single drink chit with O'Neal's name on it for the afternoons in question? If he'd really been at the NYAC, that seemed most unlikely.

"Can't you call them off, Reuben? I don't like my veracity challenged," O'Neal said. "They all but called me a liar—*me,* a director of the Police Athletic League, a trustee of the University of—"

Frost cut him off before he could recite additional character references. "Billy, I'm sure the police are only doing their job. And I'm afraid two visits, however uncomfortable they may be for you, don't constitute harassment."

"Thanks a lot, counselor," O'Neal said, hanging up.

On Monday, Frost made what had become a habitual weekly visit to the Chase & Ward offices at One Metropolitan Plaza. Despite his very real efforts to cut the ties that bound him to the firm where he had spent his active life practicing, there were still things that could be accomplished more conveniently at the firm's offices than anywhere else. Cashing checks for ready cash, for instance, or obtaining a supply of postage stamps. (Frost was not, and never had been, a cheapskate. When he had been an active partner, the firm had always supplied postage stamps for his personal mail. When he retired, he quite honorably felt that he should, like the ordinary citizen, buy his postage stamps at the local branch post office. But two trips to that grim edifice, standing on line interminably and being waited on by truly surly clerks—compounded the first time by his genuine ignorance of how much postage was required for an ordinary letter—led him back to the firm as a source of supply. It turned out that George Bannard, the firm's Executive Partner, had not countermanded Frost's right to free postage stamps. So this minor beneficence went on, to Frost's great convenience.)

And then there was the question of Frost's mail. It was all supposed to be forwarded to Seventieth Street, but very often it was not. So there was invariably a Saks Fifth Avenue catalogue of women's styles for the coming season—why couldn't these computerized stores differentiate among their customers by sex?—and a stack of unforwarded bills that, if left unpaid, would lead to exorbitant finance charges, or worse. (Letters that said "But Mr. Bloomingdale, I'm old and retired and neither the post office nor my former law firm will forward your bills" had no effect on the inexorable computers that calculated eighteen percent finance charges on the most modest purchases of an old, and generally credit-reliable, man.)

He also wanted to talk with either Ernest Crowder or Marvin Yates. Gruen's second one-week deadline was up on Wednesday; he wanted to find out what was going on and what was planned.

At the office, Frost picked up the pile of letters in the mail room addressed to him and quickly discarded the third-class advertisements and third-rate appeals for funds. He then sought out Yates, who greeted him in a friendly enough fashion, though also conveying the impression that his time was limited.

"What do you think, Marvin?" he asked, once seated in his former partner's office. "Is Gruen going to make his offer?"

"I'm sure of it. With both Sorella and Flemming out of the way, Randolph Hedley gets to name the other two Foundation directors. You've heard him talk. He's made up his mind to sell, I'm sure. Knowing him, he'll name Sally as a director, but he'll also pick someone else for the other spot who'll follow his lead. If he decides to sell, Sally could fight him in court, of course, but that might well lead to the Foundation being liquidated."

"Isn't there anything we can do?" Frost asked.

"Do for who, Reuben? The daughter wants to sell out and give the proceeds to indigenous quilt-makers. The other kid, Laurance, probably wants to sell, too, and raise his ante with those venture-capital boys he plays with in California. And I don't see that writer who was married to Sorella staying around as a long-term investor. The only one who may want to keep her stock is Mom, and she doesn't own enough to matter. Mom and the booze-head cousin. Christ knows what he plans to do. Probably depends on the time of day and what shape he's in when asked."

"So there's no way of resisting Gruen, is that what you're telling me?" Frost asked.

"There is, but there's a real question whether it's worth it," Yates explained. "The Company could hock every damn asset it owns, right down to the last can of SUPER-BOWL in its inventory, and borrow to buy back enough stock to prevent Gruen from getting control.

"When Flemming Andersen was talking about a buyback, he assumed all the family stock would stay in place," Yates continued. "The buyback he had in mind would have cost up to $440 million, you remember. With others bailing out, the ante could go up to well over a billion. I talked with Fred Stacey over at Hughes and he thinks that's too much debt for AFC to carry. It's not Brazil, after all."

"Sounds pretty grim to me," Frost said. "Is there anything else that can be done?"

"Stacey and his group are looking for a White Knight, but nothing's developed so far. Besides, if we're right that Gruen needs a win, he'll probably outbid anybody who appears."

"That's good for the shareholders, but it doesn't save the Company," Frost observed.

"Right. And every time the bidding goes up, a buyback gets less likely."

"You'll let me know when you hear something?" Frost said.

"Sure. You going to be in the office?"

"No, but you can always reach me at home or at the Gotham."

Looking out the window when he returned to his office,

Frost saw that the drizzle from earlier in the day had become much nastier. He decided to call a radio taxi for the trip home.

As usual in bad weather, he had to wait for the taxi to arrive at One Metro Plaza. But the car came eventually and began the trip back uptown. While riding north, Frost was half listening to the dispatcher's call for cabs, when one announcement piqued his curiosity, a call to pick up a person whose name he recognized at the Union League Club, going to 324 Park Avenue.

In the next few minutes, the dispatcher repeated the call several times, so there was no question about the message. He used only the last name of the customer, but that was enough to get Frost's attention. And why was there a familiar ring to the other address, 324 Park Avenue, Frost asked himself, and then answered his own question—it was where Jeffrey Gruen had his offices, where the AFC delegation had met him two weeks earlier.

As the taxi turned off the drive at Sixty-first Street, Frost changed his earlier instructions and asked the driver to head down to 324 Park. He realized he was being foolishly impulsive. The person ordering a radio taxi was probably not who he thought it was and, in any event, could be going to see one of dozens of tenants in the Park Avenue office building. And what chance was there that Frost could either spot his quarry or the quarry's destination?

Spurred by an instinctive feeling of excitement, Frost persisted and let his taxi go when he reached 324. Once he was inside the lobby, a quick inspection heightened his excitement—a gift shop with glass windows faced the lobby directly beside the bank of elevators serving the floors where Gruen had his offices.

Frost ducked into the gift shop, positioning himself by a rack of greeting cards in a way that gave him a clear view of the elevators. A clerk looked at him suspiciously and was justified in doing so, Frost thought; he was sure that in his nervous state he resembled a shoplifter. He made a pretense of looking at the "Happy Birthday/ Father" cards in front of him, while in reality watching the elevators.

After five minutes of this, he began to despair. He had been profoundly silly, he concluded. But then his instinct was rewarded—the very person he had wanted to spot appeared for a moment in the lobby and then disappeared in an elevator heading to Gruen's floors.

Frost's luck having held this far, how could he now prove that the person was visiting Gruen? He couldn't just burst in on the two of them, shouting "This is a raid!"

Then he got an idea, based on a lifetime's experience with indiscreet admissions over the telephone. Most secretaries and receptionists would guard with their lives what they thought were secrets, or what they were told were secrets. If, for example, Frost called Gruen's secretary and asked her if X were meeting with Jeffrey Gruen, there would be no way that she would reveal this private information. But if he called and told her that he understood X was meeting with Mr. Gruen, and that he wanted to leave X a message, she would invariably say, being eager to please, "Fine, I'll deliver your message just as soon as X comes out of Mr. Gruen's office."

That is almost precisely what happened. Frost went to a building across the street—no point in lingering where he might be spotted—found a pay telephone, looked up Gruen's number and placed a call, after waiting a good fifteen minutes to give his prey time to begin meeting with Gruen. He was nervous; what if Gruen himself should answer? Then he realized he was quite in control of the situation, always having the option to hang up if his scheme did not work.

But it did work. Once he reached Jeffrey Gruen's secretary, he not only was told that the person Frost was stalking was in Gruen's office but that their meeting had begun five minutes earlier. Then she asked what the message was.

Rather than hang up, Frost concocted a message. "Just tell him Albert called"—the Albert being the Prince Albert Frost remembered from childhood pranks, as in "Do you have Prince Albert in a can?"—"and ask him to call me at 799-1562."

Albert's number was made up, too. But what was very real was Frost's confirmation that Frost's prey and Jeffrey Gruen were talking. That was one Frost would have to think over very carefully.

QUESTIONS

22

Reuben Frost left the Park Avenue telephone booth with a feeling of triumph. But the feeling dissipated as he walked crosstown toward Fifth Avenue and the Gotham Club. On the one hand, he was eminently pleased with the combination of luck and guile that had established a meeting with Jeffrey Gruen; on the other, he realized that his new knowledge, in and of itself, could hardly form the basis for a murder indictment.

The trick was to build on the information he now had, to go from a random fact to an unbeatable circumstantial case. Could that be done? He was not sure, but he was certainly going to try. What he needed was an hour of absolute and undisturbed peace and quiet, of solitude. At four o'clock in the afternoon, there was no better place for this than the library of the Gotham.

"Jasper, is there anyone in the library?" Frost asked of young Darmes, at the club's front door.

"Not a soul, Mr. Frost," the young man replied. "A couple of gentlemen are taking cocktails in the bar, but otherwise the place is deserted."

Frost was pleased at this news, and headed directly for the upstairs library, avoiding the bar. The room, which contained wood paneling or books on every square inch of its walls, was almost dark and completely deserted, as promised. Frost rummaged on the top of the desk of the part-time librarian (whose duties were performed in the morning) and found a yellow legal pad. He sat down in an armchair beside a window looking out on Fifth Avenue and began writing with his fountain pen.

As he had done so often in the course of his legal career, he tried to organize his thoughts and questions and problems by writing them down in some logical order. Sitting in the library's dim light, he wrote rapidly for a few minutes and then edited what he had written, crossing out and amending as he went. Then a few moments lost in thought, his head buried in his right hand. Then more writing, more scratching out, more thought.

After an hour had gone by, he was satisfied with the product he had written and rewritten on six yellow pages. He went back to the librarian's desk and placed a series of telephone calls through the club operator: first to Cynthia, asking her to arrange dinner at their home for five people, then to Castagno and Bautista, inviting them to dine (and making very clear to them that a refusal was, if not an unacceptable answer, a not very wise one) and finally to Edith Clare, a young paralegal at Chase & Ward who had done some research work for him in the past.

Frost's wife uncomplainingly agreed to be the hostess at her husband's unusual convocation, and the two police officers and Clare accepted his invitation. This accomplished, he sat down in the library once again to review his handiwork, editing and changing it one more time.

The three guests of the Frosts all arrived shortly after eight o'clock. Reuben explained the situation to Ms. Clare, who had been puzzled by the summons to the Frost house.

"I've been working with these officers in trying to solve the killings of Flemming Andersen and his daughter

Sorella," he told the paralegal. "I'm sure you've read about the murders in the papers."

"Oh yes. And they were clients of the office, weren't they?" she answered.

"That's right," Frost said. "By the way, I'm going to have to ask you, Ms. Clare, not to discuss anything that's said tonight with anyone. Just assume that everything is confidential."

"Okay."

"Why are you here, you may ask," Frost said, addressing the group. "The answer is that up to now the search for the murderer has gotten nowhere. Is that a fair statement, gentlemen?" he said, turning to the two policemen.

"*Claro!*" Bautista said, startling Frost with his unusual reversion to Spanish.

"But we may be on the verge of a breakthrough. If we are, it's going to require a real search for detailed evidence—including, Ms. Clare—"

"Please call me Edith."

"Edith. Including some miscellaneous digging for information that I think you can help with."

"Fine," the girl said. "It's bound to be more interesting than the document-sorting I've been doing for the last month."

"Would any of you like some iced tea?" Cynthia said, coming into the living room. "Reuben has banned alcohol until after what he calls his presentation."

"I'm sorry about doing that," Frost said. "But I think we all need clear heads to help me work through my plan. I'll make up for it with an abundance of wine at dinner."

Castagno's face fell when he realized that Frost was implying that their business would have to be completed before dinner would be served.

"It's just like the medieval jury. We were just reading about that in Crim Law," Bautista observed, referring to his night school legal studies. "No food, drink or fire until there's a verdict. So what's the story, Reuben? What's the big surprise you told us about?"

"Patience, Luis," Frost said. "Before I tell you, I want to know what you've found out about people's alibis for the crucial hours on the murder days."

Bautista was disappointed, but realized that Frost was setting the agenda.

"Who do you want to hear about?" the detective said.

"What about Diana Andersen?" Frost asked.

"She claims she was at a fitness center in New York both nights, from five to seven," Bautista said. "Place called Maud's," he added, after consulting his notebook.

"What does Maud say?"

"His name isn't Maud. Big bruiser named Toby Jervis runs the place and he backs up her story. Says she comes there every other day."

"Does that eliminate her?" Frost asked.

"I dunno. The guy is obviously big buddies with her, but he seemed kind of shifty to me. We checked him out. He had a minor record some years ago, but seems to have been clean since he started his gym."

"Doesn't he have a sign-in sheet, or anything like that?" Frost asked.

"Yes, but he throws the signed pages away almost at once—or so he says."

"You think he may be covering for Diana?"

"Yes, he may be. But I can't be sure."

"So you can't rule her out on the basis of her alibi?"

"Right."

"What about Robbins?"

"I looked into that," Castagno said. "His wife corroborates his story that he was at home both evenings. He even remembers what he had to eat those nights, and so does his wife."

"Do they have a cook?" Cynthia asked.

"They said not. Mrs. Robbins does the cooking," Castagno said.

"That's what you get, Miss Clare, for marrying a husband who makes a million dollars a year," Cynthia said, addressing the visiting paralegal.

"What time do they eat?" Frost asked, ignoring his wife's interruption.

"Between eight-thirty and nine."

"So, if that's true, Casper could—just barely—have ducked over to Greenwich, committed the murders, and then rushed home in time for dinner," Frost said. "But it's not very probable."

"Yes," said Castagno.

"Do you have any reason to doubt their stories?" Frost asked.

"No, I don't," Castagno answered. "I just wish I'd been able to pin their alibi down with someone else's verification."

"How about Billy O'Neal?" Frost asked.

"His story is very fishy," Bautista said. "Claims he was at the New York Athletic Club both times, but they have no record of his being there. No bar chits, nothing."

"I know," Frost said. "He called over the weekend to complain about 'police harassment.' He's very hurt that you don't believe him."

"So we've got more work to do on him," Bautista said.

"Then there's Laurance," Frost said. "Any new thoughts on that one?"

"Well, he was in Greenwich the night his sister was killed," Castagno said. "Says he was napping and slept through the whole thing."

"But of course we know he was in California two nights earlier when his father was murdered," Bautista added.

"That leaves Sally Andersen and Nate Perkins. They

were in Greenwich on Tuesday and Thursday," Frost said, getting up to refill his iced tea from the pitcher his wife had left on the coffee table.

"And what about Jeffrey Gruen? What did you find out about him?" Frost asked.

"He wouldn't talk to us," Bautista said. "Absolutely refused."

"On lawyer's advice?"

"He didn't say that. Just said he was goddamned if he'd talk to a goddamned cop about anything."

"How could he be the murderer?" Cynthia said. "He'd never been to the family estate, had he? How would he know about the whirlpool and the Dobermans?"

"As far as we *know*, he'd never been there," Frost said. "It's very unlikely he ever was there, and Sally Andersen said that as far as she knows he never was. So we're punching feathers once again. But now let me tell you something that happened today that was *not* punching feathers."

Frost recounted the afternoon's events, and his success in finding out with whom Gruen had met. The two policemen, his wife and the newly involved paralegal listened with amazement as Frost described his afternoon's work and the conclusions he drew from it. They were further surprised when he pulled out his six-page battle plan prepared earlier at the Gotham.

"Our task is threefold—to uncover every possible clue, to pin down the murderer or murderers and to rule out the others from suspicion. This means you gentlemen have got to go over the ground you've covered already—this time not with a magnifying glass but an electron microscope. I'm confident that will eliminate most of our suspects and blast apart the alibi of the guilty party."

Castagno and Bautista looked perplexed.

"But, Reuben, we've been working like dogs on this

thing, with no success. We appreciate your pep talk, but I don't see what more we can do," Bautista said.

"Let me make some suggestions," Frost said, consulting his sheets of yellow foolscap. For the next few minutes, he doled out tasks for Castagno and Bautista, and Ms. Clare as well.

"What are *you* going to do?" Bautista asked finally.

"Unfortunately, there's very little I can help with. The one thing I probably can do better than you fellows is find out where Billy O'Neal really was during those hours he claimed to be at the NYAC. Otherwise, it's up to the rest of you."

His listeners remained dubious, even after they had absorbed their assigned duties.

"Cheer up, my friends," Frost said, sensing their doubts. "I tell you if you pay attention to every little detail, we'll get this thing licked."

"Can we eat now?" Cynthia asked, sensing that the business portion of the evening was winding up.

"Yes," her husband said. "And drink as well."

Cynthia had prepared a roast of beef. Her guests all ate with relish and drank deeply of the good-quality burgundy Frost served. They continued to talk "business" through the meal, more relaxed now after food and drink.

"Reuben, if your scheme works, I'd say you're a damn genius and ought to be the Police Commissioner," Bautista said.

"And if I'm wrong, I'm just another silly old fool meddling in other people's business," Frost answered.

"I hope I'm married to the would-be Police Commissioner and not the silly old fool," Cynthia said, raising her glass. "Good luck to all of you."

After dispersing his small army, Frost became increasingly restless.

"You're as nervous as a witch," his wife said to him the next night, as they were having dinner at Elaine's.

"Why shouldn't I be?" he snapped. "I've got people tearing all over trying to prove my theory about the Andersen murders. The problem is, I may be totally wrong. In which case I'll look damn foolish."

"But no one will know except your friend Bautista and that policeman from Connecticut. And the paralegal from Chase & Ward."

"She's the one I'm worried about," Frost said. "If I'm wrong, she'll broadcast it all over the firm in five minutes. 'Let me tell you what Reuben Frost had me doing last week. He's completely gaga. . . .' Do you know how happy George Bannard would be to hear something like that?"

Frost shook his head vigorously, as if trying to expel from it all images of Chase & Ward's Executive Partner.

Frost's mood improved as a glamorous Debra Winger swept past his table, and Pepe, the place's cheerful maître d', offered him and Cynthia a *digestif*.

"Who is that?" Frost asked his wife. He could tell

Ms. Winger was a movie star but, as was usually the case, could not place her.

"Debra Winger," Cynthia said. *"An Officer and a Gentleman, Black Widow . . ."*

Oh yes," her husband said. "She's quite good-looking, don't you think?"

"Yes, Reuben."

"I mean, she's *very* good-looking."

"Yes, Reuben."

"Who's that kid with her?"

"Her husband."

"Good heavens."

As the Frosts finished off their drinks (Cognac for him, Port for her), Cynthia tried to capitalize on the uplift Ms. Winger appeared to have given to her husband's psyche. "I'm sure your team is out there even as we speak," she said. "And they're going to prove you right and solve the murders."

Early Wednesday, Jeffrey Gruen called Casper Robbins—Frost would have given a great deal to have heard their conversation—to tell the AFC executive that he had waited long enough and that the tender offer by Gruen & Company would be announced that afternoon. Absent support from AFC's Board, the offer would be irrevocable, "subject only to finalization of bank financing," at thirty-eight dollars for each AFC share.

Frost kept in nervous contact with Castagno, Bautista and Ms. Clare, getting progress reports on their activities. Then, on Saturday morning, two vital pieces of the puzzle Frost had constructed fell into place. He called Sally Andersen immediately and asked her to assemble the group he named that very night at her home in Greenwich.

"Does this mean you know who the killer is?" Sally asked.

"I'm ninety-five percent sure," Frost answered.

"And your idea is to confront the killer at my house?"

"Yes."

There was a long pause on the other end.

"Are you sure this is the best thing to do, Reuben?" she finally asked.

"I think it is."

"Then I'll do it, even if it means inviting Casper Robbins into my house," Sally said. "But what about spouses? Are they invited?"

"It doesn't matter," Frost said. "Though I suppose it would be hard to leave them out on a Saturday night."

"Will Cynthia be coming?"

"Yes," Frost said. "I want her there for moral support. And because she'd never forgive me if she were left out."

Frost asked Sally to let him know who accepted her invitation. Within the hour, Sally Andersen called back to say that all who had been invited had done so.

Frost had earlier checked with Castagno and Bautista; Bautista would remain in Manhattan, but Castagno would assemble a team to make an arrest at the Andersen estate. The lawyer now called Castagno back to tell him everything had been settled and that the detective and his group should muster outside the Andersen home at eight-fifteen that evening, a quarter hour after Sally Andersen's soiree was to begin.

Frost rented a limousine to go to Connecticut and left Seventieth Street, with his wife, shortly after five o'clock. Cynthia could not get over how much the events of recent days had energized her husband. Always vigorous, at least relative to his age, he was now positively bursting with energy. He was quite sure that he had solved the puzzle, though there were still some nagging doubts.

Trapped now in the backseat of the large black Cadillac he had hired, he began to show his uneasiness.

"Do you realize if I'm wrong I can be sued for slander?" Frost asked his wife.

"Oh, Reuben, everything's going to be all right," she said, refraining from adding that she would have intervened with Bautista if she had thought her husband's theory of the killings was half-baked.

"And if the tabloids ever got hold of what I'm saying, I suppose it would be libel as well."

"*Reuben*, please. Just be calm. It's almost over."

Frost fell silent, though the occasional movement of his lips indicated that he was practicing his remarks to the Andersen family group—and his confrontation with the murderer.

Once in Connecticut, he asked Sally if he could rest until the evening's participants arrived. Cynthia tactfully remained downstairs, allowing her husband to rehearse his role for the evening alone in the privacy of one of the Andersen bedrooms.

By five minutes after eight, all those expected had arrived: Diana Andersen; Billy O'Neal, not surprisingly without his wife; Casper and Ditsy Robbins; and Nate Perkins. Laurance Andersen was the last to arrive, strolling across from his house accompanied by Winston, his Rottweiler.

Frost was about to begin speaking when Billy O'Neal interrupted.

"Reuben, is this damned gathering your idea? What the hell is it all about?" he asked, an angry edge to his voice. Or was it nerves? "Making us drop everything to come over here on a Saturday night. It's outrageous!"

"Yes, Billy, I'll take the blame," Frost said, trying to calm O'Neal. "I believe we have some new information about the murders of Flemming and Sorella, so I asked Sally to call all of you together."

"Oh my God," Diana interrupted. "I don't believe this—one of those tense confrontations in the family library where the killer gives himself away. Mother, how can you be a party to such foolishness?"

"Your description is not quite accurate, Diana," Frost said firmly. "We know who the killer is. It's not a question of tricking him or her into an admission. I requested this meeting. I thought you would all want an explanation of the crimes, and I thought the murderer might as well hear that explanation, too."

Frost's deliberately cold tone, as he justified his actions, created a palpable tension in the room. The others were totally silent and looked expectantly at the lawyer, as if he were about to begin a Sunday sermon.

"My explanation will take some time. I apologize in advance for that, but I hope you'll be patient," Frost began. "Let's go back three weeks, or almost three weeks. Flemming Andersen is killed right outside this house. Two days later, Sorella is killed outside the neighboring house. Each time a note is found, indicating that the killings may have been the work of a psychotic. And each time a second note is delivered to AFC's offices in New York.

"The first thing we were able to eliminate was any connection between the two sets of notes. The ones delivered in New York were written by an embittered former employee of the Company and the family named Oscar Brothers. I was able to talk to him and I satisfied myself that he knew nothing about the content of the notes left here in Connecticut.

"The police both here and in New York continued to search for a deranged killer, but without any leads at all. Finally, we all decided that there probably was no such killer: our working assumption then became that the murders were somehow related to Jeffrey Gruen and his desire to take over AFC. When Sorella was killed within hours after announcing—announcing for the first time,

I might add—that she would never let the Andersen Foundation sell out to Gruen, that assumption seemed more than justified.

"And if we were right, the killer was someone at the family meeting where Sorella announced her opposition to Gruen, or someone very close to a person at that meeting. Such as Jeffrey Gruen himself."

No one questioned Frost's linkage of the family to Gruen, though Casper Robbins looked distinctly uncomfortable.

"That means that I had to view all of you in this room who were at Sally Andersen's lunch that day as suspects, painful though that was to me. Most of you had alibis. You, Diana, said you were at your New York gym when the murders happened. You, Billy, said you were at the New York Athletic Club. You, Casper Robbins, said you were at home in Katonah with Ditsy. And you, Laurance, said you were in California the night your father was killed, though you were back here in Connecticut two days later when your sister was murdered.

"That left only three people unaccounted for at the time of both murders: you, Sally; you, Nate, and Jeffrey Gruen. Gruen has consistently refused to talk to the police at all. And Sally and Nate readily admitted that they were at the scene of the two crimes. Indeed, Sally allegedly found her husband's body and Nate allegedly found his wife's."

Frost's audience stirred at his use of the word "allegedly." Was this just careful lawyer's talk or was he leading up to some revelation about Sally or Nate?

"That's where things stood last Monday," Reuben went on. "Then a totally fortuitous event, which I'll describe in due course, took place and led me to rethink where we were.

"At my suggestion, the police retraced in minute detail the ground they had covered and tried to affirm or deny the alibis they'd been given. With greater or lesser difficulty, the police eliminated several of you as suspects.

"For example, your presence at the time of both murders, Diana, was finally established at your gym in New York by other users of the place." (He did not go into detail about the pressure Bautista had put on Toby Jervis, the manager of the gym. A not-so-subtle mention of his police record had overcome his earlier hostility and with his help four other customers had been found who recalled seeing Diana at the gym at one or both of the murder times.)

"Billy, your presence was accounted for as well." (Frost had delicately and tactfully handled O'Neal. After Frost's repeated assurances that his statement would never be revealed publicly, O'Neal had admitted that he had spent idyllic matinees on the murder days with his new on-the-side girlfriend, one Esther McGrew. Frost was now honoring his bargain, and O'Neal's face brightened noticeably as he realized Reuben was doing so. His latest dalliance was not going to be exposed to family censure.)

"As for you, Casper, the Jehovah's Witnesses came to your rescue, at least for the night when Flemming was killed," Frost said. He explained how Ditsy Robbins had remembered that two Jehovah's Witnesses had come calling in Katonah early that evening, and that Casper had sent them away peremptorily. He said that Bautista, working through the Witnesses' world headquarters in Brooklyn, had located the door-to-door evangelicals and confirmed Casper's alibi.

"Now to the event of last Monday that changed my thinking," Frost said. "By sheer good luck, I was riding uptown in a radio taxi when a call came over the radio to pick up 'Andersen' at the Union League Club and to take him to three twenty-four Park Avenue. Totally innocent, I know, but it stuck in my mind that this was Jeffrey Gruen's business address. I diverted my dialcab there and saw you, Laurance, go up in one of the elevators leading to Gruen's office." As he spoke, Frost turned to Laurance, sitting in the corner with Winston.

"Reuben, this is ridiculous," Laurance interrupted. "You're insulting everyone's intelligence here. Don't you realize there are *other* offices on that elevator bank besides Gruen's? Christ, I could have been going to my dentist."

"Quite true," Frost said. "And I was painfully aware that what I had discovered was hardly proof of a conspiracy between you and Gruen. But I seriously doubt, Laurance, that you go to Jeffrey Gruen for your dental work." He explained, though not in explicit detail, how he had found out from Gruen's secretary that Andersen had been there.

"Once I had this obvious arrow pointing at you," Frost continued, now talking directly to Laurance, "I began to question your alibi—your story that you had been in California—"

"My *confirmed* story, as you know very well!" Laurance interrupted again.

Frost, with calculation, ignored the interruption. "—and to look very carefully at you, Laurance Andersen, suspected murderer. As I tried to concentrate my thoughts, I reviewed what I knew of you and your character—after all, I've known you practically since you were born. I was assisted in this by the manuscript of your sister's book, which contained several details about you I had not known before."

The mention of Diana's manuscript provoked an outburst from her, directed as much at her indiscreet editor as at Frost.

"I don't mean to suggest I developed any great Freudian insights into you," Frost went on, "but several incidents fell into a pattern. There was, for example, your gambling in college—hushed up when your father paid off your debts. Then the totally unnecessary knee operation that kept you out of the draft—an operation you had the ill grace to brag to me about some years ago in this very room." Frost, the navy veteran of World War II, had not been sympathetic then, nor was he now, to Laurance's rich-man's subterfuge.

"Then there was the embarrassing pregnancy of the secretary in the AFC office where you worked, terminated by an abortion—then quite illegal—and a lifetime stipend from your father for the unfortunate girl. And then three marriages, each followed in short order by divorces that I think can be fairly characterized as sordid and messy. And then a close call with bankruptcy, with Flemming again coming to your rescue.

"I repeat all these past deeds not to be censorious, but to indicate a pattern that can be interpreted as showing an evasion of responsibility and some easy escapes from hard problems. And, just perhaps, a contempt for the rules that the rest of us may feel bound to play by."

Laurance sat gripping the edge of his chair with white knuckles as Frost spoke. But he did not interrupt.

"Once I came to this conclusion, Laurance, I did three things: I asked a very inventive legal assistant from my office to find out just as much about you as she could. I asked my friend Luis Bautista, a New York homicide detective, to recheck, in the most meticulous manner he knew how, your story that you were in California when your father was killed. And I asked Arthur Castagno to re-examine, with a great deal of skepticism, whether Sorella had been killed by her two Dobermans."

Frost was speaking deliberately but rapidly, and his narrative created an electrifying reaction among those in the Andersen living room. All eyes, which had been focused on Frost, had turned to Laurance Andersen.

"Do you wish to hear the results of my inquiries in any particular order?" Frost asked Laurance.

There was no response, only a slightly drooping jaw

and a look of profound I-don't-believe-what-I'm-hearing doubt.

"Let's start with my paralegal, Ms. Clare. She didn't discover anything earth-shaking, Laurance. No 'smoking gun,' as they like to say in Washington. But some small details of an accumulative nature. Such as the fact that your senior thesis at Yale contained, three times, a misuse of the word 'principle,' just as in the note found after Flemming's murder. 'Principle ingredient,' as in the note, means principal with an '-A-L,' Laurance.

"Or the fact, Laurance, that the biography you wrote for your tenth-reunion book at Yale said your hobby was karate—a useful skill when knocking out your father, I should think. And in your twenty-fifth-reunion book, it had changed to dog breeding and training."

"Jesus Christ, Reuben, you really are around the bend," Laurance interjected. "How much longer am I going to have to watch you convince everyone here you're totally out of it? You forget I was in California, C-A-L-I-F-O-R-N-I-A—California, the Golden State, the night the old man was knocked off."

"Can we go over that?" Frost said. "Several of us were present when you left the AFC board meeting the day your father was killed, announcing that you were going to Los Angeles. When the police questioned you, you told them you had indeed gone to L.A., on the noon American Airlines flight from Kennedy, and had stayed at the St. Martin Hotel. You said you hadn't had a chance to see any of your business contacts there before you got word that your father had been murdered. The hotel personnel confirmed that you'd been there and American confirmed that you'd been on the airline's noon flight, traveling first-class.

"As I said, I asked Bautista to go over these details again. This proved to be a most rewarding exercise. Yes, indeed, someone calling himself Laurance Andersen had been at the St. Martin Hotel—a hotel, by the way, where you were a complete stranger, unlike the Wilshire or the Beverly Hills. Yes, indeed, someone calling himself Laurance Andersen had been on the American midday flight that Tuesday. But it was not you, Laurance—it was Jeffrey Gruen. The room clerk at the St. Martin identified his picture—identified Gruen as the man who had stayed there as 'Andersen.'

"After finding out about your meeting last Monday, I was not surprised to learn that Gruen was involved. Even without that meeting I shouldn't have been. Looking back, why didn't the superconfident Gruen announce his threatened tender offer the day Flemming was murdered? Wasn't it because he *knew* Flemming would be murdered? There was no point in starting a tender offer if he knew it would be complicated by Flemming's death.

"Just to nail things down, Laurance. The ticket to Los Angeles in your name was issued by a travel agency in midtown for Gruen's account. And then there was an unbelievable exercise in cheapness, much like Gruen turning out the lights in his multimillion-dollar apartment, a little quirk I observed when I met with him there. Your friend Gruen, Laurance, at the risk of exposing the plot to kill your father, used his American Airlines AAdvantage number with that ticket in your name! Just think, Laurance, he not only got you to rid him of his biggest adversaries at Andersen Foods, but he got credit for what I'm told are four thousand three hundred thirty-two miles toward a free trip on American Airlines! Now there's one clever—not to say cheap—fellow! It's only too bad American doesn't fly to where he's likely to be going!"

Laurance Andersen was seething as Frost continued his narrative, yet at the same time he seemed all but mesmerized by what the lawyer was saying. Frost realized this and did not pause.

"Finally, Laurance, let's turn to the matter of dogs.

Nate Perkins, you will recall, was totally baffled by the attack the Dobermans made on Sorella. She had worked with those dogs since they were puppies and, as far as anyone knew, there had never been any sort of ugly incident involving them. Oh sure, one of them had once nipped a delivery boy, but there had never been anything whatsoever to suggest that they would turn on their mistress and kill her. I believed Nate, and I think everyone else here did, too.

"So once I had you in my sights, Laurance, I asked Officer Castagno to review the circumstances surrounding Sorella's death, starting with a comparison of the teeth marks in her flesh with wax impressions from the teeth of the Dobermans. Fortunately, by the way, this could be done without exhuming Sorella's body. The discrepancies turned out to be so obvious the police could establish them easily from the coroner's photographs of her body—once they knew what they were looking for."

Frost seemed nervous for the first time as he pressed on. He paused, swallowed hard, and then continued. "So if those Dobermans were innocent, what animal killed Sorella? A little more investigation gave the police the answer—the Rottweiler sitting there next to you. Winston, I believe his name is, killed Sorella at your instigation. After which you led him away and released her own dogs from their kennel. Seeing the blood of their mistress—indeed, licking it off her dying body—they appeared totally crazed when discovered and everyone assumed they'd attacked Sorella.

"Need I say any more, Laurance? Except you should know that your friend Gruen has been arrested in New York and has admitted everything—about your plot to kill your father and your sister and your joint plan to take over Andersen Foods."

Frost had paced the floor the entire time he spoke.

He now sat down, well-distanced from his quarry, and grasped the arms of the chair. He stared unblinkingly at Laurance.

"All right, all right, I've heard enough, Reuben," Laurance said. "Right now I'm going to leave, and if there's any trouble, I'll give that dog the same signal I gave it in Sorella's backyard. He may not show it, but he's been trained to kill. I'm getting out of here. And I don't want any of you to follow. I've got a little money left, parked in Switzerland. I'll go and be a beach bum in Brazil. There's enough money for that, and that suits me just fine right now. So sit still and I'll just leave quietly. And Winston will, too."

Laurance got up and went out, leaving stunned onlookers behind. Then the front door slammed and, within seconds, Castagno was heard ordering Laurance to put his hands up. Laurance screamed out "Kill, Winston, kill!" and those inside heard an unearthly growl, followed almost at once by two gunshots.

The police had killed Winston, one of the murderers, but had his master and co-felon in handcuffs.

Frost, his narrative of truth—and the lie about Gruen's arrest—having produced the result he expected, went to Sally Andersen and put his arms around her.

"I'm sorry, Sally," he said.

"So am I, Reuben," she answered. "But thank you for bringing my nightmare to an end." She pulled herself together as best she could and addressed the subdued band in her living room:

"There's food if anybody wants it. We really ought to eat, you know. The family fortune won't survive very long if people don't eat."

EPILOGUE

24 While Laurance was being arrested in Greenwich, Luis Bautista and two colleagues took Jeffrey Gruen into custody in New York. He was arrested while eating Saturday night dinner at Walter's, a highly touted East Side restaurant favored by the newly rich, especially ladies with nicknames that sounded like kitchen-floor coverings (*i.e.*, Keeka, Shashty and Tiley). Gruen did not go quietly, and Walter's regulars talked of little else for weeks except his colorful exit.

Early in the week after Gruen's arrest, Norman Cobb announced that Gruen & Company's tender offer for shares of Andersen Foods had been called off. Under all the circumstances, a predictable hitch had developed in the bank financing.

Reuben Frost took great satisfaction in describing to his former partners the events leading up to the arrests of Laurance Andersen and Jeffrey Gruen.

"I don't understand how you put it all together, Reuben," Marvin Yates said, with grudging admiration.

"Sometimes things are done better in small groups, Marvin," Frost replied.

The irony was lost on Yates.

*   *   *

Contrary to all expectations, Billy O'Neal *did* go to the Betty Ford Clinic and returned a new man. So reformed was he that he even abandoned Esther McGrew and effected a reconciliation with his wife. He became Chairman of AFC and, without the threat of his Uncle Flemming looming, succeeded in raising the Company to new levels of profitability. O'Neal often took counsel with Sally Andersen, whose shrewd behind-the-scenes guidance was of great value in governing the Company.

Sally Andersen took control of the Andersen Foundation. To no one's surprise, she fired Randolph Hedley as the Foundation lawyer, replacing him with an eager and attractive young lawyer from Rudenstine, Fried & D'Arms. And she named Laurance's young daughter, Dorothy, and Cynthia Frost as her fellow directors. Drawing on Cynthia's foundation expertise, and young Dorothy's naïve but real concern with contemporary social problems, she turned the Foundation into a vital and relevant institution that made many older, better-known and larger foundations look stodgy by comparison. But here, too, she avoided being in the public eye and did her work offstage; a highly visible Executive Director, not at all averse to publicity, willingly took credit for the Foundation's rejuvenation.

Casper Robbins, within days after the arrests, resigned as President and as the newly appointed Chairman of the Board of AFC "to pursue other interests," as the corporate press release put it. Since no raider had forced him out— and the misconduct clause in his contract would have probably done him in anyway—he never got to claim his lucrative golden parachute. Every time Reuben went to the Foreign Affairs Forum, he seemed to run into Robbins, still without a job, and busily glad-handing and circulating among the members. And despite his abundance of free time, Robbins no longer played tennis with Sally Andersen.

Diana Andersen, predictably, sold her holdings in AFC. She used part of the proceeds to repay her advance to Miller's in order to withdraw *Women's War* from publication. She claimed to be too busy applying her wealth to Concerned Women's worthy projects to finish it, but Frost thought some late-blooming compassion for her mother might have been involved, too. Her mother was relieved and never asked to see the manuscript, which was just as well, because Diana had burned it. (Unbeknownst to her, Christopher Terry at Miller's had retained a copy, just in case she should ever change her mind about publishing.)

And Nate Perkins finally gave up novel writing altogether, claiming that he was bereft of a creative idea for one. He decided to try nonfiction, though at last report he had not yet found a suitable nonfiction subject, either.